Michelangelo Schwartz and the Mystery of the Illuminati

The First Michelangelo Schwartz Mystery

Dr. Frank Bryce McCluskey

ISBN-13: 9781499231694
ISBN-10: 1499231695
Library of Congress Control Number: 2014907645
CreateSpace Independent Publishing Platform
North Charleston, South Carolina

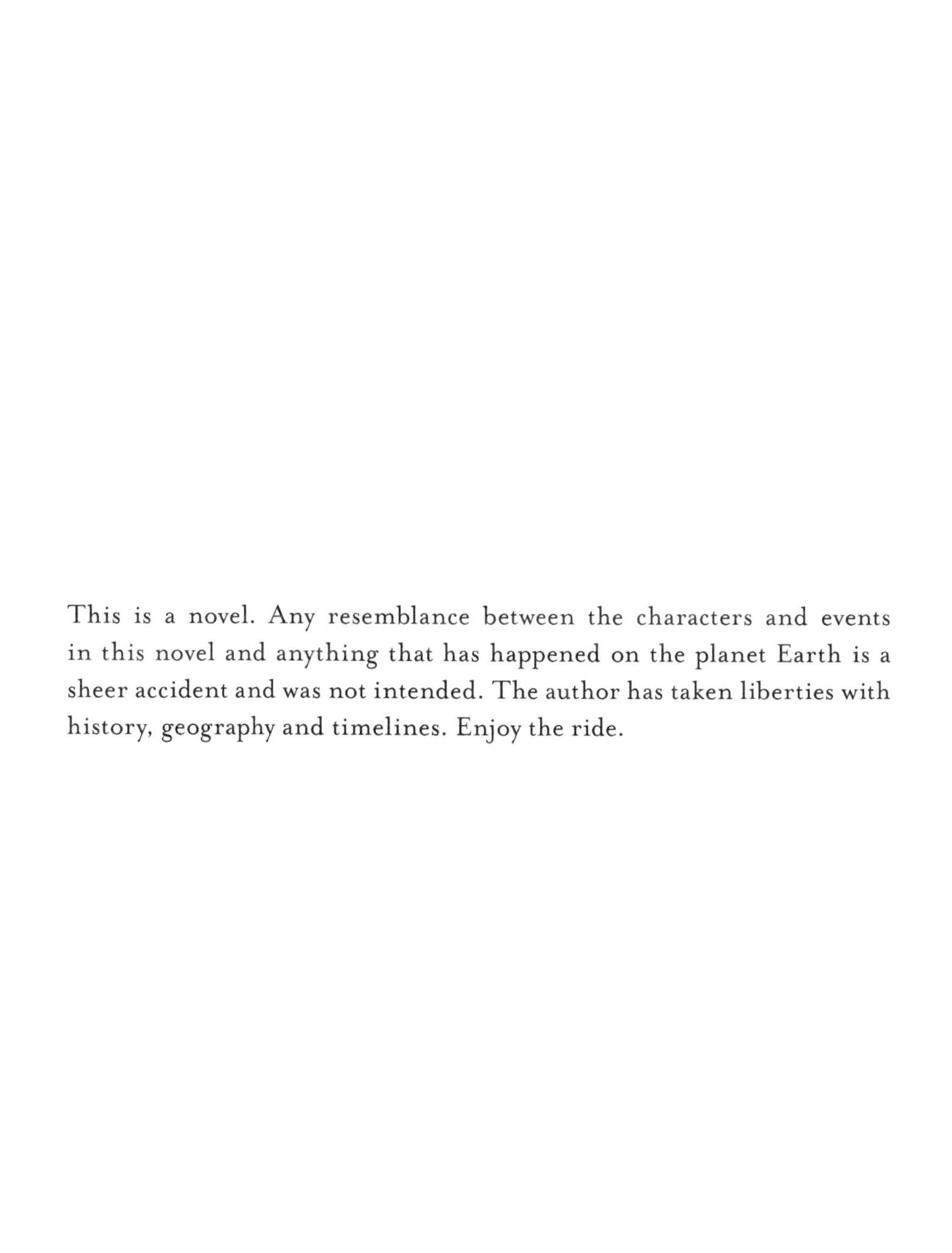

This is a novel. Any resemblance between the characters and events in this novel and anything that has happened on the planet Earth is a sheer accident and was not intended. The author has taken liberties with history, geography and timelines. Enjoy the ride.

Acknowledgments

This book was researched in the greatest universities, libraries, and museums in the world and was written, in large part, in the Hurricane Bar and Grill and Benny's Pool Hall. The author gives special thanks to a former professor of Russian at Harvard University and Smith College without whom this book would not have been written. While some of the world's most renowned professors, deans, and college presidents have read and edited this manuscript, they have universally implored me, no, *begged* me, not to mention their names in connection with this project, as they wish to maintain their reputations, their friendships, and their pensions.

Dramatis Personae

Bone, Earl Larry. Head librarian at the Bodleian Library at Oxford University. He is a hard-drinking Scottish laird with a penchant for campus gossip and good Scotch. He wears bow ties and tortoise-shell glasses as a signal of his high intelligence.

Brannigan, Luke. The foremost authority on the history of baseball. He has written dozens of books on the game and its lore. Although he has struck out with women and never made it to first base, he is a friend to Dr. Michelangelo Schwartz and will go to bat for him.

Braunschweiger, Biff. The director of the Anti-Catholic League of Brooklyn. He is heir to the fortune built up by his great-grandfather, who was known as the Bratwurst King of the Midwest.

Callahan, William, formerly known as Sister Bill. William Callahan spent the first thirty-five years of his life as Sister Bill, dean of discipline and softball coach at a Catholic college for young women, before having the operation that turned her into the man God had always intended for her to be. He is now the muscle behind the Anti-Catholic League of Brooklyn and a friend of Biff Braunschweiger.

Chip, Joe. CIA analyst and company man who grew up playing racquetball on the Upper East Side of Manhattan and would never wear a polo shirt without the right label on his chest. He is blond and blue-eyed and didn't go to Wall Street because he realized he could get away with more in the CIA.

Cuccinelli, Antonio. Curator of the Capitoline Museum, Piazza del Campidoglio, Rome. He is a man of erudition and high learning who has the wrong idea about Dr. Michelangelo Schwartz. He is a true Italian academic, who shows up at ten o'clock in the morning, has espresso till eleven, takes a two-hour lunch at noon, goes home after that for a two-hour nap to sleep off the two bottles of Chianti, and wakes up at four, just in time to get ready for dinner at nine.

Giovanni. Bartender at Harry's Bar on the Via Veneto in Rome. He is a master of cocktails and witty repartee who is well-known to Dr. Schwartz.

Greco, Salvatore. An overweight Sicilian assassin who takes his orders from the Vatican when he is not doing food demonstrations for Bubba's Burgers at the Piggly Wiggly in South Detroit. He takes pride in both of his occupations.

Jade. A beautiful bartender at Hooters of Wayne in New Jersey, who, for a short time, was Dr. Michelangelo Schwartz's object of affection. Jade's goal in life is to get into Carla's College of Cosmetology, but, so far, she is the only cash-paying applicant ever to be refused admission.

Horos, Don Carlo. A blind librarian who lives in Buenos Aries. Enough said.

Lulu Lefay. Tall, blond, and athletic. "Big Lulu" is popular and not just with the boys. She is a former student and lover of Professor Michelangelo Schwartz. When she left him to run off with another woman, she left a note stating: "I will never love another man."

Orrogante, Lindsey. The Richard Fox professor of New Testament Greek at All Souls College, Oxford. She is a stuck-up Oxford don who is sure she is God's gift to academia. Writing books that show her ability to work in six languages, which almost no one will read, has allowed her to achieve high status among professors.

Pope, the. A ninety-five-year-old master of Vatican politics who always wins at Texas Hold'em, even when he is holding a pair of threes and his opponent has a royal flush. But when argued with, he simply says, "I am infallible," and he gets the pot every time.

Reunite, Cardinal Stanley. The dean of the College of Cardinals, who has the goods on Dr. Michelangelo Schwartz and misses the Medici popes and the Inquisition. He refers to the time when the Vatican could use the spiked boot and the "red-hot poker of truth" as "the good old days."

Runciter, Glen. Director of the CIA, who has spent his adult life lying to almost everyone about things they are sure he is lying about. He lies so much every day that when asked for his name at a recent cocktail party, he had to take out his driver's license and look it up. He is considered a great patriot.

Schwartz, Bridget. A dainty lass from County Clare in Ireland, who worked as a chambermaid in New York City. The mother of Dr. Michelangelo Schwartz. She is devoted to two things—the Holy Mother Church and the New York Yankees.

Schwartz, Michelangelo. A hard-drinking and womanizing professor with an expertise in Dante, who descended into the same circles of hell he bored his students with. With leather elbow patches and a stained tie, he has been fired from every college he's taught at. One charge he faced was showing up for his Monday morning class on Tuesday afternoon. Because he has been fired from every job he's ever held, he is now searching for a new academic home. His chances of finding one are less than those of a blind man in a dark room looking for a black cat that isn't there.

Schwartz, Shlomo. A Jewish pickle salesman from Minsk, who was famous for his kosher dills. He is the father of Dr. Michelangelo Schwartz. It is rumored that spending your days in a room with fermenting pickles has a deleterious effect on both the intellect and your sense of humor.

Schwartz, Sherwood. The creator of *Gilligan's Island* and uncle of Michelangelo Schwartz. This man was once at the center of the remark that "Television is a vast wasteland." He is the man that gave the world the question that can determine every man's ideal mate for life: "Mary Ann or Ginger?"

Serrureacle, Angelique. A Parisian expert in crossword puzzles who has connections in Rome and Buenos Aires and seems one step ahead of our hero in a way that is hard to explain. She is unusual for a Parisian, in that while she is fluent in English (as are most of them), she actually speaks it when asked.

Snowden, Edward. A high-school dropout the US government entrusted its most sensitive information to. He told the truth that the US government was illegally spying on all of its citizens every day in violation of the Constitution, and for that he was branded a traitor and had to flee the country. After he was nominated for the Noble Prize and the Pulitzer Prize, the American government made every effort to put him in solitary confinement for life.

Wolf Eyes. A Norwegian assassin who was employed by the Illuminati to keep their secrets safe. He spent his life trying to avoid detection, because a single mistake could blow his cover. He is a master of planning and details and is always three moves ahead of any mark he has set out to neutralize. But one event in an airport bookstore will change all of that.

1

In a secret conclave in the Sistine Chapel, the pope and his aged and sleepy cardinals give us a humorous history of religion, and we are introduced to Professor Michelangelo Schwartz. Along the way, we find out Wal-Mart has satanic connections. We learn the link between the National Rifle Association and the Knights of Columbus and speculate that Goofy might be gay. We also learn not to play poker with someone who considers himself infallible.

The Sistine Chapel, Vatican City, Rome, Italy

His face flushed scarlet with anger and frustration, the pope hurled his crystal goblet of thirty-year-old Chateau Margaux Premier Grand Cru against the wall of the Sistine Chapel and screamed, "I know he is a man of low morals, questionable character, and bad judgment, but sometimes, my dear brothers, yes, sometimes, the Mother Church needs a man who is capable of anything, and, my dear brethren, Michelangelo Schwartz is that man!"

The pope, who was an energetic ninety-five, was dressed in a white cassock and white beanie, with a two-pound gold cross around his neck—enough bling for a gangster rapper. He was a small man who had long since lost his hair, but he still had sparkling blue eyes and had retained his ever more prominent nose. He always wore glinting gold metallic glasses.

A select group of cardinals had convened late that night inside the Sistine Chapel, the only place in the Vatican they were sure was not being bugged by the CIA, the NSA, the KGB, MI6, or Google. The chapel was lit only by flickering candlelight. On occasion, a glob of hot wax would fall from the candles in the chandelier overhead and land on the necks of the aged cardinals, suddenly waking them out of their slumbers. If they turned on the lights, it would alert the intelligence agencies around the globe that something worth listening to was going on, something big. Security had been a matter of increasing concern from the moment Julian Assange of WikiLeaks informed the world that the pope wore boxers and not briefs. There were rumors that WikiLeaks had a paper trail a mile long showing the Vatican's financial involvement in the last Justin Bieber tour, and if that were made public, it would be hard to explain, very hard to explain.

The pope was pale and perspiring as he stood up. It was rare for him to show his agitation, but he could not hide it. "What some of you don't know, my brothers, is that a document has surfaced, a very singular document. This document points the way to recovering the Holy Grail and the power that it bestows upon its holder. What we do not know is how many others may already be on this trail. So it is essential we move as quickly as possible. There is no time to dither, my brothers. The Holy Grail, the cup that our Lord drank from during the Last Supper, was in the Vatican's possession from the earliest days of our church until February 6, 1920. On that fateful day, my brothers, it was removed from our hands, and as you know, we priests are hands-on, and since that time, the Holy Mother Church has been in decline. In 1920, we were at our prime, with millions of faithful Catholics never questioning a word we said. Today, my brethren, we are but a shadow of our former glory in a world obsessed with *Keeping Up with the Kardashians* and *America's Got Talent*."

The pontiff did not need to explain, as most of the cardinals never missed either show. He took a swig from a chilled San Pellegrino bottled water and went on.

"Most of our greatest minds agree that the Illuminati must have been behind the theft. Since the removal of the Grail, the Illuminati have grown stronger, and we have grown weaker. There was a time when we could rest easy in the knowledge that everyone would say grace before dinner, bless themselves while passing a church, and never dare to suspect our priests of hanky-panky. How the world has gone downhill since that fateful day when the Illuminati used the power of the Holy Grail to make the secular world turn away from the faith of their fathers. Now, for those of you who are new to this secret conclave and doubt there is such a thing as the Illuminati, be assured there is. They are more powerful than you can imagine. Much of the evidence about them is secret, but trust me, my brothers. They are real, and we now have a chance to catch them with their pants down, in a manner of speaking.

"We believe that the document, which recently came into our possession, is from a dissident faction of the Illuminati. It indicates, we believe, a path to recovering the Holy Grail! But the document itself is not a straightforward text; it is a palimpsest, consisting of a poem that contains a puzzle. It is the puzzle that shows the location of the Grail. Once we have cracked this puzzle, we shall be able to retrieve the Holy Grail and, with it, the power to make us, once again, the force in the world we once were! We have turned that document over to the scholars at the Pontifical Institute here in Rome, who will keep our secret under oath and threat of excommunication. Alas, to date, we have discovered only one thing of which we can be certain."

The pope stopped and gulped. He knew the next thing he would say would not be popular.

"Whoever sent the document told us that there is one man, and one man alone, capable of following the signs to the Holy Grail. That man is Michelangelo Schwartz."

Cardinal Reunite, who at eighty-four was by far the youngest man in the room, furrowed his brow as he stood and walked up to the jewel-encrusted throne that the pope was standing in front of. Behind Reunite sat row upon row of tottering, old clerics. It appeared as though one or two had either fallen off the bench or merely gone to sleep.

Cardinal Reunite was plump from too many years of Roman pasta. His full head of white hair and large brown eyes, however, gave him the appearance of an impish youth. He had a Roman nose and jowls from years of frowning. When you are the number-two man to someone whose opinion you cannot question without committing a sin, you tend to frown a lot. Reunite was wearing a scarlet skullcap and a scarlet cassock over his white robes. Over his white robe, he had several layers of Valenciennes lace. It was a bit excessive and barely permitted by the church. He had a large, golden pectoral cross draped around his neck. Cardinal Reunite always wore shining black Gucci shoes. He tapped them quietly on the floor to pass the time while the pope went on and on. When he became a priest and gave up women, he figured that he deserved some return for that loss. For him, it was the lace and the shoes.

Reunite handed a thick manila folder to the pontiff. "Professor Michelangelo Schwartz: The Untold Story" appeared on the front in red letters. The pope looked at the name on it and tossed it back over his shoulder. It landed behind the pontiff, and the papers spread all over the floor. Cardinal Reunite scurried behind the pope and began to pick up the papers and stuff them back into the folder.

The pope hated for anyone to disagree with him, and he especially hated when he heard arguments from Cardinal Reunite, who objected to almost everything he said. The pope wanted to move this along. They were in a race they could not lose. He directed a long stare at the cardinals before he began again.

"Cardinal Reunite, I respect you as the dean of the College of Cardinals. We have known each other for over sixty years, and I can guess what this file will tell me. I imagine you have chronicled the drinking and the dalliances, showing a career in shambles and a man who might well be called a 'lost sheep.' But I contend that it is he alone who can save the Mother Church in her hour of need. I want him on this case in twenty-four hours. And don't argue with me. I am infallible!"

Cardinal Reunite was not to be deterred. He hurriedly came back in front of the chair, holding the papers stuffed back in the folder. He was breathless and nervous as he began.

"Your Holiness, this is a crucial moment for the Holy Mother Church, and I would beg you and the other cardinals present to hear my case as to why Professor Schwartz is, in fact, the wrong man for this task. This is a matter on which the future of our church and, quite possibly, the future of Western civilization hangs. We have only one chance to stop the Illuminati and bring the world back to God. We can't afford to make a mistake."

The Holy Father was clearly not pleased and had a faraway stare as he waved his index finger in the air in a little circle, like quarterbacks do when they want to speed up the game because there is little time left on the clock, indicating that he would listen but not with much enthusiasm.

Cardinal Reunite turned to the audience and walked toward a lectern in front of the altar and put down the file. He put the pages back in order before he addressed them.

"Your Eminences, we start by admitting that we are all sinners. As the sons of Adam, we have inherited his sin. I, myself, am a sinner, but, my holy brothers, there is a limit to what God can forgive. And I believe that limit is Professor Michelangelo Schwartz."

The pope was already showing his impatience. "Skip the 'sons of Adam,' the 'descendants of Abraham,' the 'Temple of Solomon,' and get to the point, Stan!"

Stan was Cardinal Reunite's first name, and the pope almost never used it in public, as that name was reserved for their Wednesday-night poker games in the papal chambers. The pope almost never lost at Texas Hold'em. When your boss keeps going on that he is infallible, you don't argue when he insists his pair of threes beats a royal flush. Cardinal Reunite nodded to the pontiff as the good cardinal opened the folder. He placed it on the desk and took out a pair of black reading glasses.

"Michelangelo Francis Bryce Schwartz was born to Shlomo Schwartz, a pickle salesman from Minsk, and Bridget O'Shaughnessy McGuiness of County Clare, Ireland, in Newark, New Jersey, United States, in 1948. When Bridget married Shlomo a number of years before Schwartz was born, her family, as you might imagine, shunned her. Her father, a hard-drinking Newark policeman, expected her to marry a drunken Irishman from County Clare. If she had married a Dublin man or someone from Donegal, that would have been bad enough, but Shlomo Schwartz?"

A cardinal shouted out from the back of the room, "Are you telling us Shlomo Schwartz was not Irish?"

Laughter erupted in the room. The cardinals thought that was a good one. It was way past their bedtimes, and, as a group, they had a very short attention span. To make things worse, several cardinals in the back rows were texting humorous comments about everything that had been said so far to each other on their smartphones. But you know what they say—boys will be boys.

Reunite gave an icy stare, and slowly the room returned to silence.

"But, in time, Bridget found a way back into the heart of her family. Some years after she was married, she had a son, and she raised that son, Michelangelo Schwartz, Catholic. But what none of her relatives knew, and what they could not know, was that Shlomo Schwartz was, at the very same time, raising him as a Jew. So he was raised both Jewish and Catholic. Imagine the shame, secrecy, and confusion that came from not telling his Jewish uncles he was Catholic and hiding his Jewish learning from Bridget's family. The shame!"

Cardinal Chianti, the Camerlengo who could sign documents in the pope's absence, was 105 years old and had been at the Vatican for eighty years. He had been senile since Eisenhower was in the White House. But, like the US Supreme Court, a cardinal could lose his mind and still keep his job for a couple of decades before anybody noticed it. Cardinal Chianti stood up, using his cane, and wobbled as he did.

"Cardinal Reunite, how is it possible for someone to be both a Catholic and a Jew?"

Reunite smiled. "Cardinal Chianti, of course, it is impossible. But, nonetheless, his parents could not agree. Bridget and Shlomo were both difficult and argumentative people who had trouble focusing. It is rumored that working in a shop filled with the fumes of fermenting pickles can have a detrimental effect on the intellect. Like almost every religion tells all of its members, both of them were utterly convinced that they had the only true religion, and everyone else was out of luck.

"For Bridget, this meant only Catholics are saved and will get into heaven. This idea brought some solace to her, as she realized she would not be stuck with Shlomo for all eternity. For Shlomo, it meant that only the Jews were God's chosen people and knew where the good bagel shops and Chinese restaurants were. Each believed the other either was going to hell or had to eat in bad restaurants, which, for the Jews, is like being in hell. Bridget and Shlomo could not agree, so they compromised and decided to raise him as both a Catholic and a Jew. They took him to Temple Beth Shalom, ten miles away in Nutley, New Jersey, on Friday nights and to Saint Barbara's Catholic Church in their neighborhood on Sundays."

Cardinal Chianti had another question. He got to his tottering feet again. "It is unusual to have a church named after Saint Barbara. Her story is a strange one. When she became a Catholic against her parents' wishes, her nasty, heathen father, Dioscorus, tortured her and then personally cut off her head. Later that same day, when he was walking back to the castle, a lightning bolt struck and killed him, because ours is a loving God who cares for his children and often gets revenge on their behalf. That, my dear brothers, is why Saint Barbara is the patron saint of both lightning and fireworks."

Reunite knew the old cardinal was on his last legs, so he forced a fake smile and went on. "Because Catholics and Jews hated each other so much in those days, these two worlds never collided, as long as young Michelangelo played ball and kept his mouth shut. Nobody was the wiser. Now and then, he would blurt something out in front of the wrong grandparent, but Shlomo would just smash him in the face, and that was the end of it. Parenting, my brothers, was so much simpler in those days and more in keeping with biblical precepts.

"So Schwartz grew up hearing bad things about the Christians from the Jews and worse things about the Jews from the Christians. He had a most confusing childhood. By going to CCD, the Confraternity of Christian Doctrine, every Wednesday afternoon, he learned that the Jews killed Christ, were not getting into heaven, and may have been drinking the blood of Christian babies, and, for this, he felt secretly ashamed. Later that same week, he went to synagogue, and he learned about the Inquisition, pogroms, and the Holocaust, and he also felt guilty about them. After all of these confusing claims, he became a nihilist, a man who believes in nothing. But at the same time, because he was constantly in religious-education classes, he became immersed in both traditions. Schwartz grew up reading Hebrew, Latin, Greek, French, German, and Italian. It turned out he had a talent as a scholar. After receiving his PhD, he published articles that got him noticed. He went on to become one of the world's leading experts on the hidden symbolism in Dante and late medieval literature."

The elderly Cardinal Chianti again arose. "How did a good Catholic woman turn from our Holy Mother Church and raise a son exposed to Judaism? How could she raise him in such a sinful way? Didn't she know that Jews are corrupt bankers?"

Cardinal Reunite adjusted his glasses. "Cardinal Chianti, I would not go on about corrupt bankers if I were you. You can't use Visa in Vatican City because our accounting practices are suspect. One of our bankers was found hanged under a bridge in London not too long ago, and two others are missing in action, along with about a billion euros. But let me get back to my story. Shlomo Schwartz and Bridget McGuiness did not share any traditions, any foods (with the sole exception of corned beef), or any spiritual beliefs. They apparently argued constantly and barely managed to get along with one another. There are even stories of physical violence perpetrated by Shlomo. He came home from a frustrating day at the pickle store only to find that Bridget had drunk the last of his Manischewitz kosher wine. Loss of temper at such a moment is understandable but not to be applauded. They only had one thing in common. They were both rabid New York Yankees fans."

Cardinal Chianti did not understand. "If that is all they had in common, how could they stay together?"

Reunite was a master of exposition. "Cardinal Chianti, as a simple man of faith, who has spent his life in prayer and contemplation, it is possible you have missed a few things about the modern world, such as television and sports. The Yankees are the winningest team in all of sports. There are thirty American baseball teams. There have been fifty-three World Series and one team, *one team*, the Yankees, has won twenty-seven of those. They use suitcases full of money to buy the best players and stack the deck against all of the other teams. Once they get these super players, they are still not satisfied. They lead the way in injecting their athletes with steroids, vitamins, and supplements. This made the 1990s team look like the cover of a Marvel Comics book. They are bullies who play dirty. But, boy, do their fans love them!

"Before they were married, Bridget would go into the pickle store where Shlomo worked and they would talk Yankees for hours. Bridget knew all the players, knew her baseball statistics, and listened to all of the games on her old radio. Shlomo knew almost as much. But, in those days, money was tight, and Bridget had never been able to see the Yankees live at Yankee Stadium in the Bronx. When Shlomo got two free tickets from a grateful customer who drove all the way from Brooklyn every week for his delicious kosher dills, Shlomo asked the dainty, young Irish lass to accompany him to the game. She, of course, could not tell her parents the truth, so she lied and told them she was going to novena at Saint Marsha of the Swollen Kidney in the Bronx. Together, they took a bus to New York City then the subway to the stadium on that fateful day. That game ended with a bases-loaded, walk-off grand slam by Joe DiMaggio, and the Yankees came from behind and won in the last second. As the crowd went wild, Shlomo became overwhelmed with emotion, got on his knees, and proposed to Bridget, using a ring from a Cracker Jack box. In the excitement and confusion, Bridget thoughtlessly said, 'Yes,' and, because she was an Irish Catholic and knew it was a mortal sin not to keep your word, they were later married in secret at city hall."

Cardinal Chianti was old school. "Doesn't it say somewhere in our church teachings that if the person you give your word to is a Jew, you can cross your fingers behind your back and it doesn't count?"

Cardinal Reunite ignored him and went on. "They were married in secret, and Bridget went home to her family and never mentioned a thing. Once a week, she would meet with Shlomo in his small room over the pickle store to fulfill her wifely duties. Eventually, her family got suspicious, because she smelled of pickles all the time. You can imagine what happened the first time she brought Shlomo home to meet her drunken Irish brothers, all of whom were cops in Newark, Maplewood, and Irvington. It was not pretty. The two eventually got a small apartment nearby and started living together. Shlomo worked in the pickle store, and Bridget got a job as a chambermaid at some of the better hotels in New York. She would take the bus into the city and come back late to New Jersey. Some years later, God saw fit to bless this couple with new life. Although, when I tell you more about Michelangelo Schwartz, you may think God had little to do with it."

Cardinal Chianti was wobbling on his cane. "He doesn't sound like such a bad fellow."

Reunite frowned. "Oh, yeah? Well, let us now look at the man to whom we are going to entrust the future of our church. After he got his PhD, he became an English literature professor, and you know what they are like!"

At this point, the elderly Chianti just started shouting random things at the top of his lungs. "Yes, literature professors teach sinful and obscene works, like Joyce's *Ulysses*, the sinful *Tale of Two Cities*, and the pornographic *Little Prince*! Oh, for the days when Anthony Comstock was postmaster general of the United States and would not allow any of these books into his country! All these books should be burned and their authors turned over to the Holy Inquisition!"

Cardinal Reunite released a deep sigh and moved on. Cardinal Chianti had been acting out like this since the sixties. And you can't really put a muzzle on a cardinal. Although in the old days, the Borgia popes sometimes did, literally. Cardinal Reunite wondered, where have all the good times gone? Then, he returned to his reading of the file.

"Michelangelo Schwartz has been fired from every college that hired him. The charges you ask, my dear brothers? He has been charged with sleeping with female co-eds, atheism, showing up for his eight o'clock Monday-morning class on Tuesday afternoon, drinking during his office hours (the few times he actually showed up for them), violation of the campus chapel, and unauthorized nocturnal visits to the convent."

Several of the elderly cardinals lowered their eyes and blessed themselves by making the sign of the cross when they heard this, but the good cardinal was just getting going.

"He questioned the infallibility of the Holy Mother Church when he taught in Catholic schools and raised doubts about the phrase 'chosen people' during a lecture at B'nai B'rith. He has argued in his career, if you can call it that, against African American studies, women's studies, and Chicano studies. He once wrote that the 'whole discipline of political science is certainly political, but it has nothing to do with science.' In short, he is persona non grata, not only in many of the universities in his home country of America but all over the world. He has even written some unflattering articles about the Vatican, but that is the least of our worries. My fellow cardinals, this man is such a menace that our own intelligence organization, Opus Dei, as well as the Knights of Columbus, Disney, the Mafia, and the Jesuits have been keeping an eye on him for years."

Cardinal Chianti shouted out again, "Sounds like a normal professor to me!"

Cardinal Sin, who oversaw the Catholics in the Philippines, stood with a question: "Cardinal Reunite, I am new to this secret conclave and am unfamiliar with some of its traditions and methods. This file seems very large, and you know a lot. Do you have files this size on all Catholics?"

"Cardinal Sin, we have files this size only on the most interesting Catholics. While we have been doing this for thousands of years, our intelligence work heated up in the 1950s, when we found out that the Rat Pack had admitted Sammy Davis Jr., whom we mistakenly believed was, at that time, a Freemason committed to satanic practices. What people don't know is that we are like the Mormons or Scientologists. We like to keep an eye on our flock. To do so, we have developed ways of making sure they don't go astray. We are masters of public relations. In the 1950s, we drew upon the Madison Avenue ad agencies to clean up our past and manage our image. Remember, Don Draper was a man of God! So we are like these modern cults; only we are older, have better artwork in our churches, and have a more respectable exterior.

"You may have heard that Protestants, in the old days, were fearful that the pope wanted to rule their country. In order to make them convert, so the Mother Church could manipulate their politics, we used whatever means necessary to force them to convert. The rack, the wheel, the thumbscrew, and the red-hot poker were all used for the virtuous purpose of expanding the influence of the Holy Mother Church. Well, let's tell the truth, and, my brothers, let's be honest. They were right. In the old days, those were popes!"

The pope coughed to show his displeasure, and Reunite blushed.

"Forgive me, Your Eminence. I did not mean to offend. But, to answer Cardinal Sin's question, we have many files. We have relations with and share information with the KGB, CIA, NSA, MI6, and the Mossad."

Cardinal Sin was amazed. "The Vatican has a working relationship with the Mossad, the Israeli intelligence agency?"

Reunite smiled with the pride of one who knows. "Yes, we have worked with the Mossad for years. It is true that the Holy Mother Church has spread hatred of the Jews for centuries, but now we both hate the Muslims. You know the old chestnut: 'The enemy of my enemy...'"

Cardinal Sin had one more question. "As I said, my brother, I thought I had been briefed about all of our front organizations, but I did not know about Disney. Do you mean Walt Disney?"

Reunite smiled. "Yes, Cardinal Sin, Disney is one of ours. You know we all love the wholesome entertainment, the commitment to goodness, and good, old-fashioned family values. I know every once in a *while* former Disney child stars, like Britney Spears and Miley Cyrus, get a screw loose and go over the deep end, but, mostly, they are on our wavelength. What you might not know is that we have worked with Disney over the years and had our seal of approval on many of his productions. Remember that scene in *Bambi* where his mother gets blown away? That was our idea. How about that scene in *Old Yeller* where the twelve-year-old boy has to shoot the family dog that he raised from a puppy? That was our idea again. Do you remember when they tortured Dumbo, the baby elephant, for a full twenty minutes in the film after he witnessed the death of his mother? Our idea yet again!

"These films were meant to traumatize children, and, in their terror and confusion, we hoped they might seek refuge in the church and would turn away from the sinful and painful world and turn toward heaven. When you think of how disturbing those images are to children, you will understand how they took comfort in the idea of heaven, where Bambi's mother, Old Yeller, and Dumbo's mom would be reunited. Walt Disney showed children the fear of God, no doubt about it. The films of Disney showed children how to be good. What do they have today? We have directors like Francis Ford Coppola, Brian De Palma, Martin Scorsese, and Quentin Tarantino! And I would add, all four are Catholics. I've always wondered why so many Italian Americans are so obsessed with violence and crime. Shame!"

Cardinal Chianti yelled out again, "De Palma? I quite liked *Scarface*. Do you remember when he takes out that huge gun with the grenade launcher on the front and says, 'Say hello to my little friend'?"

After Chianti imitated the motion of spraying the cardinals with bullets, using his cane while making a machine-gun sound, he collapsed back into his seat and immediately started snoring.

Cardinal Sin ignored Chianti and posed another question. "Cardinal Reunite, are you sure Disney was one of ours? I have read somewhere on Google that Disney was in league with the Illuminati and was called the Dark Prince of Hollywood. They have gay-pride parades at Disneyland. If you look at the Disney signature, some say you can clearly see the number 666 in it. He has cartoons where Mickey Mouse, while in a magician's costume, conjures up the devil. In the cartoon *Aladdin*, the title character says plainly, 'Teenagers, take off your clothes.' In the *Lion King*, the letters *S E X* appear in the stars as a subliminal message.

"Drugs are very big in the Philippines, where I come from. In Manila, cocaine is known by many names, but the most common is 'Snow White.' You snort Snow White, and, pretty soon, you get sleepy, grumpy, dopey, and bashful, and then you end up at the doc. Just don't get sneezy when the Snow White is in front of you. Remember when Woody Allen blew cocaine all over the room in the movie *Annie Hall*? Think about the seven dwarves going to work in the diamond mines. Could that be a reference to crack rocks? Note the number seven, like the seven deadly sins. And what would we say about a young girl living alone with seven dwarves, who are known in mythology for their lusty, Pan-like natures? What is the so-called medicine that Mary Poppins feeds the children before they pop into paintings and start hallucinating? Do you recall the song lyrics 'a spoonful of sugar makes the medicine go down'? What is that fairy dust Peter Pan uses to help himself fly? Angel dust? Why does Alice eat the mushroom that makes her go into Wonderland? Finally, I have seen that Donald Duck does not wear pants, and I have read that Goofy is gay."

The pontiff rose to his feet. He often wondered how they had dominated the world for so many of the past centuries when most of his brothers had the same IQ as a bag of rocks. He clearly had heard enough from Cardinal Reunite. The pope spoke in a voice that wavered between conviction and anger.

"The vice-president of the National Rifle Association in the United States, Wayne LaPierre, once said that 'the only thing that stops a bad guy with a gun is a good guy with a gun.' You may not know it, but Brother Wayne, of French descent, is a good Catholic and a high-ranking officer of the Knights of Columbus. Now, while I have rejected his suggestion that the Knights of Columbus carry semiautomatic weapons in church on high holy days, I take his wisdom as guidance in this particular case. Using the argument from an analogy developed by Aristotle and perfected by Saint Thomas Aquinas, we can adopt Brother Wayne's principle for our use here. Thus, verily I say to you, my brothers, the only way to battle the unscrupulous and unethical people who are steeped in medieval symbols is with another unscrupulous and unethical man who is also steeped in medieval symbols. Again, my brothers, while I respect your opinions, we will go ahead as planned. Michelangelo Schwartz will help us unmask the Illuminati and bring the Holy Grail back to Saint Peter's, where it belongs."

With that, the pontiff collapsed onto his throne and sighed. The cardinals all nodded in agreement. He held out his hand as a young priest nervously handed him another glass of wine. The pontiff smiled. He thought, it is good to be the pope.

Cardinal Reunite stood again. "Your Holiness, are you absolutely sure it calls for Michelangelo Schwartz? That is a very common last name."

The pope had thought the argument was over, and he was getting frustrated. "It is he and only he. We have checked and double-checked. We cannot hesitate, because time is too short. Only he can decipher this poem. I am not sure why he is the one, but that is what the document indicates."

Cardinal Reunite was insistent. "But we have cryptographers, symbologists, astrologers, and historians of ideas. What does Schwartz know that they don't?"

The pope was at the end of his patience. "I am not sure of the combination of skills that are unique to him. But here is what we think. There is something about him that will allow him, and him alone, to find the Holy Grail and answer questions that have been asked for ages. We must find the Holy Grail, and the key, the only key, is Michelangelo Schwartz. We are in a race here, and there is no time to waste. My brothers, sometimes an imperfect messenger is called for, and no one is more imperfect than Professor Michelangelo Schwartz." The pope nodded to indicate the argument was over.

Cardinal Reunite stood up and walked to the back of the Sistine Chapel. He took out one of the disposable phones that the Vatican purchased by the case from Wal-Mart. That was how powerful and far-reaching the Vatican actually was—they actually knew how to get the Wal-Mart extra discount. He was only going to use that phone one time; then he would take out the SIM card and crush it, hoping it could not be tracked. He dialed a number known only to the most powerful in the church. It was a number in New York that was listed in the phone book as "The Anti-Catholic League of Brooklyn," which was, in reality, a clandestine Jesuit operation directed by the Roman Curia.

Faraway, in a run-down brownstone on Twelfth Street in Brighton Beach, Brooklyn, New York, a cell phone was blaring to the ring tone of "In-A-Gadda-Da-Vida."

2

We visit the Anti-Catholic League of Brooklyn, where we meet William Callahan, formerly known as Sister Bill, previously the mother superior of the Sisters of Little Mercy, and Biff Braunschweiger, whose great-grandfather once warned him: "You don't want to see how the Bratwurst King of the Midwest makes the sausage." We learn why you should not marry a Russian supermodel and how New Jersey has come to be called the "Garden State."

A run-down brownstone, Brighton Beach, Brooklyn, New York

The Anti-Catholic League of Brooklyn was the perfect cover for what the Vatican referred to as its "wet work" in America. It was located in Brighton Beach, which was so full of Russian immigrants it had the nickname of "Little Odessa." The Russian men of the neighborhood were so busy manufacturing fake Rolexes, fake Levis, and fake Coach handbags that they paid no attention to the Anti-Catholic League of Brooklyn. The Russian women all looked like supermodels, were often over six feet tall, were outfitted in black miniskirts, and were fluent in four languages. The typical "Ultra-Natasha," as they were known in Little Odessa, had a PhD in physics, theoretical mathematics, or aeronautical engineering (on rare occasions, they had all three degrees) from Moscow State University; was a chess grand master; was proficient in all sixty-four positions of *The Kama Sutra*; and was busy looking for a rich American husband. Five years after an Ultra-Natasha landed and married that rich American husband, the groom often found himself broke, exhausted, and alone and knew that after the divorce, when the Russian mob had cleaned him out, he would never have "Russian gymnastic sex" again for the rest of his life. He may love again, but he would never have what the Ultra-Natashas promised, the fabled "Chernobyl Orgasm." And that was the worst part.

Brighton Beach was far enough away from Manhattan to be a little run-down but still have affordable rents. The outer boroughs of New York City were full of frustrated and angry people. Wouldn't you be angry if there was no Krispy Kreme store in your borough? Many were mad because they wished they were living in Manhattan with a view of Central Park East and were married to either a Russian mobster or a Russian supermodel. They would place the blame for this sad situation on anyone else.

The most unimaginative of these neglected, depressed people blamed their loving mothers and fathers, who had worked themselves to the bone for their children, whom these losers now saw as responsible for the failures they had become. "Mommy didn't love me," or "Dad hit me," or "Big Brother bullied me, and that is why I am on the public dole today." It was all sad, very sad.

The many Irish, Poles, and Italians that went to Catholic schools had another class of villains on whom they could blame their failed lives. The nuns, brothers, and priests who taught generations of children were now blamed for everything that went wrong as those children grew into unhappy adults. It was natural for Catholics, even good practicing Catholics, to hate and despise the church while never missing mass on Sunday. This combination of anger, disappointment, and total loyalty to Rome always made Catholics a little questionable to the Bible-clutching Protestants. So the Anti-Catholic League of Brooklyn did not attract an ounce of attention, even though it was right down the street from the Little Church of Saint Mary Magdalene.

The Anti-Catholic League of Brooklyn had exactly two employees—Biff Braunschweiger and William Callahan, neither of whom were who they appeared to be. Biff Braunschweiger was in his late fifties, had long, flowing white hair, and an aristocratic demeanor. Raised in one the wealthiest families in Saint Louis, he was heir to a fortune built by his great-grandfather, the Bratwurst King of the Midwest. His great-grandfather was a ruthless tycoon, and he never discussed his dark business with the family. As he used to say, "Believe me, kids. You don't want to see how the Bratwurst King of the Midwest makes the sausage."

Two major competitors had sold bratwurst in Saint Louis at the beginning of his great-grandfather's career. Both disappeared within six months of each other and were never found. The only thing that aroused people's suspicions was a two-week period during which the Bratwurst King's sausage tasted funny, no matter how much mustard you used.

Over generations, wealth allowed families to appear refined, and it covered up the sins of the ruthless bastards who first accumulated that wealth. The same guys that busted the heads of union organizers now had hospital wings and college buildings named after them. Later generations of the robber barons built libraries, orphanages, and fed the hungry. And believe me, these were not the businesses Biff's great-gramps was in when he was "making the donuts," so to speak.

Wealth and privilege had certainly made Biff refined. He knew his opera, his antiques, and his art. He was well traveled, witty, and urbane in conversation. At an early age, he had joined the Jesuits, but he'd supposedly quit, allegedly over disagreements about theology. He then went on to found the Anti-Catholic League of Brooklyn. What no one knew was that Biff was not the ex-Jesuit, angry ex-Catholic he pretended to be. In reality, he was the Vatican's go-to guy in Brooklyn. His refined dress—ascot, no white shoes after Labor Day, straw hats, and designer Gucci sunglasses—hid the fact that, in his private life, he was still a Jesuit who would do whatever was needed, anything and everything, for the Mother Church. In this run-down section of Brooklyn, none of his down-on-their-luck neighbors knew that Biff was, in his spare time, a scholar of church history, iconography, and ritual.

His coworker, William Callahan, had an even more twisted and secret past. Just a few short years ago, he was Sister Bill, dean of discipline and a physical-education teacher at Saint Christopher College for Catholic Women in Cleveland, Ohio. She had been a mother superior for her order, the Sisters of Little Mercy. William had the operation and taken the hormones necessary to become the man that God had always intended him to be. He was a little overweight, short, and stocky, with brown eyes and hair and a thick moustache. He frequently sported a three-day growth on his chin. But he looked younger than his seventy-one years. William was not a stylish or spiffy dresser. He usually wore jeans with a sport coat over an unbuttoned Oxford shirt. Sometimes, his undershirt would stick out in places it should not.

William Callahan, driven by guilt, had combined an odd loyalty to the Catholic Church with a deep resentment of it. He displayed a ruthlessness exhibited in a few serial killers and some of the most savage dictators in the third world. Unlike the refined and cultured Biff Braunschweiger, William Callahan was a street fighter raised on the streets of South Chicago, where when a bully asked for your lunch money, the only answer was a Lone Ranger metal lunch box to the face. And that was among the girls.

William Callahan and Biff Braunschweiger did share a love of good Scotch (their agreed-upon favorite was a thirty-five-year-old Glenlivet) and cigars—Cuban, of course.

The Anti-Catholic League of Brooklyn was designed to not attract attention. The first floor of the old brownstone was furnished with bad office furniture bought from Goodwill. There were signs that read "No pope here!" and "Justice for Altar Boys," and "Catholics for Contraception." Of course, this was all a ruse. A locked door separated the first floor from the rest of the town house, which was much more upscale, in keeping with the taste of Biff Braunschweiger.

The upper floors of the town house were closed to the public. Up there, the rooms were lavishly decorated; a few Impressionist originals, on loan from the Vatican Museum, even graced the walls. The Vatican had dozens of Van Goghs, Caravaggios, and Rembrandts, which hadn't been viewed for years, lying around, covered with dust, in the basement. So it was always ready to loan a few here and there. The second floor of the town house was decorated with Louis XIV original furniture, and, by original, we mean actually owned and rubbed threadbare by Louis XIV's copious bottom at Versailles. A table and mismatched chairs were scattered in the middle of the heavily mirrored room. Braunschweiger had the mirrors placed opposite each other so that in each reflection was the reflection of a reflection and so on to eternity. For him, it was a reminder that his true home was in eternity, not in Brooklyn. Thank God.

In the living room, the sound of "In-A-Gadda-Da-Vida" could be heard with the bass thumping. Biff Braunschweiger opened his cell phone and listened obediently. William Callahan sat smoking a huge Montecristo, waiting for the call to be over. Biff was the brains of the operation, and William was the brawn. They both knew their roles and got along just fine.

The call lasted for well over an hour. When Biff hung up the phone, he poured two glasses of Scotch into cut-crystal glasses and handed one to William as he settled down across from Biff in a red velvet chair.

"William, I have some good news and some bad news."

William took his first drink of Scotch before he answered. It was smoky and smooth, with a hint of the salt air that made the island malts distinctive.

"OK. I'll bite. What's the good news?"

Biff stood up, drink in hand, and began pacing with excitement as he talked. Biff did not converse so much as he lectured. "What we have prepared for and talked about all these years has come to pass. Our superiors in Rome are going after the Illuminati and hope to find and return the Holy Grail, that source of power and world control, back to its rightful home in the Vatican. Here is the good news. It turns out that the trail starts here. William, you and I are going to be the point men, so to speak."

William Callahan took a long sip of his Scotch and twirled the ends of his thick brown moustache. "The trail starts here in America?"

Biff smiled. "Better than that. It starts not just in America but right down the road in Jersey."

William laughed and sat up. "New Jersey! So how ironic is that? Who would have guessed that the quest for the Holy Grail would begin in New Jersey? You know that the most traveled way from Jersey into New York is by the Holland and Lincoln Tunnels that go under the Hudson. And that is where the old joke comes from."

Biff had heard the joke a thousand times but figured he would go ahead and ask. Sister Bill had become a true man. And true men, real men, still found the jokes they'd first heard in the third grade to be hilarious.

"OK. What joke?"

"They say for New Yorkers, there is good news and bad news. The good news is that there is light at the end of the tunnel, and the bad news is it's New Jersey."

William always laughed at his own jokes, but he wasn't done. "I have a million New Jersey jokes. There is something funny about New Jersey. Don't you find it funny that some states make you laugh and others not so much? For example, how often do you hear jokes about Iowa or Missouri? Almost never! But Texas, West Virginia, and New Jersey are rich fields to be mined and all for different reasons, of course. Let me do a few more. Why don't gays live in New Jersey?"

Biff sipped his Scotch and played along. "I don't know, William. Why don't gays live in New Jersey?"

"Because they have taste! OK. Why is New Jersey called the Garden State?"

"Please do tell, William. Why is New Jersey called the Garden State?"

"Because the Oil, Petroleum, Nuclear, Landfill, & Toxic Waste State didn't fit on a license plate!"

Biff was feeling the Scotch, and he was enjoying himself, so he let William continue.

"How about this one, Biff? What is the only thing that grows in Newark?"

"Do tell, William. What is the only thing that grows in Newark?"

"The crime rate! Here's another good one! Why does California have the most lawyers and New Jersey the most toxic-waste dumps?"

"I don't know, William. Why does California have the most lawyers and New Jersey the most toxic-waste dumps?"

William smiled. "Because New Jersey got first pick."

Biff began to get itchy. He wanted to get back to the business at hand. "We have to get serious. We are about to embark upon the most important quest in the history of mankind. We need to return the world to balance, and you are making New Jersey jokes!"

William nodded in contrition as Biff went on. And William knew Biff always went on and on and on. Even on the fifteenth telling of a tale, he never omitted a single detail.

"This is the mission for which we have trained our whole lives, and we must be absolutely clear about our goal. We need to restore the balance. We have said many times that the world was a moral and good place for most of human history, with a few exceptions, like Sodom and Gomorrah and the second Bush administration."

William was enjoying his Scotch, swooshing it back and forth through the gaps in his teeth. Its beauty lingered after he swallowed. He listened as Biff went on. And on.

"The battle between the Illuminati and the Holy Mother Church is ancient and ongoing. We simply cannot coexist. When Paul arrived in Rome, he encountered Simon Magnus, sometimes called Simon the Sorcerer. It was said that Simon could strike people dead with a wave of his hand. Simon also claimed he could fly over the city of Rome, which was only useful during peak rush hours. Paul defeated Simon, and, since that time, the struggle between the forces of good and evil has gotten more and more vicious.

"People think the Medici and Borgia popes were wicked and sinful. There are those Protestant historians who accuse those popes of nepotism, just because they had a few nephews who needed jobs as cardinals. But those popes fought against evil and destructive forces, such as Leonardo da Vinci and Galileo—"

William interrupted. "You always say Da Vinci and Galileo were destructive, but that is not how they are remembered by most people. They are looked upon as heroes, as martyrs for the advancement of science."

"I am not interested in what most people remember. What I remember are the words of that great Irish writer Charles Halpine: 'The masses are asses.' Most people think that Da Vinci and Galileo were in the first rank of the good guys advancing science and reason. In reality, they were selfish bastards. Hey, as long as people believed that the earth was flat and the sun went around us, they were fat and happy. Well, maybe the peasants in those days were not quite so fat, but they were happy. They believed everything the church said, never missed mass, and behaved themselves, so they could eventually get into heaven, and they gave the church enough money to build the Vatican. Do you think we would have all this marble and gold and these jewels if people had been watching *Three's Company* or *Married...with Children* every day? No! I say bring back the Inquisition! Bring back the Holy Roman Empire! Bring back the thumbscrew, the spiked boot, and iron maiden, but please, not the heavy metal band. Those were the days! Those peasants, uh, that is impoverished souls, believed every word we said and never thought for themselves. They would have been perfect viewers of Fox News!

"But, no! Science and logic made people doubt the wisdom of the Holy Mother Church. Did you know there was a time when every other Catholic household in America had a personally autographed picture of the pope, for which they had forked out fifty bucks? Plus, think of all of those Vatican rosaries, from the sweatshops of Haiti and Mexico, with the pope's special blessing for two bucks each. It was a short walk from the great thinkers of the Enlightenment to Madonna squirming around on the floor in her bra and panties, singing 'Like a Prayer.' The battle between the forces of faith and morality on the one hand and science and immorality on the other has been the greatest source of strife in our world ever since time began. On our side, we have the Holy Mother Church, and on the other side, we have MTV, *Jackass*, *Seinfeld*, and Mel Brooks, all laughing their asses off as the world spins out of control—"

William interrupted. "You say science and progress are not always good things. I pray to our Madonna, but you have to admit it, the new Madonna is not bad."

Biff was getting worked up. William was often a little slow on the uptake, and Biff wanted to get this parade on the road. "Yes. In the Renaissance, it was the so-called men of science that mesmerized the people and drew them away from the Mother Church. It was Galileo who showed us that the universe was not sacred but a random rolling of stars. Now reruns of *The Three Stooges* and *Benny Hill* show us that there is no sense or order in the universe. It is a short walk from the publication of Galileo's famous book *The Starry Messenger* to *The Love Boat*.

Finally, William, in my opinion, Western civilization hit rock bottom with the appearance of Andrew Dice Clay. God! Did you see his movie *The Adventures of Ford Fairlane*? I tell you, it has gone too far! It has gone much too far. The balance must be restored.

"These so-called men of reason were the enemies of our basic faith, plain and simple. As the Middle Ages ended, an ancient enemy, the Illuminati, used the new science and took a more active role than we had ever thought appropriate for ourselves. Many of us are still unaware that the most famous and influential people in history held the role of Supreme Ascendant Illuminated Master of the Illuminati. Those who held this title include Isaac Newton, Washington, Jefferson, Victor Hugo, Rasputin, and P. T. Barnum. Remember when Barnum said, 'Never give a sucker an even break,' and 'There is a sucker born every minute'? Of course, he was right! But why tell the world? Following the advice of P. T. Barnum, the Illuminati invented the stock market and, through that sham, bankrupted every hardworking person in the world and all of our loyal donors. Instead of investing in building a new church so that their wicked sins can be forgiven by buying their way into heaven, people now put their cash into Apple, GM, gold futures, and pork bellies. We fought science and progress with everything we had. In the old days, the Mother Church was strong. With our own intellectual thinkers, from Thomas Aquinas to John Cardinal Newman, we were able to keep the world close to faith and loyal to our Holy Father. Threats regarding the hereafter and promises that only we could forgive sins made our flock comply with every single one of our ideas. But then it happened—February 6, 1920!"

"Biff, you have gone on about the date February 6, 1920, for years. But, surely, we can say that many things were eroding long before that?"

William took a puff of his Montecristo while Biff answered. "We are clear about what this means for the church. An army of scholars from all of the great Catholic universities has worked on this. The archives make it clear. Catholic political scientists, Vatican astronomers, our astrologers, and our greatest minds have looked at that date and what happened. They are all in agreement that 1920 was the year that the twin tragedies happened on the exact same day. That was the day that we lost track of the Supreme Ascendant Illuminated Master of the Illuminati, and it was on that very same day that the Holy Grail disappeared from the Vatican Museum."

Biff thought for a minute while he twirled the ice in his glass. He resumed his lecture. "Once those two events occurred, things moved fast. The church fathers and elders have gone over every historical event, every astrological sign, every earthly and celestial event, but there is still controversy about exactly what happened and what it means. Did I ever mention that at midnight on January 16 in 1920, shortly before the Grail was stolen, the Volstead act went into effect, which began Prohibition in America? Prohibition, the women's movement, and the temperance movement were all backed by those stuck-up Protestants who thought outlawing booze would make America more moral and upright. It had the exact opposite effect. It only made things worse. You see, we Catholics didn't want to outlaw booze. We know that Jesus's first miracle was changing water into wine."

William smiled. "Yes, and good wine, too! You priests start every day with mass, and what do you do at mass? You drink wine. And some of you drink plenty of it. Hey! That is one perk of being a priest—you have to drink as part of your job description."

Biff always fumed at priest-hating nuns and ex-nuns. He continued his lecture—he always lectured. "We Catholics were never in favor of Prohibition, but those damn Bible-thumping Baptists, those holier-than-thou jerks, they had to do it. No more booze. They assumed a sober America would be a moral America. They imagined the formerly drunken American male would return to his family, kiss his wife on the cheek, and sit down in a jacket and tie with his pipe and *The Saturday Evening Post*, and never wander again. Boy, did they call that one wrong! With Prohibition came the Jazz Age, organized crime, bootlegged liquor, the tommy gun, flappers, *The Great Gatsby*, widespread atheism, and skepticism about the Holy Mother Church. When Americans sobered up, they realized they weren't as great as they had thought."

Biff stopped for a sip of Scotch and then went on. "Before Prohibition, everyone believed in 'American Exceptionalism.' But that was just a booze-fueled illusion kept afloat by gallons of colonial whiskey. Just look at our history—not the one you learned in school but our real history. The Founding Fathers pounded down more booze than those guys in the movie *The Hangover*. Why do you think George Washington's teeth fell out? Jefferson was on the sauce, because he wrote the line 'all men are created equal' while at the same time he was raping his female slaves. Talk about a hypocrite! They say he had to have his slave shave him, because he was too ashamed to look in the mirror to do it himself.

"Do you know why they called them the Founding Fathers? Because every single one of those drunken, horny slave owners had about five hundred offspring each. Every night, it was about six glasses of cherry brandy, a few mugs of whiskey and sodas, and then it was off to the slave quarters to play 'hide the salami' with the wives of the field hands. What became of the genes of the Founding Fathers? They say George Washington was sterile, but they lie! He had plenty of descendants. They walk among us today. How about Denzel Washington, Booker T. Washington, George Hamilton, and who do you think was the great-great-grandfather of George Jefferson? People talk about the Founding Fathers, but, in reality, nobody really cares about them anymore. Forget about John Adams and John Quincy Adams. The only Adams that Americans care about today is Sam Adams's Boston Lager. Oh, and don't forget William Jefferson Clinton. How those genes got from the aristocratic plantations of Virginia to Hope, Arkansas, is another sad and twisted tale. Read what the Founding Fathers really thought about religion. Half of them were Masons, and none of them ever attended church. So don't lecture me about the Founding Fathers. But it didn't stop with them."

Biff was turning a little red and spitting as he spoke. William just sat there, listening. He had heard it all before, a dozen times, but he feigned interest. It was like listening to that drunken uncle who, at Thanksgiving, launches into a "Why America is no longer great" speech year after year.

"Let's move on in history to Andrew Jackson. He had fifty-two gallons of Tennessee whiskey at his inauguration, for anyone who wanted a toot, and then he drunkenly rode a horse through the White House. Ulysses S. Grant, president of the United States, wasn't sober for one single day in his adult life. So, when people talk about the 'wisdom of the Founding Fathers,' what they don't know is that those drunken sots, whose portraits are on our coins and bills, were just front men for the Illuminati and their Masonic foot soldiers. The Catholic Church was always suspicious about the American Revolution. You may not know it, but the fat, drunken, cleric-hating-atheist Ben Franklin actually was the inventor of flipping the bird."

William smiled. "In Chicago, where I come from, we call it 'giving them the finger.'"

"Yes, it was his response to John Hancock when Hancock accused Franklin of schtupping Hancock's wife while he was away, founding our great country. You won't read that in *Poor Richard's Almanac*! Do you know the institution called the Franklin Mint in Philadelphia? That is named after a candy that old Ben used to carry in his pocket to hide the liquor on his breath whenever he went into a breakfast meeting. I tell you the only moral man in the whole bunch was Benedict Arnold. But who am I to say?"

William finished his Scotch and got up to pour another. "Biff, do you really believe that all the presidents are members of the Illuminati?"

Biff sat back in his chair. "Brilliant and skilled politicians, like George W. Bush and Jimmy Carter, are actual voting members of the Illuminati. They are masters at hiding their light from the masses. But the stupid ones, like Abraham Lincoln and Franklin Roosevelt, just follow orders without knowing too much."

William nodded, as he had heard this story many times before. But Biff was not done.

"After the immorality of the 1920s, things continued to get worse. Along came the beatniks, Bill Haley and the Comets, the hippies, free love, William Shatner's singing career, *Rocky I* through *XXII*, the Singing Nun, anarchism, Ringo Starr, and public television, and chaos followed in their wake. There were messages from the Illuminati about how this was being done, but the world either could not interpret these messages or did not believe them."

"Biff, OK. Let's agree that starting sometime around 1920, the world began going to hell, but can you blame it all on the Grail and the Illuminati? Could it be that the world just changed?"

Biff was getting aggravated. "The Holy Mother Church is a pure and ancient institution. But it has succeeded in becoming an ancient institution because it, sometimes, knows the score, so to speak. We had undercover agents who penetrated deep into the Illuminati, and those double agents stayed undetected for centuries. In 1919–1920, two things happened that changed everything. First, in what then looked like a series of coincidences, three Supreme Ascendant Illuminated Masters of the Illuminati died in rapid succession. Pierre-Auguste Renoir, Theodore Roosevelt, and Henry John Heinz. Each, for a short time, held the position of Supreme Ascendant Illuminated Master of the Illuminati, and all passed away within a very short time span."

William put down his glass and squinted. "Henry John Heinz? You never mentioned him before."

"Yes, the ketchup mogul of Pittsburgh. The Illuminati have hidden themselves well. If you read any biographies of Heinz they claimed he died of pneumonia on another date. But that is just to hide what really happened. I have heard from a good source that on that fateful day, February 6, 1920, the same explosion, in the ketchup factory at the confluence of the Ohio and Monongahela Rivers that killed Heinz also killed our two undercover brothers in the Illuminati. So we lost our ear to the wall. This was thought to be a simple accident. But on that same day, at that exact same time, it was noticed by the head curator in the Vatican Museum that our security had been breached, and one single item was missing from inside a double safe in the heart of the museum. The Holy Grail was gone and with it the grace of God and his protection for the Mother Church.

"From 1920 until today, we have not known the identities of any of the new Supreme Ascendant Illuminated Masters of the Illuminati or where the Grail is hidden. We need to know who took over the leadership of the Illuminati in 1920, so we can follow the trail. Each Grand Master should help us determine the identity of the next. If we are able to follow that trail, the hiding place of the Holy Grail will be obvious. It is the

Grail that gives the Illuminati power and protection. But a new clue has come to light that may lead us to retrieve this treasure and restore the church to its former glory."

"What is this new clue?"

"William, I have learned today from Rome that a poem has come to light. Our brothers high up in the Vatican believe this poem is from a dissident faction inside the highest ranks of the Illuminati. This dissident faction senses that things have gone too far in the wrong direction for us. With so much stupidity, wickedness, and scandal, they fear that it will not be good for business, and the Illuminati are all about controlling world finances. The Illuminati need business to move along to fund their illicit activities. They have been behind some of the biggest business scandals ever, such as the Pet Rock, the Hula-Hoop, Chia Pets, and Wal-Mart."

"Wal-Mart?"

"William, don't you see it? The little smiley faces and the brain-dead zombies that repeat 'Welcome to Wal-Mart' over and over again without any enthusiasm in a kind of hypnotic trance? In terms of evil influence, it ranks up there with Johnson & Johnson and Apple. Did you know that Wal-Mart plants RFID chips in many of their products so that they can track where they go and who has them? Everyone knows Wal-Mart is making a ghost town of small-town America and replacing good jobs and family owned businesses that are generations old with low-wage, no-benefits jobs. The employees need food stamps to get a meal at the end of the workweek.

"But here is something you may not know. When Wal-Mart opened their 666th store in the United States, they held a black mass in Bentonville, Arkansas, where it was reported that a human sacrifice was required. Some say it was an elderly greeter from their Nashville store. She was boiled in oil while being forced to yell, 'Welcome to Wal-Mart.' You recall the Biblical line from Revelations? 'He also forced everyone, small and great, rich and poor, free and slave, to receive a mark on his right hand or on his forehead so that no one could buy or sell unless he had the mark, which is the name of the beast or the number of his name. This calls for wisdom. If anyone has insight, let him calculate the number of the beast, for it is man's number. His number is 666.'"

Biff Braunschweiger was sweating as he continued. "Do you remember the five-pointed star in between the *Wal* and the *Mart*? Did it ever occur to you that it was the pentagram, the symbol of Satan? Some say it was the Star of David, but to me, it meant the same thing! Sam Walton supposedly taught Sunday school and was a Bible-believing, modest businessman. Nothing could have been further from the truth. Once inside his plain-looking Arkansas home, he would dress in outfits that would make Liberace blush. He would wolf down jars of beluga caviar that cost ten thousand dollars an ounce. He once had the Rolling Stones give a private concert for him and five of his Arkansas hillbilly friends. Of course, the Stones, who are also on Satan's payroll, would never admit to this. I can just see Sam laughing when Mick began, 'Please allow me to introduce myself. I'm a man of wealth and taste.' When Sam Walton, who was a Wicca-inspired witch, died, they changed that pentagram to a radiant sun, signaling their allegiance to Ra, the sun god, and the pagan magic of ancient Egypt. That new sun symbol has six points. Yes, six, six, six! If you draw two pyramids through the midpoints of the six lines, you will get a pentagram. Beginning to make sense?

"Under the guidance of Wicca-devotee Sam, Wal-Mart proceeded to destroy the manufacturing sector of our country and replace it with sweatshops in other countries. The result? Children chained and beaten just to get more Ralph Lauren jeans produced in each fourteen-hour shift. They are even prevented from having bathroom breaks. Sam paid his workers almost nothing and made sure they didn't work enough hours to qualify for basic health care. Yes, Sam fulfilled his purpose."

William was not convinced. "If there were an Illuminati, why would they be so obvious?"

Biff was getting more and more agitated. "Obvious! I will tell you about obvious. They are throwing it in our faces! There was once an entertainment company known as the World Wrestling Federation or WWF. They were followed by millions of Americans. A group of unsanctioned wrestlers arose to take over the federation. What was the name of this tag team? The New World Order! I mean, talk about bold! And, if you notice, the New World Order group always gives the hang-ten sign, where the pinkie and index finger are extended but the rest of the hand is in a fist. But did you also know that is the sign of the evil eye? In Italian, it is called the *malocchio*. The Spanish call it *mal de ojo*, and, in German, it is called *böser blick*. What most people do not know is that Saint Bernard of Clairvaux, founder of both the Cistercian Fathers and the Knights Templar, called it the *signum diaboli* or 'sign of the devil.' So we have the New World Order showing us the sign of Satan, and blue-collar workers and their children all over America tune in, cheer, and approve. President Obama makes this sign all the time."

William objected. "He is not making the sign of Satan. President Obama was born in Hawaii, and that sign is the *shaka*, which is the Hawaiian greeting, hang ten, and a kind of cool sign. It's not Satan; it's surfing."

Biff smiled and continued. "Hey! Only the most rabid, left-wing Democrats believe Obama was born in Hawaii. On the day he was born in the jungles of Kenya, a council of voodoo priests, Communists, Muslims, Democrats, feminazis, neighborhood organizers, and serial killers had to decide what state they would use for his fake birth certificate, so he could run for president forty-seven years later. They recognized his potential early—I mean within about fifteen minutes after he was born. Listen, Obama was a man who was born with a plan, literally. They considered many states where they could plant false documents, bribe nurses, and take out fake birth notices in local newspapers. If he claimed he was born in Mississippi, he could get the southern vote. They looked at California and Texas, because they had the most electoral votes. Then, they realized two things about Hawaii that made it the best choice. First, because almost all of the doctors, hospital workers, and state workers are stoner surfers, anybody could get a birth certificate with fifty bucks and a bag of Maui Wowie. Second, if he claimed he was from Hawaii, he could give the sign of Satan every day from the White House, and nobody would be any the wiser. It was brilliant. Boy, Obama had great advance planning on the day he was born!"

William was still not convinced. "But isn't that the same sign they use for Hook 'em Horns for the University of Texas football team? Don't tell me they are in league with the Illuminati, too."

Biff had thought long and hard about these things. "Texas, the Bush family, Kinky Friedman, Lyle Lovett, big oil. Need I say more?"

Biff was now nearing the end of his argument. "There is a faction inside the Illuminati that believes restoring the balance will be good for all. It seems that they have realized the world has spun too far off course and that it might be bad for business. The Illuminati encouraged a certain amount of crime and depravity, but when they realized that the movie *Anchorman* had spawned a sequel entitled, unimaginatively enough, *Anchorman Two*, they realized something had to change. This dissident faction believes that if the Holy Grail were back in the hands of the Vatican, humanity might be returned to a state of greater morality. Then, the average person would be less inclined to cheat, thereby giving the Illuminati the upper hand all over again. The top scholars at the Vatican believe this document will lead us to unearth the Grail, restore balance with the Illuminati, and make the playing field a little more even. Our mission is to interpret that poem, go where it leads us, and put an end, once and for all, to the unrestrained reign of the Illuminati."

William put down his drink. "So much for the good news. So we have a mission. We also have a direction, and I bet we even have driving directions. Now I must ask you a simple question. What is the bad news?"

"The bad news, William, is that you will have to work with your old nemesis. While our scholars cannot untangle all of the code contained in the poem, they did come up with one name, the name of the only man who can solve the riddle—Dr. Michelangelo Schwartz."

William Callahan made the sign of the cross, closed his eyes, and muttered a quiet "Our Father." He opened his eyes and spoke. "Saints preserve us, and may God be with us. With Michelangelo Schwartz involved, we will surely need God's protection."

"I will get the car. We can go over the George Washington Bridge and take Route 80 to Route 23 in Wayne, New Jersey. I just got a text from one of our young priests there, who told us where Michelangelo Schwartz will be for the next few hours. The Vatican wants us to move quickly on this one."

William smiled. "I am afraid to ask, but where will Dr. Michelangelo Schwartz be for the next few hours?"

"Hooters of Wayne."

3

William and Biff travel to a strange and distant land, New Jersey, where they find Professor Schwartz pursuing his favorite hobbies at Hooters of Wayne. We meet Salvatore Greco, an assassin for the Vatican who does food demonstrations at Piggly Wiggly in his spare time. A bartender named Jade gets into the act, and the chapter ends with Professor Schwartz falling off his barstool.

Hooters Bar and Grill, Wayne, New Jersey

"Michelangelo Schwartz, you are a sexist pig!"

That was exactly what one of the Hooters waitresses had just shouted as she stormed away to be harassed by another drunken customer. As she tottered off on her five-inch heels, Michelangelo Schwartz looked at the menu to see what he might order to eat. He was partial to bacon double cheeseburgers with an order of cheese-and-bacon-covered French fries that had been prepared in boiling trans-fat oil that hadn't been changed in a week. But, before he ordered, he always took a look at what other unhealthy choices there were. He drooled as he read about the chili dogs, chicken wings, and potato skins filled with sour cream, bacon, and Hamburger Helper. As he read the offerings, he noticed, for the first time, that Hooters had a children's menu. A children's menu at Hooters? Yes, that was how great America was!

Happy hour was in full swing at Hooters of Wayne, and middle-aged, balding, red-blooded American males, wearing New York Giants T-shirts that didn't quite cover their hairy potbellies and baseball caps that hid their receding hairlines, were doing what they did best—making total fools of themselves in front of beautiful, slim women half their age with whom they had zero chance of getting a date. You could look, but you could not have. It was similar to Catholic Purgatory, where you could see heaven, but you couldn't get there.

The jukebox was cranked up and blasting Bob Seger's song "Katmandu," and the theme song of New Jersey—Bruce Springsteen's "Born To Run"—was next in the queue. The well-endowed Hooters waitresses were sporting tight-fitting white shirts where the *O*s of the word *Hooters* were sewed on in the right place.

Michelangelo Schwartz was seated alone at the bar, dressed like the professor he most certainly was. His lucky jacket, with the leather patches on the elbows, was threadbare, and his woolen woven tie, the kind only college professors would dare wear, had seen better days or, at least, seen a few better days before that mustard stain had taken its toll. He was in his midsixties and was not in the great physical condition on which he had once prided himself. He was dividing his attention between the well-endowed female employees and a Yankees preseason baseball game on the big-screen TV.

Schwartz never missed a Yankees game if he could help it. Since his grandfather had taken him to his first Yankees game as a six-year-old child in 1954, he'd been a dedicated fan.

He knew more about the Yankees than almost anyone he knew. He had even written a few articles on the history of the great team.

Michelangelo Schwartz was not at his most dapper that night. As a matter of fact, the term *dapper* could not have been used to describe him since *Easy Rider* had been the number-one hit at the box office. His thin black hair was almost gone, and he was sporting a stubble beard out of laziness.

For the last three martinis, a twenty-two-year-old blond Hooters bartender from Hoboken who claimed her name was Jade had entranced Michelangelo Schwartz. But he had noticed, in the four or five times he had been there before, that all the good-looking barmaids claimed to have names like Jade, Asia, and Goldie. He had been trying to convince Jade to give him her cell-phone number, an idea that four other men had proposed to her more than a dozen times already that day. She came down to his end of the bar, and Michelangelo Schwartz waved his empty glass. As she began to make him yet another martini, he snagged the opportunity to talk to her.

"Jade, do you know you look just like my fifth wife?"

Jade was taken by surprise by that statement. She put down her glass and walked over to him. "Exactly how many wives have you had?" she asked Schwartz. He smiled.

"Four."

It took her a few minutes to process that complicated exchange, so she just smiled and went back to making his martini.

Michelangelo Schwartz was not out of pickup lines yet. He had devoted much of his life to chasing women, although lately it was getting harder and harder to catch them. He looked down at his wrist. "Jade, my magic watch here tells me you are not wearing any panties."

She turned in anger. "Then your magic watch is wrong. I am wearing panties!"

Schwartz looked back at his watch. "Oh, yeah. I just realized it's running an hour fast."

Jade didn't get that joke either. As Schwartz was contemplating his next move, two men sat down on the barstools on either side of him. If you are sitting alone at a bar and suddenly the two barstools on both sides of you are taken at the exact same second, this is never a good sign, especially in New Jersey. He turned to his right and saw a well-dressed man wearing a blue blazer, a blue-and-white-striped Oxford shirt, a wide-brimmed straw hat, and a purple ascot. He was wearing cologne that had a faint trace of lilac. The man was in his fifties and was obviously a child of privilege. He held out his hand to Michelangelo Schwartz.

"Professor Schwartz, my name is Biff Braunschweiger, and I have an interesting proposition for you."

Michelangelo Schwartz was thinking of another proposition at that moment and, again, tried to get Jade's attention. "Jade, do you have the time?"

"I thought you just said you had a magic watch."

"No, I meant the time to write down my number."

Biff Braunschweiger was having a hard time getting the professor's attention. "Doctor Schwartz, how would you like to go on the adventure of a lifetime?"

Schwartz grimaced, because the adventure of a lifetime was what he was trying to set up with Jade.

"I am here to offer you an opportunity to embark upon a journey that you could only have had in a dream. You have been a scholar of Dante, medieval symbols, and secret societies. We need your expertise on one of the most interesting adventures of our millennium."

Schwartz was too drunk to agree to anything, but he was also too drunk to say no.

"Dante, yes!" Schwartz agreed. "Medieval symbols, yes! Secret societies, yes! But you forgot my real passion—the Yankees." He turned and looked up at the game. It was a pitching duel in a preseason game between the Yankees and their crosstown rivals, the Mets. The game was still zero to zero in the sixth inning. He was hanging on every pitch. It was going to be another great year for the Yankees. He turned back to Biff Braunschweiger.

"Did you know that I can name every Yankee shortstop in order, from Jeter all the way back to John Knight, who played the position in 1909?"

Biff was not interested in Yankee trivia. There was something more important here than sports. "We are not here to talk baseball. As a matter of fact, baseball is the last thing we need you to think about right now. We need your help, Professor. We are beginning a quest to return the most sacred artifact in Western civilization to its rightful home."

Schwartz smiled. "The most sacred artifact? Hmm. Let me see now. Where have I heard that one before? Let me think. I can guess where this conversation is going. Let me tell you something. I have spent a lifetime studying medieval legends, and there is only one thing people want to talk to me about, and you know exactly what I am referring to—this so-called, alleged thing that no one has ever seen—the Holy Grail. The Holy Grail is a myth. It is all bullshit. Any scholar of repute who is in his right mind knows that. The only people who think that it is real have been spending too much time watching the History Channel or that show *Finding Bigfoot*. By the way, that show has run for six seasons and, so far, no sign of Sasquatch!"

Biff was going to close the sale. He didn't care how much it would cost or what he would have to do. He got in close to Michelangelo Schwartz and whispered, "It is not a myth. I can assure you. The Holy Grail was in the possession of a certain institution from earliest times until it went missing on February 6, 1920. I represent that institution. From that time on, the world has changed and not for the better."

Schwartz was still sober enough to be a little curious. "If that certain institution you are referring to is what I think it is, that means you are here representing the Vatican. And to be honest, my friend, that leaves a rather bad taste in my mouth, like an all-you-can-eat sushi buffet in New Jersey!"

Schwartz was beginning to see double. But, in his drunken state, he began to recall a faraway memory of something that happened to him many years ago. The date of February 6, 1920, rang some kind of bell in association with the Grail. Why did that date seem so familiar? It started to come back to him. It was then that Schwartz recalled from his historical reading that February 6 was the birthday of the most famous Illuminati Master, Adam Weishaupt, founder of the Bavarian Illuminati. He reasoned that must be why they chose that particular day. But there was a more vivid memory now coming back to him.

He remembered a conversation he'd had with a drunken Dominican monk at a conference on Dante held in Siena, Italy, more than thirty years ago. After the scholarly papers were presented and speeches made, there was a cocktail party. At that party, Schwartz started drinking heavily with a monk who was attending the conference and had also presented a paper on Dante. The monk taught at the University of Padua. After the cocktail party, Schwartz and this monk found themselves alone at an outdoor table in front of a small restaurant, away from the other conference attendees, feasting on freshly made pasta and consuming more wine. They sat for hours, and the empty bottles of Montepulciano started to pile up. As the evening wore on, the restaurant gradually emptied out, leaving only the two scholars. The owner finally brought out a bottle of grappa, a very strong and fruity after-dinner liqueur, and went back inside the inn. The two men were totally sloshed. Suddenly, the monk, in halting English, began to relate a story too strange to be believed.

When he was studying to be a Dominican priest many years ago, he'd spent time with an old monk, who often alluded to the fact that he was the keeper of a great secret. As the old monk was dying, in a delirious state, he confessed a story to Michelangelo's companion that was shocking. This old Dominican was working in the Vatican Museum in 1920, helping to catalog paintings. He was working on the night of February 6, 1920, when the head of the Vatican Museum came screaming that something important had been stolen. The museum was immediately shut down, and the premises were searched. The monks and priests were never told what it was they were looking for, but soon it was rumored, among those in the know, that the Holy Grail had been stolen. Schwartz had dismissed that story as a drunken fiction. But now, here was this man, who might be from the Vatican, telling him a very similar story.

"And why exactly are you telling me this?"

"I was going to keep our employer secret, but, obviously, that is impossible. The Vatican is interested in obtaining this artifact, and certain members of the church believe you have a particular set of skills that could prove useful. We are prepared to make it worth your while financially."

Michelangelo Schwartz had always spent more money than he made, no matter how much he made. He was a semiretired professor, who only did the occasional night or weekend course at Bloomfield College, Caldwell College, or Montclair State University, all in New Jersey. His career was washed up, and his local reputation was terrible, to say the least. He didn't know exactly what they wanted him to do, but he had the time, and he was getting bored. To say his finances were in a state of disrepair was to put it mildly. He turned to his left to get a good look at the second man seated on the other side.

He looked at William Callahan for a while and began to squint and lean in closer. Finally, he widened his eyes in both shock and surprise.

"I may be drunk...no, let me amend that. I am drunk, very drunk, but are you any relation to a nun they call Sister Bill?"

The man smiled. "Michelangelo Schwartz, I did not think we would meet again in this lifetime."

Michelangelo Schwartz's eyes opened wide as he turned back to the bar. "Holy shit! Sister Bill is a man! Jade, bourbon on the rocks! Make it a double! No! Make that a triple!"

Jade was not sure this was a good idea. She had noticed he was wobbling an hour ago, but she decided to pour it anyway and make it his last of the night.

William leaned over to Biff. He spoke quietly but loud enough for Michelangelo Schwartz to hear. "Biff, I told you that Professor Schwartz here and I had a history, but, when I said that, I probably did not include all of the colorful commentary that the statement deserves."

"Here we go," said Michelangelo as he pushed back from the bar without much enthusiasm.

William went on. "Yes, Biff. Professor Schwartz here taught at Saint Christopher College for Catholic Women in Cleveland when I was the dean of discipline there, and believe me; I had my hands full with him. In those days, I also coached girls' softball and was the mother superior of the Sisters of Little Mercy."

Schwartz was used to being put on the spot, and he had a simple reply that he used without fail in situations like this. "Sister Bill, I deny everything. I was framed. Those co-eds all lied!"

"Those co-eds all lied? All of them? Schwartz, do you remember what I found going on in the stall of the ladies' room during the freshman BBQ? How about the grow lights on your kitchen table? How about that confrontation in the faculty senate, when a secretary in a miniskirt stormed in, in tears, and slapped the pipe out of your mouth? How about Mildred, the lunch lady? Yes, Schwartz, a lunch lady with a hairnet! We found out about her after you had left. Did you know she was a grandmother? Schwartz, have you no shame?"

Schwartz drank down his last drink in one gulp and turned toward William. "In times like this, I like to remember my motto: 'Nobody is perfect!'"

William's disgust was obvious as he shook his head. "This is not going to be a picnic."

Schwartz was woozy and was staring across the bar. "Sister Bill, I know I am not the same man I was when we first met. The years have not been kind to me." He pointed across the bar. "See that guy on the other side of the bar? I am going to look like that in about twenty years. Pathetic."

William laughed. "Schwartz, take a good look across the bar. That is not another customer. You are looking at a mirror."

Schwartz squinted. "Hell, Sister Bill! You're right! Shitski!"

Biff wanted to get the train back on the tracks. "Professor Schwartz, recently a poem was discovered in an old book, which Rome believes gives us a way into the Illuminati and will lead the way to the Holy Grail."

Schwartz was drunk but not that drunk. "The Illuminati? So now we are talking about the Holy Grail *and* the Illuminati? How about throwing in the JFK assassination and the most elusive lost artifact of all—Barack Obama's birth certificate? Listen, Biff and Sister Bill...William...whatever your name is now. Let me make myself clear. I may be drunk, but I am sober enough to know that there is no Holy Grail and no Illuminati. These are myths, plain and simple, written to keep the simpleminded in line. Believe me; I know all the literature, and there is nothing there."

Biff smiled. "I will admit, by all appearances, the world seems chaotic with no plan and no blueprint, but what if things are more logical than they seem? What if there were some sign that God made the world and keeps an eye on it as if it were a well-oiled machine? Let me demonstrate to you that the world is actually unfolding according to a flawless plan. Let me ask you a few simple questions that might illustrate my point. If you were going to write a novel about a congressman who would take pictures of his own genitalia and have it on the front page of every newspaper in America, what would be the most humorous and unbelievable name you could make up for him?"

Even Jade, the bartender, knew that one. She leaned over and answered, "Weiner!"

Biff smiled with satisfaction. "Do you think it is random that a man named Weiner would become famous for flashing his wiener? If you were to write that character into a work of fiction, your literary agent would throw that manuscript out of an adjacent window and say, 'Weiner? Too obvious! Too over the top! No editor would publish this! Make it more believable!' The whole world is like this, if you think about it. Vladimir Putin wrestling the tiger with no shirt on. Do you really believe that was random? Governor Rick Perry of Texas going jogging, and, during the run, he shoots and kills a coyote. Random? Hey, listen; the Illuminati are good.

"Let me take a single example from one of your less inspired jokes. Let us speak of an Indonesian Muslim named Barry Soetoro, known to you under one of his numerous aliases, Barack Obama. The guy was born in a thatched hut in Kenya, about three hundred miles east of Mombasa. He was delivered by a witch doctor. His half brother is an African warlord, who, in order to attain manhood in the Masai tribe, to which he belongs, killed a lion when he was supposedly only twelve. His mother is a card-carrying Communist. His uncle is a voodoo priest. He went to a Muslim school in Indonesia, where he learned to read the Koran. He attended Occidental College as a foreign-exchange student. He has more false passports than the entire team of *Mission Impossible*, and not a single one of his classmates or professors at Columbia or Harvard recall laying eyes on him once. He has a dozen social-security numbers. He is best friends with SDS bombers and black racists, goes under about fifteen assumed names, has never voted in his life, can't get on a plane because he does not have a US driver's license, and, the next thing you know—*Kaboom!*, *Bam!*, *Boom!*—he is president of the United States, commander in chief, and leader of the free world. Coincidence? I think not. I will tell you how tightly the Illuminati control the world. They already know next season's winners of both *Dancing with the Stars* and *The Bachelorette*. You must know those rose ceremonies are fake!"

Schwartz had a question. "If the Illuminati know everything, do you think they know who Carly Simon was referring to in the song 'You're so Vain'? I always figured it was every man ever born."

Biff smiled. "Even I know that one. And let me just say, it isn't Warren Beatty or Mick Jagger. But let me give you another example. You are one of the world's leading experts on symbols and codes, but I bet you have never looked at some of the most famous names or symbols in history to see what they are really telling us. Let us make anagrams out of just a few. Remember we are just scratching the surface here.

"Rearrange the letters of the name 'George Bush,' the forty-third president of the United States, and you get 'he bugs Gore.' Now, if that is a little surprising, let's try this one on for size. Nat King Cole can be turned into 'lacking tone.' Guy Fawkes tried to blow up the English Parliament, but the powder kegs failed to ignite, and his name gives us the anagram 'gawky fuse.' Boy, how much more obvious can you get? The suave Shakespearean actor Alec Guinness gives us 'genuine class.' Britney Spears can be read as the 'best PR in years.' Richard Milhous Nixon's letters can be rearranged to give us 'his climax ruined honor.' Lee Harvey Oswald becomes 'revealed who slay.' President Clinton of the USA gives us 'he finds interns to copulate.'"

Schwartz was truly impressed. But it was hard for him to get his words in edgeways. "Biff, are you sure these anagrams are real? This seems too fantastic to be true!"

Biff just smiled and continued. "Keep in mind steroids when you see that Arnold Schwarzenegger becomes 'he's grown large n' crazed.' The United States of America tells us about capitalism and consumption when we read it as 'Dine out; taste a Mac, fries.' Christopher Columbus has been shown for who he is by becoming 'He is a much corrupt slob.' Sir Edmund Hillary, the first man to climb Mount Everest, can be arranged to give us 'I'd murder any hills.' Jennifer Aniston, a favorite of the Illuminati, can give us 'fine in torn jeans.'"

Schwartz could not believe it as Biff went on.

"Margaret Thatcher can have her name spelled out as 'that great charmer.' Clint Eastwood is an anagram for 'old West action.' Hillary Clinton, a well-known follower of the Illuminati, can have her name anagrammed as 'Only I can thrill.' Princess Diana can give us two phrases 'Ascend in Paris' or 'End in a car spin.' The Statue of Liberty becomes 'Build to stay free.'"

Schwartz was hypnotized, and he was trying to add up the letters to make sure this was all the way it seemed. He stopped Biff again. "Yes, these letters add up, but how can this be?"

Biff didn't break his string. He just went on. *How the West Was Won* becomes 'What we shot, we own.' The American dream can become 'Meet a dear rich man.' How about the Declaration of Independence that gives us 'no finer deed, an ideal concept'? But the most interesting is Leonard Nimoy, who played an alien on *Star Trek*, only to hide the fact that some claim that he is, in fact, a real alien who came here to Earth to propagate his species with Earth women. The letters of his name give us 'on my alien rod.'"

Michelangelo Schwartz's attention span was at an end, and his thirst was now getting in the way. He was doing his best to get the attention of Jade by waving his glass.

She shook her pretty head. "No!"

Biff Braunschweiger was not deterred. He went on. "You may have been a scholar on the symbolism of secret societies, such as the Illuminati, but I bet you couldn't guess the identities of some of the people we have identified as belonging to the Illuminati."

Schwartz thought it was all hooey. But he figured he would bite. Jade was beginning to look like a lost cause. No. These two twerps were putting a spanner in his otherwise perfect pitches. Schwartz had always had the ability to lie to himself. But he had to answer Biff. "OK. Wow me. Who are the modern Illuminati?"

"Tony Blair and the Bushes."

Michelangelo Schwartz yawned. "We have all heard those rumors."

"The Clintons."

"Again, an old charge. I've heard that a dozen times."

"OK. How about Rodney Dangerfield?"

Schwartz sat up straight. "Are you talking about Rodney Dangerfield, the New York comedian? Do you mean the *Caddyshack* and *Back to School* Rodney Dangerfield?"

Biff smiled, as he knew Michelangelo was getting interested. "You remember when Rodney Dangerfield would pull on his collar nervously while telling us that he 'doesn't get any respect'? Well, you may not understand the true meaning of that phrase. Since February 6, 1920, we have not known the identity of the Supreme Ascendant Illuminated Master, but we have identified some of the lower-level functionaries in the Illuminati elite. One such man was the Nazi officer Rudolf Hess. Rudolf Hess was the deputy führer backing up Hitler. He was a Freemason and a well-known member of the Illuminati. As you recall, he parachuted into Scotland in 1941 to try to negotiate an early end to the Second World War. He did it not for humanitarian reasons but because it was costing the Illuminati too much money. His negotiations were unsuccessful because the Brits did not believe he had the power to negotiate a treaty. He was not given the respect of someone who had the power to negotiate peace. He was imprisoned, and, many years later, he was found hanged. Some claim it was suicide, while others bet on the British Secret Services."

Jade was listening, and she was a little confused. She walked around the bar and stood next to the three. She had a question. "So why Rodney Dangerfield?"

Biff was smooth in his presentation and in the way he pulled a stool over for Jade, using just one foot. "When Rodney Dangerfield pulled at his collar, he made the universal symbol of hanging. When he said he didn't get any respect, he was honoring his fellow fallen Illuminati Rudolf Hess!"

Jade didn't get that one either. Schwartz was breathing at twice his usual rate, but he was still suspicious. This all sounded like bullshit. His attention span was at an end, and so was his ability to stay on his barstool.

But Biff was going to close the sale no matter what. "Professor Schwartz, in my briefcase, I have a computer and a projector. I would like an hour of your time, in your apartment, to show you this information. If you are not convinced, we can all go our own ways. If you feel like it is something you want to get involved in, I have fifty thousand dollars in cash with your name on it. I'll even initial every bill. All you have to do is help us solve a simple riddle."

Michelangelo Schwartz raised his finger in the air as if he had something profound to say. Instead, his eyes rolled up into his head; he slipped off his barstool, and he collapsed, in a drunken stupor, on the floor.

Jade looked down and shook her head. "I guess the professor is done drinking."

Detroit, Michigan

What Schwartz did not know was that other wheels were already in motion. The recovery of the Holy Grail would tip the balance of power for the whole world. So the Vatican was not taking any chances. They were going to play both ends against the middle, a tactic they had mastered over the span of two thousand years, under the rule of the Borgia and Medici popes, one of whom strangled his own son. A little known fact was that the Vatican was built with the stones from the exterior of the Coliseum. But that was not all the Vatican borrowed from the Romans. The Vatican had dispatched a hit man that very day. The hit man was already en route from Detroit to New York. There were to be no loose ends.

If Michelangelo Schwartz heard all of this secret information and decided he did not want to go along, he would not be around to tell his story. This quest was far too important to have anyone who might blab the story hanging about. The hit man's name was Salvatore "Two Fingers" Greco, who, when not serving as the number-one killer for Rome in America, spent his free time doing food demonstrations in supermarkets. It was an avocation of which he was justifiably proud. That very morning, before he left Detroit, he'd sold $150 worth of Bubba's Burgers at a Piggly Wiggly in South Detroit. It was a good thing to take pride in your work.

Salvatore was a fat Sicilian who liked pasta and meatballs too much and dressed like he was much older than his fifty-five years. He was a humble soul whose frugal nature caused him to shop at many of the seedy secondhand shops so prevalent in and around Detroit, a city never famous for fashion. He had been involved in some of the biggest hits in America. Most of these hits looked like natural causes, and his face was unknown to most local police departments. Most of his hits never made the papers. His work on Kurt Cobain and Michael Jackson certainly made the papers, but his name never came up in the long list of possible perps that the police investigated. But he was known to another government agency. His orders now were to head for New York and wait for instructions.

Route 23, Cedar Grove, New Jersey

A little while later that same night, back in New Jersey, William was driving Michelangelo Schwartz's 1980 Toyota Corolla with 850,000 miles on the odometer. The muffler had been held up with a coat hanger for the last three months, the right taillight had been out for a year, and you had to get in through the passenger-side door, as the driver-side door had not opened since Clinton was in the White House.

Michelangelo sat in the passenger seat, still with a good buzz on. To get him into the passenger seat, they had to toss out a dozen wrappers from McDonald's Happy Meals, a fistful of ungraded student essays written in blue books, and another dozen empty Budweiser bottles. As they did that, Michelangelo Schwartz was reminded of the line from a Leonard Cohen song—"Wasn't it a long way down; wasn't it a strange way down?" He was sad that his life had led to this, and he was "bottoming out," as the saying goes.

Biff was following the two in his Ford Fiesta. William looked over at the drunken and woozy Schwartz as they sped down the road. "Schwartz, I have tried to forgive you for everything but that last little adventure you had."

"William, are you referring to Big Lulu?"

"I never called her by that name. I only knew her as Lulu, Lulu Lefay."

"William, I did wrong, but so have you. You are no angel. I know things about you that would not exactly make nice reading."

William remembered how much he hated Michelangelo Schwartz. "To what exactly are you referring?"

"On Saint Paddy's Day, you always hosted Irish coffee in your office at Saint Christopher's College. If you recall, during my second year you and I stayed after everyone else had left, and you broke out the straight Jameson. You always said you never drank Protestant whiskey. After a little while, you got a little tipsy, and you said there were some things in your life you regretted."

William was not quite sure where this was going. "Schwartz, I remember us drinking, but I am a little fuzzy about what I might have made up."

"Oh, you did not make it up. Do you remember a clandestine organization in 1960 known as 'Nuns for Nixon'?"

William, now remembering he was once Sister Bill, went pale. "I told you about Nuns for Nixon?"

"You did, in all of its gory detail."

William thought for a while before he spoke.

"You have to understand what was happening back then," William began. "In 1960, the first Catholic was running for office. John F. Kennedy was young, handsome, charismatic, and loved by the public. He seemed like a fine and moral young man. But the Sisters of Little Mercy had a kind of underground network where we all shared our secret thoughts. While we often ate and prayed in silence, once a month we had an evening of cocktails and gossip at the convent we called 'Bar Nun.' We took the vows of poverty, chastity, and obedience, so all that was left were the pleasures of Scotch whiskey, gossip, and sadism. So, as we talked, we found out things about Johnny Boy that the papers were too polite to report in those days."

Schwartz was interested. "What kinds of things did the nuns of Massachusetts and Washington, DC, tell you?"

"It was not just we Sisters of Little Mercy but a drunken Franciscan priest who had been attached to the Kennedy compound in Hyannis Port. He heard JFK's confessions. But, after they found out he couldn't keep his trap shut, they exiled him to Cleveland, which for many people is like being in hell. Schwartz, you may have heard Kennedy had a bad back because a Japanese destroyer rammed his navy boat, *PT-109*. You may remember he swam ten miles and saved his shipmates' lives. I have it straight from the priest, who heard his confession, that JFK threw his back out on a water bed with an exotic dancer named Fifi La Fromage at the Golden Nugget on Fremont Street in Las Vegas."

Schwartz was having a hard time believing this. "I thought the seal of confession couldn't be broken under any circumstances."

William smiled as he educated Schwartz on the dark side of JFK. "Well, some believe it is OK to tell nuns, because that is sort of like keeping it in the family. Also, priests drink heavily, and you know what happens to secrets then! Anyway, Kennedy never let the pain of his bad back keep him from the parade of hookers that would sashay into his congressional office every day at closing time, which, for JFK, was about two in the afternoon. His sham wife, Jackie, was just for show. JFK was doing more three ways than an electrical wall outlet.

"The pope had secretly instructed all of us to do everything we could to help elect a Catholic president. The pope knew what a slimeball Ol' Jack was, but hey, he was in the club. Pope John XXIII is often seen as a soft reformer, but let me tell you, that man knew how to crack the whip when nobody was looking. So, on the one side, you had Nixon, who was a Quaker, a man of peace, faithful to his wife, a nondrinker, and averse to swearing, or so we all thought before we heard the Nixon tapes years later. On the other side, you had JFK, jacked up—by the way, the expression 'jacked up' is named after Jack Kennedy—on bennies, steroids, uppers, and downers and boinking everything in a dress. Hey, forget about the sexual exploits of Jim Morrison and Sid Vicious. The real Johnny Rotten was going into the White House in 1960. So we sisters had a meeting and secretly convened an organization we called Nuns for Nixon to keep America moral.

"After hours, we would lower the shades of the convent and unroll the poster of Richard Nixon hidden under my bed. We would tack it up and then get on our knees and pray. At the bottom of that poster, it read: 'Nixon is the One.'"

"So you kept this secret?"

"Yes, but during the famous debate, Nixon, known to his enemies as Tricky Dick, broke out into a sweat. You see, he was not really tricky. When an honest man lies, he shows it, because it is unnatural. But not JFK! During that famous debate, Kennedy was as cool as the scoundrel that he was. Lying to his wife and all those angry husbands over the years taught him to look like the most trustworthy guy on the planet.

"The election happened. Mayor Daley's machine in Chicago had everybody in the cemetery vote five times each, and it was over. Then came the Bay of Pigs, *Ich bin ein Berliner*, which really means 'I am a

German pastry,' and finally Marilyn Monroe singing 'Happy Birthday, Mr. President' in Madison Square Garden. And you don't want to know what happened to her that night on a boat anchored at the boat basin on the Hudson River, surrounded by secret-service agents. Think about Eisenhower, Truman, and other giants. Then think about JFK getting it on with three call girls in the White House swimming pool. Sacrilege!"

"Listen, Bill, I mean William, I want to get back to talking about Big Lulu. Hey, she was a good-looking student. She was in my poetry class. When she and I started our relationship, I had no idea you two had been an item. She never mentioned it, and you had to keep it under wraps yourself. You were the dean of discipline and a nun! How could you be mad at me?"

William looked down at the speedometer and noticed he was speeding. He slowed down and turned to Schwartz. "Lulu Lefay was the love of my life, Schwartz. I was crazy for her."

"Yes. And when you caught us fooling around during my office hours, you made sure I was fired. And then you went on your merry way. Is that ethical? You may not know it, but the day I left there, Big Lulu sent me a perfumed note in a purple envelope. Do you know what that note said?"

William was afraid to ask, but he did. "What did that note say?"

"'I will never love another man.'"

4

We meet the Illuminati and find out their connection to reality television. We spend a good bit of time on an episode of *The Jerry Springer Show* called "A Backwoods Surprise." We meet Wolf Eyes, a Norwegian assassin who is tasked with stopping Michelangelo Schwartz at all costs. Finally, we meditate on the humor of Donald Rumsfeld.

A run-down motel, Eyota, Minnesota

A thousand miles west, another contract killer was about to Skype into a virtual session with one of his employers, known to him only as the Firm. Wolf Eyes, as his employers knew him, was the perfect assassin, with one exception. He was a tall man of Norwegian descent, with striking gray eyes that were almost translucent. Those eyes would sometimes attract the attention of those he did not wish to see his face, which was not a good thing when your main aim in life was to remain anonymous. And for those who looked and made any gesture of recognition, it was a dark day. He was tall, pale, thin, and had a shock of blond hair. He often wore sunglasses to mask his unusual eyes. He dressed only in black. He had no accent, no history, and he was from nowhere. He was the best there was.

Three times previously in his career, he had worked for this same employer. They had called themselves the Firm each time they had used his services. Because he had connections and knew how to follow leads, he determined quickly that the Firm was, in reality, some branch of what some thought was the Illuminati. When he had finished his contracts on the previous three occasions, he had always gotten a cold feeling. He dreaded dealing with the Firm, but he was not in a position to refuse them anything. The Firm did not like any loose ends. After the money was deposited in his account, Wolf Eyes always took precautions. In this business, he couldn't afford to make a single mistake.

Wolf Eyes wanted to live in a place where he would not be recognized and where there would be no one he would recognize. For this reason, he made his home in Eyota, Minnesota, a small farming community just an hour southeast of the Twin Cities. Eyota was the perfect place for Wolf Eyes to live and work. First, half the people in the town were Nordic, blond, and six foot four. Because of the miserable weather and lack of any tourist attractions, no one in their right mind would go there, so it was out of the way. There would be no one around who would give him a second thought or a second look. Eyota was a one-horse town with no traffic lights. "One-horse town" was one of those odd metaphors that Wolf Eyes often meditated on. If it were a one-horse town, why would it need traffic lights, unless there was, at least, one more horse?

Eyota was settled when the wheels fell off of two wagons belonging to a drunken German pastry cook on the way to California in 1844. The sodbuster never had the ambition to either fix the wheels or move on. The nearest "city," and this was stretching the definition, was Rochester, Minnesota, which was ten miles away. The flourishing downtown of Eyota featured Bert's Meats, American Legion Post 551, Amy's Beauty Shop, the Eyota Country Café, and the Green Door State Liquor Store and Bar. It was the perfect town for Wolf Eyes. It was said that Eyota, like the rest of Minnesota, had two seasons, winter and the Fourth of July. Oh, yes, and the Fourth of July was stifling hot.

As he prepared for his video session, Wolf Eyes thought about what he had learned, not only in his research about the Illuminati but also what he'd learned from his three previous meetings with the Firm.

He laughed as he thought about all the so-called secrets of the Illuminati that people read about. These "secrets" were surreptitiously handed out by the Illuminati to a cooperative press in dark parking garages to confuse people. They were masters of misinformation and misdirection, he thought as he remembered one example of how they could direct attention away from the obvious.

He recalled one example of how cleverly the Illuminati hid their purposes from the general public. It was believed the United States invaded Iraq in 2003 because they were sure they had weapons of mass destruction and were about to unleash them on the United States. Donald Rumsfeld, then secretary of defense, gave a speech explaining the invasion, which was to cost over a hundred thousand lives and spend two hundred billion dollars of US tax revenues, which would, in some future time, help bankrupt the nation. So, when it turned out that Iraq had nothing to do with 9/11, had no weapons of mass destruction, and never had any atomic yellow cake, you might think the United States would have egg on its face. It had bombed Iraq into the ground anyway, unleashing a torrent of sectarian killings and bloodshed that would go on for generations.

It got worse. Vice-President Dick Cheney's company, Halliburton, got no-bid contracts for billions, with him smiling and nodding. When Bush and Cheney were caught red-handed with their hands in the cookie jar, they sent out Rumsfeld to confuse the American people, so they would not get upset. They told the American people that the war would be over quickly, with few casualties, and that it would pay for itself. Wolf Eyes remembered that Bush had even given a speech on an aircraft carrier under a banner reading, "Mission Accomplished."

In a press briefing on February 12, 2004, Rumsfeld said the following words:

"There are known knowns. Things we know that we know. There are known unknowns. That is to say, things we know now that we didn't know. But there are unknown unknowns. There are things we do not know we don't know."

Wolf Eyes wondered if anyone knew how brilliant that was. He figured if Plato or Aristotle had heard that, they would have hung themselves halfway through the second sentence. He remembered the IBM supercomputer, Watson, that defeated all of the *Jeopardy!* champions and throttled chess grand masters. They said it was smarter than the smartest thousand humans combined. One night, a smart-aleck computer programmer fed Rumsfeld's lines into Watson and asked the supercomputer to interpret it. Watson blew out all of his circuits, melted his core, and they lost half the electric grid in Palo Alto. Just think. That was the guy that argued for and planned the whole war. So he could see why the Illuminati referred to former Secretary of Defense Donald Rumsfeld as "Rummy, our main man." Oh, and to put a cherry on this sundae, when he said that, he was smiling.

Wolf Eyes understood that the Illuminati liked to have as many nuts with wacky conspiracy theories running around as possible. By muddying the waters with talk of aliens, UFOs, reptilian ruling classes, fake birth certificates in Hawaii, shapeshifters, and Obamacare, they could keep their real aims hidden. This was one of the main reasons the Illuminati liked Fox News and the Oprah Network. By linking the Illuminati with every possible wacky scenario, people failed to see that just a handful of powerful individuals controlled almost everything. At the same time, because of this campaign of disinformation, almost nothing was known for sure about the Illuminati.

But Wolf Eyes had gotten a library card to the Library of Congress under an assumed name, so they would not know who he was. He assumed, correctly, that a single reader would raise a red flag if he took out a certain combination of titles. And Wolf Eyes was not about raising red flags. Because he had worked for them himself, he quickly separated out those works about the Illuminati that were accurate. He could almost feel their truth, like electricity, in his fingertips. But in all of his research and all of his reading, he had come across one, and only one, book that mirrored what he knew to be true from his experience. It was not found in the Library of Congress but someplace very, very different.

He found that particular book in a place that doubled as a bar and bookstore in Charles Town, West Virginia. No, not Charleston, the state capital of West Virginia, but Charles Town in the same state. You can imagine the confusion this caused for mail carriers and would-be assassins. He was in West Virginia, taking care of a little item involving two characters named Whitey and Hollywood. And take care of them he did.

One night, while he was enjoying a salad and a bottle of water in this out-of-the-way pub, he'd noticed some old books on the shelves. They had obviously been left to entertain customers who had wandered in alone and did not want to be disturbed. Wolf Eyes was a compulsive reader. He ventured over and picked up a spiral-bound volume. This was not what most people would call a book, but a Xeroxed copy of a typewritten manuscript put together in the most amateurish way. The manuscript in question was entitled *Every Statement about the Illuminati is False* by Lee Roger Glow. Wolf Eyes was smart. He mused on the title. The title said 'every statement about the Illuminati is false,' and this was a statement about the Illuminati; therefore, by applying the rules of logic, it could only be false. The opposite of that false statement would be the true statement. That meant the book title *Every Statement about the Illuminati is False* must itself be false for it to be true. So, that would indicate that this book, at least, held some grain of truth. If he were a drinking man, which he wasn't, he would have needed a drink by now.

He took out his cell phone and ran the name Lee Roger Glow through an anagram generator on the Internet and quickly came up with the name George Orwell. George Orwell, the author of *1984* and *Animal Farm*, was famous for shining a spotlight on things that the powers that be would rather have left hidden.

Wolf Eyes knew this manuscript was authentic, because on page one, the author mentioned something so odd that it could not be a coincidence. In his acknowledgments, Lee Roger Glow oddly mentioned *The Jerry Springer Show*. Wolf Eyes recalled that whenever he Skyped into a meeting with the Firm, they intentionally timed it around a showing of *The Jerry Springer Show*. They instructed him to have the show on a television set in his room and to turn it up loud so that any bugging device would not be able to pick up the conversation. But there was something Wolf Eyes did not know. Not only did the loud volume of *The Jerry Springer Show* protect the privacy of the conversation, but, apparently, embedded in that show, and that show alone, was a hidden signal on a very low frequency that neutralized the most sophisticated listening devices. This disruptive technology was known to very few. If anyone was listening in, they would just get a buzzing sound. All three times he had worked for the Firm, he had *The Jerry Springer Show* turned up to full volume in the room. He even recalled the names of the episodes that played during his last three communications: "Woman in Labor Confronts Mistress," "Pregnant by My Brother," and "I Slept with 125 Men in Ten Hours."

He had often wondered why the Illuminati would be obsessed with *The Jerry Springer Show*. Wolf Eyes theorized that once you had power over the world, unlimited funds, and unlimited access to carnal and gourmet pleasures, you eventually became jaded and lost interest in almost everything. The process of becoming jaded goes through a number of stages, but somehow for them, it had ended up with *The Jerry Springer Show*. After a lifetime of the most sensuous and skilled love slaves, exquisite gourmet meals prepared by Michelin five-star French chefs, thousand-dollar-a-bottle forty-year-old Bordeaux, and unlimited access to the most exclusive resorts on the globe, one eventually tired of these things. You might argue they could turn to chess, but that, too, loses its allure over time. Eventually, they hungered for simpler pleasures.

How the Illuminati became involved with reality television was unclear, but it had often been noticed by sociologists and social psychologists that certain groups historically exhibited common tendencies. For example, it had been noticed that an inordinate number of the world's greatest mathematicians, geometers, and astronomers had been Polish. It had been noted that four of the five greatest violin players of all time had been Hungarian and Japanese people were born with a strong urge to have leather straps around their necks, often attached to cameras. In the book *Every Statement about the Illuminati is False*, the author mentioned that Illuminati meetings began not with a prayer or the Pledge of Allegiance but a DVD of a particularly vulgar episode of *The Jerry Springer Show*. The book mentioned that a TV was often on in the room, and the rulers of the world were watching *Jerry*.

When the Illuminati got together in person, they made sure they did not stir any curiosity. Secrecy was their first, middle, and last name. To keep their privacy, they tended to stay out of the world's great cities, like Venice, Monte Carlo, Nice, or Geneva. They, instead, preferred run-down motels in the hinterlands that made the Bates Motel look like Caesar's Palace in Las Vegas. They liked places like Trudy's Roadside Inn on a lonely country road outside of Keokuk, Iowa, The Big Bear's Den in Polson, Montana, and Bertha's Clean Motel (which wasn't very) in Truth or Consequences, New Mexico. Somewhere, in some out-of-the-way place, three members of the Firm had gathered in order to Skype into this session.

Wolf Eyes turned on his television set and changed the channel to *The Jerry Springer Show*. In a little while, the show came on. This episode was entitled "A Backwoods Surprise." This particular episode of *Jerry Springer* featured a severely overweight woman with a thick southern accent, whose age was somewhere between twenty-two and fifty-nine. Frankly, it was hard to tell. She had a really bad 1950s-type hairdo, was wearing a dress that used to be called a muumuu, wore flip-flops, and had bad teeth.

Jerry Springer, the host, ran a show that featured the poor and maladapted. He himself preferred the latest glasses, sports jackets, and open-necked shirts. He always had a deck of cue cards in his hand, so he could keep track of the action. This was a fake out, because all hell would break loose long before he ever got to the cue cards. This show was not based on charity. His specialty was surprising his on-air guests with the most horrible news anyone could imagine, live on television, and watching their reactions, which were frequently violent.

The live studio audiences were connoisseurs of *The Jerry Springer Show*. They were young and vulgar blue-collar Irish and Italian toughs from New York and New Jersey, and they smelled blood. The audience would howl, clap, and chant, "Jerry! Jerry! Jerry!" as the contestants would, almost on cue, cry, shake, bash each other in the face, or fall on the floor in a struggle, only to be forcibly separated by burly bouncers with headsets, who were also required on every show.

Jerry Springer was now setting the stage. "Now, Elvira, you are here today because you think your boyfriend is going to propose to you here on stage."

She answered Jerry in a thick accent right out of rural Mississippi. "Yes, my Jethro loves me, and I guess we are here to find out if he is going to propose to me on national television." She then smiled and squealed with delight as she clapped while bouncing up and down in her chair.

The Firm had not Skyped in yet, so Wolf Eyes was forced to watch and could not believe what he was seeing. If Elvira, if that really was her name, had seen one single episode of *The Jerry Springer Show*, she would have known that nobody gets married. It never turned out well, and there were no happy endings. Could she be so naïve, or was she there for her horrible fifteen minutes of fame?

At this point, his computer screen came alive with the message for an incoming call on Skype. It was a scrambled private number that could not be traced, even by the most sophisticated tracking software. When the best hackers in the world were caught, they didn't go to prison; they went to work for the Firm. The screen showed three men in masks, sitting on a sofa, watching a small black-and-white television. They were wearing Venetian carnival masks—one silver, one blue, and one red. The one in the silver mask was obviously the boss. The voices were also altered, so voice-recognition software could not detect any voice pattern that could be saved and reconstructed. Wolf Eyes smiled. These guys were good, very good.

Jerry Springer moved the show along, according to a tried and true formula. "OK, Elvira, we want to bring out your boyfriend, Jethro."

The audience went wild as an obese man in his late twenties waddled out. He had blond hair, a scraggly beard, and, for his appearance on national television, wore a white T-shirt with a big brown stain on the front and jeans that looked like they were four sizes too big and had seen better days. He had a rope for a belt. The shoelace on his right sneaker was untied. One toe had made its way through to the outside of his sneaker.

Wolf Eyes wanted to get his business done and get out, so he addressed the three men. "Can we take care of business, so you can get back to your program?"

The man in the silver mask waved at him to be quiet as Jerry introduced Jethro.

"Now, Jethro, you work as an auto mechanic in Dogtown, Mississippi. Is that correct?"

"Well, I ain't exactly what you might call an auto mechanic, but I do help around the garage part time. I sweep up and get stuff that the boss needs to fix the cars that come in."

The audience was getting restless, so Jerry had to get it going.

"And you have been dating Elvira here for about three years?"

Jethro was sweating. "Yes, sir. I guess."

Jerry Springer turned toward the audience with a bemused look on his face. "You guess? Don't you know?"

Jethro was really nervous. "I mean, yes, sir, three years. Elvira and I have been dating for three years."

"And you have something to tell her on national television?"

The audience sensed blood.

Jethro got up and got close to Elvira. He got down on one knee, and she began to giggle and clap. He clasped his hands together as if in prayer. Her dreamboat had come in, but she was about to find out it was a garbage scow.

"Elvira, I have something to tell you."

She was smiling with delight. She was, apparently, the only one in the studio who did not know how the script of a typical *Jerry Springer Show* unfolded.

Jerry waved his finger, encouraging Jethro to speak up. So Jethro went on.

"Elvira, I know we have been going out for three years, but I have to tell you something."

He took a long, deep breath. "I am sleeping with your sister Jo Ellen."

Elvira had a momentary look of shock on her face. But, like a wounded rhino, she was not stunned for long. As if on cue, Elvira tore out of her chair and started to administer a beating to Jethro as the audience went wild. It took some time for the tall and muscular bouncers, in their black T-shirts and headsets, to get the tangled couple separated. Elvira was crying loudly but winning hands down. But Jerry was not done.

"Elvira, we have another surprise for you today. It is your sister Jo Ellen!"

As Jo Ellen came out, she looked like a carbon copy of Elvira, only uglier and dressed worse, if that were possible. She also had bad teeth. Jo Ellen came in and sat close to Jethro. At that moment, Elvira jumped out of her chair and began to punch Jo Ellen. It took some time to restore order as the audience chanted, "Jerry! Jerry! Jerry!"

Wolf Eyes felt like he was trapped in a bad dream. The Illuminati seemed so glued to the TV that they had no interest in the business at hand. Whatever they had in mind was supposedly pressing, but they seemed distracted. Now the show had gone to a commercial break. There was some guy with an Australian accent selling a cleaning rag for fifteen dollars, which he claimed was somehow a hundred-dollar value, and you could get two rags for a special price if you phoned in during the next five minutes.

Wolf Eyes tried to get their attention. "Excuse me, but can we talk business now?"

The man in the silver mask waved him off. "Wait. *Jerry* is coming back on in a minute. Our business won't take long."

Sure enough, *Jerry* came back on. And, at this time, Elvira was sitting alone, and Jo Ellen was sitting next to Jethro, holding his hand. Jerry looked at his cards for the next cue.

"Jo Ellen, you are here to tell your big sister Elvira something today. Go ahead."

The camera panned in on Jo Ellen's ugly face.

"Elvira, you have been mean to Jethro, so he is going to marry me. I am carrying his baby."

With that, Elvira jumped on Jo Ellen again, and they rolled around some more on the floor, items of clothing and costume jewelry flying all over the set, all to the delight of the audience and the Illuminati. When the ladies, and we use this term generously, got back up and were seated, the camera zoomed in on Jerry.

"We have one more surprise guest. We have Jethro's father, Billy May, who was flown in secretly from Mississippi to be on the show."

At this point, an old hillbilly in overalls, who was bald and in very bad shape, came on the stage. He sat down with Elvira, Jo Ellen, and Jethro. Jerry gave him the floor.

"Billy May, today is a day for telling the truth, and I understand you have something to confess to your son Jethro."

The camera zoomed in on Billy May, who also had bad teeth.

"Jethro, I have to come clean with you. I have been sleeping with both Elvira and Jo Ellen for the past year, and that baby ain't yours; it's mine!"

At this point, all hell broke lose. The beeps covering up the profanity were coming fast and furious as the four rolled around on the floor. As the show went to commercial break, the Illuminati began to analyze the show. You could see they were connoisseurs.

Finally, Wolf Eyes realized the first segment was over. He turned to the Illuminati on his computer screen. "What's the job?"

The man with the silver mask did all of the talking. "At this point, all we want you to do is shadow a man. For now, we only need you to do that. If he gets too close to what he is looking for, we may require the services we have purchased from you in the past."

Wolf Eyes wanted specifics. "Who is he, where is he, and what do you not want him to get too close to?"

Silver Mask answered, "His name is Michelangelo Schwartz, a college professor."

Wolf Eyes could not believe his ears. "Michelangelo Schwartz? This is seriously his name?"

Silver Mask was not amused. "His name is, indeed, Michelangelo Schwartz. He lives in New Jersey, and we will tell you as you follow him when he is getting close to what he seeks. Right now, you are to stick to him like glue and let us know his movements. We cannot tell you right now what he is looking for, and we also cannot tell you what it means to get close to it, because the whole issue is beyond your need-to-know clearance. In addition, it would not be healthy for you to inquire more about what he seeks and where it might be. Are we clear?"

Wolf Eyes nodded, as he was absolutely clear what the consequences of a negative response would be. He also thought, if they had this much information, that meant that someone on the other team, someone close to and trusted by Michelangelo Schwartz, was playing on both sides of the fence. That meant this job was going to be a tricky minefield. Wolf Eyes would have to watch his step.

Silver Mask continued. "Half the usual fee is already in your account by the agreed upon means. In addition, an e-mail with all of the information and habits of Professor Michelangelo Schwartz has been sent to your secure e-mail account. Contact us in the usual way. It is essential, I repeat, absolutely essential, that Professor Schwartz not be successful. If it seems to us he is getting close or has made some essential connection, we will ask you to intervene to prevent his ultimate success. If this becomes necessary, we will so indicate by using the phrase 'Episode 432: Guess What? I'm a Man!'"

Wolf Eyes smiled. Naturally, the code phrase would be the title of a *Jerry Springer* episode. He thanked them and made ready to disconnect. Before he did, Red Mask interrupted.

"Be sure to stay tuned to the second part of the show. It is entitled 'Midgets of the Ku Klux Klan.'"

5

The chapter goes into the Kennedy assassination, humorous anagrams, and the mystery of Obama's birth certificate. Biff Braunschweiger demonstrates the reach of the Illuminati by showing how they have used television shows like *Gilligan's Island* to brainwash citizens. Finally, we learn the real reason why the question "Mary Ann or Ginger?" never arose during the three years the castaways spent on the island.

The apartment of Michelangelo Schwartz, Prospect Avenue, Bloomfield, New Jersey

The run-down apartment building was built before the Second World War, and, like its resident Michelangelo Schwartz, it had seen better days. William, Biff, and Michelangelo walked up to the third floor. There was no elevator. You could hear children crying and playing and smell the cabbage and tomato sauce cooking. The tile on the floor of the landings between the stairs was yellowed and cracked. The railings were worn. On the third floor, they arrived at an old wooden door with the sign "Chez Schwartz" on it.

Schwartz took a couple of swipes while trying to get the key into the lock and was finally successful. The inside of the apartment was in total and complete chaos. The walls were lined with old bookshelves that were overloaded with books. More books were piled everywhere. There was a beat-up desk, and on it there was a huge, old computer that you might find in a museum. All over the apartment were piles of paper. The kitchen, which was attached to the living room, was a wreck. The sink was overflowing with dirty dishes.

Schwartz had already pulled out a bottle of cheap Scotch and filled a dirty glass as he settled down to watch Biff's presentation. He didn't offer any to William or Biff. He was not that generous. He could not afford to be.

Biff Braunschweiger set up the projector, aimed it at a blank wall, and stood in front of the room. As he did, William looked through the mail that was piled on a table by the door. William looked up at Schwartz. "A lot of unopened mail here, with the words 'Final Notice' on it."

Biff wanted to get going with his presentation. "Professor Schwartz, before we can begin, we want to take you through a little slide show to show you just how pervasive the Illuminati have become in our culture."

Schwartz was not sure what to say, so he did what he always did in such circumstances—he said nothing. The Scotch tasted terrible, and it burned as it went down. Michelangelo Schwartz shivered as it hit him. But, then, he thought to himself that it didn't taste that terrible.

Biff went on. "You may not know it, but the Illuminati have become so powerful that they are able to broadcast their messages to society. They dress it up likes news and entertainment and, thus, make their schemes more palatable to an unknowing population. Like the frog that is slowly boiled in water, so it doesn't think to jump out until it is too late, the Illuminati have been softening us up for a long time, in preparation for the New World Order. Then they can, finally, publicly rule us all. As you may have heard, they already control banking, education, and politics. But things went into high gear when they decided to use the full power of Hollywood and that Satan-inspired box of sin and depravity we call television to spread their insidious message. My God, Schwartz, have you ever tuned into QVC? It is demonic."

Schwartz was not buying any of it. "You sound like you have been listening to too much Rush Limbaugh and Glenn Beck. Those whack jobs see a conspiracy around every corner. They think FEMA, the Federal Emergency Management Agency, made up of fire fighters and EMTs, is setting up concentration camps for loyal Tea Party members. They think that there is a homosexual agenda in kindergarten and that Obama is going to outlaw guns. So what do they do? They tell people Obama is going to take away their guns, so everybody runs out and buys every gun and bullet that they can stash away. After about a year of this stampede, ammunition is in short supply. And guess who they blame for it? Obama!"

Biff Braunschweiger laughed. "We have believed for a long time that Glenn and Rush actually work for the Illuminati. Then, Glenn went over the top last year and told his listeners not to check up on him or Rush on Google and other fact-checking websites, because they, too, were part of the big conspiracy. Think about it. 'Don't check what I say on Google, because Google is giving you the wrong answers.' Glenn is a thing of beauty."

Biff looked at his watch and wanted to get this going. He didn't have time to banter with the good professor. "But let's get back to the story of how the Illuminati got control of the media. They wanted to do it, but there was a problem with their plan. They had powerful enemies. As you may recall, Joe Kennedy Sr. made his money bootlegging whiskey during Prohibition and heading up the Irish Mafia in Boston. He was as dirty as a mine worker at quitting time. Joe Senior was a ruthless criminal who let nothing stand in his way. But, like the *Godfather* movie, he wanted a better life for his sons. You remember the line: 'Michael, I never wanted any of this for you.' In this case, it was 'Jack, Bobby, and Teddy, I never wanted any of this for you!' That was Joe and the Kennedy boys. Although Joe Kennedy Sr. was known to move in the inner circles of the Illuminati, his boys didn't want to play ball, as we say, and that was bad for them, very bad. His sons, John, Bobby, and Teddy, wanted to do away with the Mafia, the old guard, and, with them, the Illuminati. Those boys were brash, young, horny, and idealistic. You may recall Teddy was kicked out of Harvard for cheating. Bobby had some shady associations, and Jack never met a hooker he didn't like. These were the guys that wanted to clean up America. So they decided they would mess with the Mafia, J. Edgar Hoover, and the Illuminati.

"J. Edgar Hoover may have been a cross-dressing pervert with a predilection for little black cocktail dresses, but he was a formidable foe. So, if you play with fire, you'll get burned. On November 22, 1963, the Illuminati and their agents assassinated JFK in Dallas. They set up those poor saps Lee Harvey Oswald and Jack Ruby and, then, went about their work. Lee Harvey Oswald was innocent. Just because he had once moved to Russia and given up his American citizenship; married his wife, Marina, who was the daughter of a general in the KGB; played poker regularly with Jack Ruby; and visited the Russian Embassy twice in 1963, people thought he must be part of a conspiracy. What a laugh! How easily people jump to conclusions. Yes, the assassination of JFK was the second worst thing that happened to America that day."

This got Michelangelo Schwartz's attention. Schwartz was in high school when Kennedy was president. There was something about Kennedy he'd always liked. Little could he have guessed then how much they would have in common later in life. He thought that he was to college professors what Kennedy was to politicians. Then, he mused how sad it was that Kennedy had not lived long enough to visit a Hooters.

"Biff, did you say that the Kennedy assassination was the second worst thing that happened that day? Are you kidding? What was the first?"

Biff walked to the back of the darkened room and started the PowerPoint slide show. The first slide was the image of a tropical island with music playing in the background:

Just sit right back and you'll hear a tale,
A tale of a fateful trip,
That started from this tropic port,
Aboard this tiny ship.

The mate was a mighty sailing man.
The skipper, brave and sure.
Five passengers set sail that day for a three-hour tour,
A three-hour tour...

Schwartz could not believe what he was seeing. "*Gilligan's Island*? What has this got to do with the assassination of JFK and the Illuminati's plan to take over the world?"

Biff smiled. He knew Schwartz was hooked. "Patience, my new friend. If you give me half an hour, I will show you things you would not believe. Now let's begin our journey."

The next slide was of the *SS Minnow* heading out on a three-hour cruise.

"This is the opening scene for the pilot of *Gilligan's Island*. It seems innocent enough. A boat is serenely motoring through a harbor on its way out to sea. You, who are an expert in signs and symbols, Professor Schwartz, will be sure to notice that the American flag flying in the background of the harbor where the *SS Minnow* is pulling out of is flying at half-mast."

Schwartz had noticed that and wondered why that would be. Biff was about to tell him.

"That flag was at half-mast because this pilot was filmed late in the afternoon on November 22, 1963, the same day Kennedy was shot."

Schwartz was amazed. "Are you sure it was shot on the same day Kennedy was shot?"

Biff smiled. "Google it up, if you don't believe me. The cast had a moment of silence on the set, and then they went on with the filming. Hey! When Hollywood is on a schedule, it is on a schedule. But that is not all. Look at the name on the side of the boat, and see, its name is the *Minnow*."

Schwartz did not see the significance. "A minnow is a small fish. So would it not be a good name for a small boat?"

"Professor, it is not so simple. Let us go back to the politics of 1963. Newton N. Minnow was the man President Kennedy picked to run the Federal Communications Commission."

Schwartz was still not following the argument. "What has the chairman of the FCC got to do with *Gilligan's Island*?"

"Professor, he has two things to do with it. Newton Minnow hated the creator of *Gilligan's Island*. Minnow was also the man who called TV the 'great wasteland.' By naming the boat the *Minnow*, the Illuminati were thumbing their noses at those who wanted to keep television from reaching its full potential as a tool for propaganda and brainwashing. They were saying, 'The hell with the FCC. We will use this great wasteland to make Americans compliant zombies.' Why do you think that The Learning Channel started off with shows about science and British history and quickly came out with shows about celebrities, ghost stories, and pawnshops? How could *Ghost Hunters* go on for seven seasons? And people still tune in, hoping against hooe they might actually see a ghost. Who actually believes that line in the commercial that claims the first hundred callers will get those diet pills for free, with no obligation? In England, they have the BBC, which gives us stories of the English monarchy, complex miniseries based on Charles Dickens, and science programs that you need math to understand. In America, we have *The Bachelor*, and we know he will never marry the girl who gets the rose. But there are other reasons for this name on the boat, as you will shortly discover."

Schwartz settled back and took a swig. The next slide was of the island.

"Professor Schwartz, while the Illuminati is an ancient organization, the members began to form globally at the end of the Christian Middle Ages. Much of the symbolism they use today references that time. You are an expert on said time. Thinking like a person in the medieval period, can you name a place that you wouldn't want to be in, could be stuck in forever, and would not be able to get out of, no matter how hard you tried?"

It was beginning to dawn on Schwartz that this was getting interesting. "Hell, the ninth circle, Dante's *Inferno*."

Biff smiled. "Yes, Dante's *Inferno*. Now tell us, Professor, what does one do to end up in hell?"

"Sin, Biff. You end up in hell by committing sin."

"Yes, Professor. Now, the Catholics were very big on cataloging and dividing these sins into mortal and venial sins. But there was a special class of sins that was especially dangerous for Catholics."

Michelangelo Schwartz was in his element.

"The seven deadly sins: lust, greed, sloth, pride, envy, anger, and gluttony."

"Excellent, Professor. You are doing well. Now let us go on to the next slide."

It was a studio picture of the cast of *Gilligan's Island*. Schwartz quickly realized there were seven castaways. Thurston Howell III, his wife, Mrs. Howell, the Skipper, Gilligan, the Professor, Mary Ann, and Ginger. Seven castaways, seven deadly sins. Could it be?

Biff took out his laser pen and began to point to the characters, one at a time.

"OK, Professor, you can walk me through this. Let us match a sin with each of the castaways. Let us begin with Thurston Howell III, played by the great character actor Jim Backus, a rich and selfish multimillionaire who came aboard the Minnow with suitcases full of cash. While the name is spelled differently, we recognize the Roman god, Bacchus, god of sensual pleasure, drunkenness, and excess. Hell, Jim Backus only got the role because of the symbolic meaning of his last name. But most of all, Thurston Howell III wanted it all for himself. Do you think it was an accident that they chose an actor whose very name hints at the real sin of wanting it all for himself?"

Schwartz knew where this was going, so he decided to play along. "He would represent the sin of greed."

"Next, we have Mrs. Howell, Thurston's wife, also known as Lovey. She never lifts a finger to help on the island. She was raised in wealth and never learned to do anything for herself. She often sleeps in late, and she wants Gilligan and Mary Ann to wait on her. What sin would you say she represents, Professor?"

"That is obvious. Mrs. Howell would represent sloth or what we today call laziness."

Biff smiled. "The Middle Ages were a glorious time. Just think of it. Laziness was a sin, and now it is the goal of everybody who listens to Jimmy Buffett music or buys Tommy Bahama shirts. Next comes Ginger. Tina Louise plays Ginger. She is a movie star who oozes sexuality. She is often scantily clad, licks her lips in a suggestive manner, and makes jokes about how many men she has manipulated through her good looks. Professor?"

"Ginger represents lust."

"Next comes the innocent and wholesome Mary Ann. She has pigtails and dresses very modestly but really wishes she were more like Ginger. What do we say of someone who wishes they were someone else?"

"That's simple. Mary Ann represents envy."

"Next, Professor, we have another professor. He is a curious one. He can make a radio out of a coconut and a machine to air-condition the huts, but he can't seem to figure out how to fix a three-foot hole on the boat. He is logical. He thinks he can solve any problem, and he has no humility and knows no limits."

"So the Professor's sin is pride. Hold on. I was OK up until now. We would be OK, because there are now two sins left, gluttony and anger, and two castaways left, Gilligan and the Skipper. But there's a problem, Biff."

"No, there is no problem. I can already guess what you are going to say. You are about to tell me that Gilligan can be neither gluttony nor anger. He eats like a bird, is skinny as a rail, and he never gets mad. But think about it for a minute. The Skipper, played by Alan Hale Jr., is obese, which indicates gluttony. He also abuses Gilligan, is short with him, and frequently strikes him; thus, we have anger. So the Skipper represents both gluttony and anger."

"So you have the seven deadly sins but only six people. That is not a neat package. We have Gilligan left without a job."

Biff knew where the conversation was going. "Not at all. We have hell, where they can't escape. We have the seven deadly sins that got them there, so what is missing?"

Schwartz smiled. "Of course...Satan."

Biff went on. "Gilligan as Satan. This program was the flagship broadcast of the Illuminati to show us the New World Order, their plan, their values, and how we can all get there. It is to be paradise for those who control it, but for the rest us, shipwrecked without any hope of rescue, it will be hell. It is like Dostoevsky's Grand Inquisitor in *The Brothers Karamazov*. The Illuminati will, then, give us new values and a new world. The freedom that Americans value so much will be swept away in a police state run by peace-keepers from the United Nations, overseen by Nancy Pelosi and Hillary Clinton. First, they will take away our guns, and next, we will have to surrender our PlayStation 2s and our Xboxes, and then they will come for our iPods. It will be terrible."

Schwartz did not understand. "What values is this New World Order going to bring along? What do they want us to do?"

"Well, Professor, let me answer your question by asking you a simple question. Mary Ann or Ginger?"

Schwartz didn't understand. "'Mary Ann or Ginger?' What are you talking about? What has that got to do with the values of the new society?"

"Boy! You professors are really out of it. No wonder college sucks and your students can't find jobs when they graduate. 'Mary Ann or Ginger?' is a classic question asked of red-blooded American heterosexual males to see about their taste in women."

Schwartz got it. "In that case, I will take both Mary Ann and Ginger!"

Biff Braunschweiger smiled. Professor Schwartz was going to be a fun travel companion.

"OK," Biff continued. "So the classic question has been 'Mary Ann or Ginger?' Do you like the all-American girl next door or the sexy, wild party girl? Which one is your type? But now comes something that does not add up. While millions of American men have asked this question in bars all over the country for generations, isn't it strange that on the show the Professor, Gilligan, and the Skipper never showed the slightest interest in either one? Does it not strike you as odd that in its three seasons on the air, not once did the three single males make any play for Ginger or Mary Ann? So the classic question: 'Mary Ann or Ginger?' never actually arose on the show. And, if you think about it, there can only be one answer to explain this curious anomaly."

Schwartz refilled his glass. He was a world-class drinker. Biff went on.

"The question of Mary Ann or Ginger was never asked because they were all gay, every last one of them. That is the only possible explanation. If they were straight, after about the first two months, those boys would have gotten antsy and would have been on Ginger like white on rice. You have heard of Hollywood's gay agenda? Well, the yellow brick road to the gay city of Oz started on *Gilligan's Island*. Even Mr. and Mrs. Howell slept in separate beds. That was because their marriage was just for show. And did you ever see the way Mr. Howell leered at Gilligan when Gilligan was sweaty or swimming? It was disgusting and so obvious. Even though the island was large and there were numerous huts, Gilligan and the Skipper slept together in the same hut, in hammocks over each other like bunk beds. Gilligan fell out of his bed and into the Skipper's arms at the ends of episodes 12, 23, and 44. As the credits rolled at the end of the episodes, can you guess what was happening to the Skipper's 'little buddy'?

"And did you notice that Ginger and Mary Ann shared a hut away from the others? Why were they not interested in men? I will tell you why! Because the innocent and childlike Mary Ann, with her little pigtails and schoolgirl outfits, was being brutalized and ravished by the more sophisticated, lustful, and experienced Ginger. Imagine Mary Ann eventually giving in to her sinful lesbian impulses. Now further imagine the two of them in the bamboo shower, slowly soaping each other in a sensuous way, the way all true red-blooded American men imagine all lesbians do."

Schwartz could barely contain his enthusiasm. "This is getting good!"

At that moment, Michelangelo Schwartz looked at the expression of lust on William's face and realized that he and William finally had something in common after all.

Biff now put up a slide of a Norman Rockwell painting. It was of a happy and loving nuclear family: a father, a mother, and two smiling children, all sitting down to a Thanksgiving meal. The mother, in her apron, is serving the father, who, of course, is wearing a tie, while two well-behaved blond children smile as they look at the turkey and all of the trimmings. It was the way America used to be, a wholesome and moral country, back before the days of Rachael Ray, Axl Rose, and Sean Hannity.

"Do you see this wholesome all-American family, Professor Schwartz? That was the target of the Illuminati. They wanted to destroy the fabric of traditional values. And the battering ram they were going to use to smash in the door of morality and faith was *Gilligan's Island*. Once the Illuminati had this vehicle, they had a message, and it was not simply their homosexual agenda. Notice there is no place to use money on *Gilligan's Island*, and the Professor rules through science and technology. We now see a socialist, communal world where the controlling shepherd rounds up the sheep. No longer was it the strong American males of *Gunsmoke*, *The Rifleman*, or *Father Knows Best* but the bumbling, weak males of *Gilligan's Island* trying to serve lusty, orgasm-crazed, oversexed women. The New World Order was beginning to be laid out.

"What you may not know is that the filming of the pilot commenced with military precision when Kennedy was killed. You may have heard stories about how Lyndon Johnson quickly pushed Bobby Kennedy to the side, even during the funeral arrangements for JFK. Johnson wanted to make sure Bobby and his buddy Newton Minnow of the FCC were out of the way so that the Illuminati could do their work. President Johnson was a good old Texas boy who knew the score. Johnson was the perfect front man for the Illuminati, the Trilateral Commission, and the New World Order. With JFK out of the way, they had their blueprint, and *Gilligan's Island* began preparing the rest of us to accept it. Johnson showed us our fate. When he picked up that Texas hound dog by his ears, he was showing us in the clearest way that we needed to be subservient and compliant. That was a secret message by the Illuminati saying that we could not resist. This brainwashing began a few hours after they took care of JFK, and, shortly after that, we were all zombies drinking Bud Light and watching sports, oblivious to the shackles Mary Ann and Ginger had clamped on our minds. By the time *Gilligan's Island* ended its run in 1967, the damage was done. The Beatles and the Rolling Stones had taken the place of the Lone Ranger and Marshall Dillon as the role models to be emulated.

"In 1964, during the first season of *Gilligan*, a lot happened. Johnson declared war on poverty and began to redistribute America's wealth. Cities were burning, and the Beatles arrived in the United States. Virtue was drowned out in the screams of teenyboppers yelling "John," "George," "Paul," and, most inexplicably, "Ringo." But the impact of *Gilligan's Island* really began to be felt in 1965, when it all started to go down. Malcolm X was assassinated, Martin Luther King Jr. led the Selma march, and Johnson began to enforce the Voting Rights Act that unleashed chaos on the American South. Johnson began to bomb North Vietnam, and the first draft riots and antiwar marches started all over America. That year, Watts, a neighborhood in Los Angeles, was burning, and cities all over America experienced riots. The year 1967 was the Summer of Love. America was falling apart; the Soviet Union had begun to collapse; South Africa was in turmoil, and Europe was experiencing more riots than it had seen since 1848. Gilligan had done his work."

Biff stopped to catch his breath and noticed that Schwartz had settled down and was quiet and attentive.

Biff began again. "Something else you might not know is that Paul Simon wrote the mysterious and prophetic *Sounds of Silence* in February of 1964 in reaction to the assassination of JFK. A sensitive soul and a poet, Paul Simon sensed something in the Zeitgeist had changed on November 22, 1963. He and many other folk singers could feel the icy fingers of the Illuminati beginning to pull the strings of our society. Did you ever listen to the lyrics of 'At the Zoo'? But what Paul Simon did not know, and could not know, was that on the very same day that JFK was assassinated, the forces of darkness began their insidious plan. When the Illuminati rubbed out Kennedy to get their message out, Paul Simon sensed something new and disturbing was about to happen. What did he know when he penned the line 'Hello, darkness, my old friend'? Is it a coincidence that *Gilligan's Island* appeared on American television the same month that the *Sounds of Silence* was released?"

Biff next showed a slide of Gilligan standing next to Paul Simon. "Another thing you may not know is that there was a strong connection between Hollywood and the New York folk scene. At that time, Bob Denver, who played Gilligan, was a friend not only to Paul Simon but to Bob Dylan, as well. And you may recall that before *Gilligan's Island*, Bob Denver played a beatnik named Maynard G. Krebs on the show *The Many Loves of Dobie Gillis*. That show starred Dwayne Hickman as a red-blooded, blond, athletic, heterosexual, patriotic, hardworking American teenager. Bob Denver was his dirty, lazy, beatnik sidekick. He used to stutter on the letter *W* when he tried to say the word 'work,' which terrified him.

"How is it that suddenly Bob Denver was in a new show that was named after his character? How is it that Gilligan replaced Randolph Scott and John Wayne? How could this abomination have occurred? It has been speculated by Bob Dylan's biographer, Phil McNair, that Bob Denver suggested to Dylan the lyrics for 'A Hard Rain's a-Gonna Fall.' That song hints that the Illuminati will soon take over and that they will rule with an iron fist. If you doubt that, listen to the lyrics of 'Masters of War.' You have also heard the Dylan song 'All Along the Watchtower.' If you know that song, you might remember the line 'Outside in the cold distance, a wildcat did growl, two riders were approaching, and the wind began to howl.' Don Jenner, in his well-documented book *Dylan: The Village Years*, tells us the two riders they were referring to are Bob Denver and Alan Hale, as Gilligan and the Skipper, bringing in the New World Order."

Schwartz could not believe his ears. But Biff continued. "But we are not done yet. As a scholar of medieval symbols, you know that colors have significance. Let us look at the three single males on *Gilligan's Island*. Notice the Skipper only wears blue; Gilligan only wears red, and the Professor only wears white. They used red, white, and blue to symbolize America, the new target of the Illuminati. By 1964, Baron Rothschild and his Eurotrash ilk had bled Europe dry, and now they were on to new lands, like Dracula leaving Transylvania for the green countryside of pastoral England.

"But there are still some curiosities we need to understand. You may not have known that there are, mysteriously, two versions of the *Gilligan's Island* theme song. The first version goes: 'The millionaire and his wife/ the movie star and the rest.' But, by 'the rest,' they meant only two people—the Professor and Mary Ann. While they were mentioned in the second version, why were these two not mentioned in the first? The answer is simple. They were the two-person dyad that gave away the Illuminati's plan. It would have been too obvious, even to the casual viewer. The Professor used science and logic to control the weak and powerless. Who was being controlled? Mary Ann, a simple farm girl with pigtails, dressed like an innocent farm girl, representing the traditional, wholesome, nuclear, patriarchal family of the American heartland that *Gilligan's Island* had swept away like the storm that carried away the *SS Minnow*. The image of the strong and ruthless Illuminati masters using science and control to crush innocent and wholesome Americans may have been too much to include in the song. The image of the Professor and the lusty and overweight Mr. Howell having their brutal way with the defenseless and innocent Mary Ann is exactly what the Illuminati have in store for all of us!

"Finally, you may not know this, but both Bob Denver and Alan Hale do not have headstones. They were both cremated. Don't you find that curious? Alan Hale claimed he wanted his ashes spread at sea by the Neptune Society, and no one knows where Bob Denver's ashes were spread. Is this so that they would not be worshiped as the bringers of the New World Order? As *Gilligan's Island's* run was ending, American values were crumbling. Free-loving, panhandling, and pot-smoking loafers were the new order. John Wayne Gacy had replaced John Wayne. Shortly after *Gilligan's Island* was finishing its run, the hippies came. Now, Professor, what kind of pants did the hippies wear?"

Schwartz recalled his own hippie days. "Bell-bottoms."

"And what kind of pants did Gilligan wear? Are you beginning to get the picture? Of course, you may know that years later, the Village People's famous song 'In the Navy' was actually an homage to Gilligan and the Skipper."

Schwartz wasn't buying it. "Tell me you're kidding?"

"Kidding? Kidding about such an important subject? How about that other song 'YMCA'? Did you know that within that supposedly innocent title is the hidden Illuminati message that tells us 'You Must Change America'? It is frightening. But the Village People had the images from *Gilligan's Island* as their inspiration. As a manly, hairy-chested, dominant male, the Skipper was a 'bear,' as they say in gay culture, and his innocent and sweet 'cub' was Gilligan. If you go to a costume party in Greenwich Village, Provincetown, Fire Island, Delray Beach, or San Francisco, you will inevitably see a couple dressed as Gilligan and the Skipper, those two who did so much to tear down American family values and usher in the new age of control, government surveillance, the New World Order. These heroes to the LGBT community, anarchists, perverts, and communists are the sworn enemies of the Holy Mother Church. Gilligan and the Skipper did more to destroy morality than all of the countless generations of gangsters, heretics, and criminals that preceded them. Now, Professor, let me ask you one last question to see how much of this you have retained and what you have grasped. It is a simple question: Who do you think is buried in Grant's tomb?"

Michelangelo Schwartz thought for a second. "Gilligan?"

Biff smiled with approval. "You are on the right track. The full answer is Gilligan and the Skipper were buried in their costumes, so they could be together in death as they were in life, and, there, they could be honored by the Illuminati."

Schwartz took one more sip and turned to William and Biff. "There is one last thing I have to mention. The creator and writer of *Gilligan's Island* was Sherwood Schwartz, from Passaic, New Jersey, my uncle."

William stood up and made the sign of the cross. "This is a sign from God. May he be with us on our journey and keep us in his hands. But, oh, Lord, if you had only granted me half an hour with Ginger!"

The lights came back on as Biff turned off the projector. But he was not done lecturing. "The document initiating this search was given to a professor at Oxford University. The Vatican suggests we start there. We can catch a flight to Heathrow tomorrow night, if you are game."

Schwartz noticed the bottle was almost empty, an experience that was not new to him. He turned to his two visitors. "Gentleman, and that includes you, Sister Bill, I am just about out of Scotch, and I am down on my finances. I have zero confidence that anything you have told me tonight is true, and I have even less confidence that of all of the people in the world, I am the one and only person you need to find the Holy Grail, if such a thing exists. However, because of the constraints put on me by my landlord and accountant, I will tentatively accept your offer and will be glad to accompany you. I will be glad to serve the Holy Mother Church. I ask almost nothing in return, only half the cash down now and a seat in first class to Europe and back."

Biff thought for a moment. "We will give you two thousand dollars now and the rest when you solve the puzzle."

Schwartz smiled. "So I ask for twenty-five grand, and you give me two? But, times being what they are, I will accept. So let's see where this goes."

At that moment, William was sorry that Michelangelo had drained the bottle. He could have used a drink.

6

Professor Schwartz visits the New York Public Library to bone up on conspiracy theories. We find the connection between the Trilateral Commission, the Freemasons, and Mothers Against Drunk Driving. We hear about Ruby, who once made mad, passionate love to Michelangelo Schwartz but later stabbed him with a pair of scissors and tried to run him down with her Dodge Avenger.

The New York Public Library, 5th Avenue, between 42nd and 41st Streets, Manhattan, New York

Michelangelo Schwartz was a drunk, a lecher, a habitual philanderer, and a born liar, but there was one thing he was good at—he was a scholar. For some inexplicable reason, with all of his ex-wives, escapades, financial troubles, difficulties with stupid, control-freak deans, and pending lawsuits, he had kept up his ability to read and write scholarly texts. He knew how to research and present ideas in a way that made him a star in the academic world. It was only when people met him personally that problems arose.

Academics were not like other humans, whom they often referred to as "mere mortals." You may not know it, but the very word "school" comes from the Latin *schola,* which means "to loaf or do nothing." For example, while Julius Caesar and Augustus Caesar were being busy little beavers, conquering the world and trying to get conquered peoples, like the Jews and Irish, to color inside the lines (a task that, two thousand years later, remains undone), their descendants Caligula and Nero excelled at *schola* when they were not torturing or murdering their subjects.

Human history is based on creation and work. We have crawled out of the caves and come down from the trees by the work of industrious and hardened leaders who labored diligently to improve our condition. Men like Leonardo da Vinci, Thomas Edison, Cornelius Vanderbilt, Henry Ford, and Bill Gates worked day and night to bring us a better world. However, most professors have a different idea. Like Cheech and Chong in that classic of the silver screen *Up in Smoke*, they prefer a life of *schola* to working around the clock to cure cancer. You may ask why the typical college professor has a life expectancy that is a full six years longer than the average American male. Then you see them tottering around campuses, lecturing off the same yellow notes they took as undergraduates a full two generations ago, perfectly happy and content to live a life where their teaching load starts at noon on Monday and is over by two in the afternoon on Wednesday, and, suddenly, it makes sense.

This was the life Michelangelo Schwartz would have enjoyed forever had it not been for his major vice—women. Most often, it was co-eds. But he was very democratic when it came to his love of the opposite sex. His troubled past had highlights, such as being caught with the dean's wife in his VW Bug during the faculty Christmas party and being surprised by Sister Bill as he lowered himself down using a sheet from the convent. Believe us, you don't want to know what he was doing in there. Then, there was his most memorable event of all. He was leaving a motel at six o'clock in the morning with a married woman when he ran into another couple just coming into the same rent-by-the-hour motel. It was Michelangelo's companion's husband, a real-estate giant in the community who, by the way, was also the chairman of the college board of trustees. Upon meeting him in the lobby of that shabby motel, Professor Schwartz uttered his most famous and well-used phrase—"Whoops!" Needless to say, this did not help his career.

So he bounced from one job to another. He was hired on the strength of his vita (a vita was what academics called their résumé, because they were too special just to have a résumé). He was hired because he published books, articles, and reviews that made him look like an academic superstar. When they hired him, they always falsely believed they were raising the standards of the department and starting on the road to being an academic powerhouse. Six months later, amid scandal, lawsuits, angry husbands, and threats of public exposés, they all wondered why they'd only checked the two references he had given them on his vita, which turned out to be two phone numbers, one of a bartender in Key West and the other belonging to his younger brother in Apex, North Carolina, both of whom he had paid to lie for him.

Schwartz could not help himself around beautiful women. He could recite poetry, had traveled the world, and had a devil-may-care attitude that made women love him. When he was younger, he almost never chased any women; he just never ran away. As he aged, he had to take the first step, and, most of the time, he struck out. This new adventure promised to give him the money and leisure time to get back to his old tricks, and, consequently, he was all in.

The New York Public Library was an amazing place. It was founded by the great robber barons Astor and Carnegie. Today, most New Yorkers don't associate Carnegie with the library but rather with a deli in Times Square, which is famous for sandwiches that nobody can eat in one sitting and you are not supposed to take with you. With the exception of the Library of Congress, which began when Thomas Jefferson bequeathed his personal library to the nation, the New York Public Library was the largest library in the United States. Thomas Jefferson was quoted as saying that, after the slave quarters, his library was his favorite place to "blow off steam." But the New York Public Library was impressive. With fifty-two million volumes, it was the third largest in the world and superior to any college library in the Americas.

The building, which was opened in 1911 with a speech by none other than President Taft, was in the Beaux-arts architectural tradition and was the largest marble building in America at that time. Two stone lions stand guard on either side of the main entrance on Fifth Avenue. The legend is that they started there alive but died in position from pollution. Behind the library is Bryant Park, almost a whole city block of gardens, chessboards, cafés, and bandstands. In the heart of the city, it is an oasis of green...well, yellow-green.

Now most people only know about the New York Public Library from movies and shows like *Breakfast at Tiffany's*, *Sex and the City*, *Spider-Man*, and, of course, the classic haunted library scene in *Ghostbusters*. It had once been a fertile fishing ground for Michelangelo Schwartz's love life. It was here, in the periodicals room, that he met Ruby, with whom he made mad, passionate love, and who, later, tried to stab him with a pair of scissors and run him down with her Dodge Avenger.

Michelangelo Schwartz was in the Rose Main Reading Room. As he sat down in his usual spot at the end of a long oak table, he looked at the room that never ceased to fill him with awe. It was an amazing and majestic space that was two city blocks long. So he always could avoid sitting next to the young lady he'd picked up two weeks ago and promised, falsely, to love forever. The room was decorated to look like an ancient reading room you might find in one of the great universities in Europe, with low-hanging incandescent lamps and large windows on both sides that let in an excellent quantity of light. The room was surrounded in dark wood paneling, with bookshelves all around.

Looking up, Michelangelo Schwartz often thought he could see the sky, but that was an artful illusion. Fifty-two feet above his head, the ceiling was painted with a mural of floating clouds. Schwartz often recalled that many famous New Yorkers had researched and read in this reading room, and it would continue to be the home of tomorrow's literary luminaries. Such notables as Norman Mailer, Isaac Bashevis Singer, E. L. Doctorow, Elizabeth Bishop, and Danny Bonaduce had sat in this room. You may recall the story of how Marian Anderson was not allowed into Constitution Hall in Washington, DC, by the all-white Daughters of the American Revolution on account of her race. In a similar way, a disgraced former New York congressman was also once banned from the reading room of the New York Public Library, but for reasons having nothing to do with race.

Today, unlike so many days, Michelangelo Schwartz was on a mission. He had a first-class ticket from JFK to London that he was going to use that night. The flight would leave at six in the evening and land at Heathrow just after dawn. But, before that, he had to bone up on the Illuminati. The list he gave to the reference librarian was one she had seen before. Conspiracy theorists were regular users of libraries worldwide. They were usually hungry for information, too poor to buy the books they needed, and often liked to read in public spaces. They reasonably feared the CIA would shoot them for taking out those books.

He opened his red leather book bag, which he had bought thirty years ago at an outdoor market in Florence. It was covered with coffee stains and even had a few bloodstains from past paper cuts. He took out his notebook. As he was getting set up, the librarian carried over a stack of books and placed them next to him on the table.

The first book was entitled *Secret Societies and Dangerous Movements*. It told the story of the most famous and only agreed upon and real member of the Illuminati. On May Day in 1776, an auspicious year in many ways, an idealistic and young professor named Adam Weishaupt initiated a new organization. He was born on February 6, 1748, had been trained by the Jesuits, and the secret organization he founded was christened the "Illuminati."

Michelangelo Schwartz knew a great deal about the Jesuits or the Society of Jesus. A crazed Spanish soldier, who later became a priest and mortified his own flesh, had founded the Jesuits. If you don't often use "mortified" in casual conversation, you can still guess its meaning. The Jesuits were the pope's secret agents. In a document written in 1530, which has never surfaced but exists only in rumor, Pope Paul III stated that the Jesuits were exempt from the Ten Commandments. This meant the Jesuits were allowed to use any means necessary to accomplish their ends. They were fanatical supporters of the pope and church tradition. Jesuit members infiltrated political and religious organizations to better achieve their goals.

Weishaupt called his organization the Order of Perfectibilists, and he called himself Brother Spartacus. Schwartz had always liked that name and once knew a gay bartender who called himself Brother Spartacus and mixed cocktails at Marie's Crisis Café in Greenwich Village. The order of the Illuminati had spies and spies who spied on the spies. And, then, Weishaupt spied on the spies who were spying on the spies. Historians tell us he and his merry band joined a Masonic lodge in Munich in 1777. The Illuminati then attempted to infiltrate the Freemasons. The house of Rothschild, a name well-known to conspiracy theorists, secretly funded him. Boy, couple up the Rothschilds and the Jesuits, and you've got some serious shit.

But, eventually, Weishaupt believed that he personally was illuminated (just like most college professors), exempt from the laws of nature, and meant to rule the world as an ascendant spiritual master. He believed in a world without boundaries, where goods, without nations, without money, and without family, would be shared. It was like *Gilligan's Island*! In 1784, he was betrayed by some of his followers who thought he had gotten a swollen head, and they accused him of treason. At this point, he fled Bavaria. The Illuminati were dispersed, and that should have been the end of it. But was it?

Michelangelo Schwartz smiled as he thought about what came afterward. People love conspiracies. So, of course, they thought the Illuminati had gone underground and now ruled the world in secret through a number of other groups.

As the morning wore on, Schwartz read more books that were no longer published by Harvard University Press or Cambridge University Press but were products of Bob's Press in Butte, Montana. Eventually, he got to books that looked like they were run off on a copy machine in somebody's basement. These classics of literature and sloppy research connected the Illuminati to the Jews (hey, they get blamed for everything, so why not?), the Bilderberg Group, the Society for the Preservation of Barbershop Quartets, the Committee of 300, the old families of the European Black Nobility, Toastmasters International, the American Eastern Liberal Establishment, Planned Parenthood, the Freemasons, the March of Dimes, the Skull and Bones Society of Yale University, the Mumma Group, the American Federation of Teachers, Acorn, the National and World Council of Churches, the Circle of Initiates, NASA, the Nine Unknown Men, the Elks, the Lucis Trust, Blue Cross and Blue Shield, Jesuit Liberation Theologians, the Order of the Elders of Zion, the US Olympic Committee, the Nasi Princes, the Grand Encampment of the Knights Templar, La Leche League of America, the International Monetary Fund, the League of Women Voters, the Bohemian Club of San Francisco, the Order of Saint John of Jerusalem, One World Government Church, Socialist International, the Black Order, the Thule Society, the Rosicrucians, the Great Superior Ones, the White Lodge, the Trilateral Commission, and Mothers Against Drunk Driving.

It seemed there was little agreement among the conspiracy theorists, even though there were thousands of them. Schwartz looked at his list of those organizations thought to secretly control the world. He thought how wonderful it would be if, in fact, there were an Illuminati and there was some logic to the world. Wouldn't it be wonderful if there was somebody in charge, somebody keeping an eye on things, making sure things did not go too far off the tracks? As he thought this, he saw a newspaper on the end of the table. It was a copy of *The Key West Citizen* that someone had left in the library. He picked it up and perused the first page. There were three stories on the front page. "Fantasyfest Brings Nudity and Drunkenness to Key West," "Stripper Snorting Bath Salts Robs Armored Car," and "Baboon Attacks Man at Hog's Breath Saloon." He put down the paper. It would be nice thinking there was some logic to the world. Then, he thought about Key West.

7

We take a plane ride to Europe, sitting next to an assassin who never misses. We explore the pleasures of flying to Europe in coach. We learn the relationship between spanking the monkey and Custer's Last Stand. We see how a book can open a door. Finally, Professor Schwartz learns you can drink for free in first class, all the way from New York to London.

JFK International Airport, Jamaica, New York

The three arrived at the airport early. But they were not alone. Wolf Eyes was standing near the gate, reading a newspaper. Soon, he spotted what he guessed was his possible target. He quickly ducked into a bookstore next to the gate, while keeping an eye on Dr. Schwartz. So as not to arouse suspicion, he grabbed a book, without looking at the title, and got in line to purchase it. He had not brought a book along, and, whatever it was, it might keep him busy on the six-hour flight to Europe. Having a book was a good excuse for not engaging in conversation. It always helped to have one with you on an airplane if you wanted to be left alone. However, if he had taken the time to glance at the title, he would have seen this was the wrong book to take on a crowded flight. It was the worst book he could have purchased.

First class cabin, United Airlines Flight 511 from New York's JFK to Heathrow, United Kingdom

The United Airlines flight from JFK to Heathrow was almost totally sold out. But, with Biff's connections, the three traveling companions were in the first-class cabin.

There are two ways to fly to Europe. Most people fly coach, and this means they sit up in stiff chairs while the people in front of them tilt their seats back until they hit the exhausted travelers in the face. For the filthy rich, it is an entirely different experience. They lie down on silk sheets, drinking fine wines, and are pampered like the princes and princesses they are. They have filet mignon, served with real silverware on monogrammed white cotton napkins, while their fellow passengers in coach are thrown a few bags of peanuts for dinner. Occasionally, one of the coach passengers will cry out in anguish, "For God sakes! We are not elephants!" But then that is how the cookie crumbles. For one group, the trip is torture; for the other, it is a luxury cruise. That's what makes America great—free choice. The rich can choose first class, and the rest of us get to choose coach. In coach, you can get a meal fit for a king. Here, King! Supper, boy!

William and Biff were sitting together a few rows back, and Michelangelo Schwartz had the window seat in the first row. Back in coach sat Salvatore Greco, who, on the instructions of the Vatican, was keeping close to his mark, in case he needed to tie up any loose ends. A crowded plane was the perfect place to keep an eye on Professor Michelangelo Schwartz. Salvatore did not mind coach. He was a peasant, and he offered up all of his suffering for the poor souls in purgatory, if that place still existed.

Michelangelo was adjusting his seat belt when a man came up and sat down in the seat next to him. The man was in his midthirties and had a beautiful black leather briefcase. His shirt, pants, and sports jacket were all jet black, and they screamed "expensive." He had blond hair and was wearing glasses with a gold metal rim frame. The man sat down without looking at Michelangelo and opened up a copy of *Le Monde Diplomatique* and buried himself in it.

What Michelangelo Schwartz could not know was that this was the man known as "Wolf Eyes." By accident, sheer coincidence, Wolf Eyes had booked the last seat in first class and found himself sitting next to Dr. Michelangelo Schwartz. Wolf Eyes realized he had gotten unlucky, but it was too late now. Hopefully, he could get through the flight with as little notice and conversation as possible. Besides, he was one of those lucky people who could sleep on airplanes. This seating choice was a major mistake, and he would have to minimize its impact.

The plane took off just as the sun was setting and headed northeast over the Nova Scotia coast, where it would gently veer due east over Greenland and Iceland and eventually pass over Ireland on its way to England. About twenty minutes after the plane took off, a particularly good-looking flight attendant came to the first row and asked if there was anything they needed.

Schwartz's seatmate shook his head no and hid behind the newspaper he held up in front of him. But Michelangelo rarely flew first class and wanted to take full advantage.

"Can I order champagne?"

She smiled. "You can have whatever you like. This is an international flight."

"In that case, I will have a glass of the bubbly."

The good professor sat back and waited for his drink. As he did, he thought about all of the strange events of the past few days and started to wonder about all the pieces that had fallen into place. Sister Bill was his sworn enemy and had helped ruin his life twenty years ago. While he was often in trouble because of his constant and habitual philandering, he'd had a particularly bad fallout with Sister Bill over that student he'd called "Big Lulu." Schwartz closed his eyes and pictured her. Lulu Lefay was the tall, blond pitcher on the college softball team. Watching her throw strikes drove him absolutely wild. He usually never attended sporting events, but seeing Big Lulu covered with sweat while throwing that ball was an event not to be missed. He could not have guessed why her coach, Sister Bill, was clapping so hard as well.

Lulu made the mistake of signing up for Professor Schwartz's Introduction to Poetry class. Three weeks into the course, after spending hours on the love poems of Keats and Shelley, the inevitable happened. Lulu came to Schwartz's office hours, which he actually kept for the first time in years when he heard she was coming, for what she termed "extra help." The after-school help drifted into drinks, which drifted into dinner, and, after that, things heated up. As often happened with Professor Michelangelo Schwartz, nature took its course.

Things went wonderfully at first, and it seemed that, maybe, for the first time in his life, Michelangelo Schwartz was truly and deeply in love. Everything went along well, until Schwartz and Big Lulu were discovered almost *in flagrante delecto* in his office by none other than Sister Bill. *In flagrante delecto* is Latin for "in blazing offence." And, if you had seen what Lulu Lefay was about to do when Sister Bill kicked in the office door, you would know why this phrase has survived in the original language. What Schwartz had not known and what Lulu had never mentioned was that Sister Bill had beaten Michelangelo to what he, in his classical language, called the "Golden Fleece." The Golden Fleece was what Jason and the Argonauts sought in their quest. In the myth, Jason met Medea, an angry woman who ruined his life. In this misadventure, Schwartz crossed Sister Bill, and the outcome was the same. What does the old song say? *Que sera, sera* (whatever will be, will be).

As the champagne did its work, Michelangelo Schwartz was transported to that drunken, dreamy state where he spent much of his life. He wondered if it was a coincidence that Sister Bill, who was once his bitter enemy, was now a man and his traveling companion. Was it a coincidence that Sherwood Schwartz, the creator of *Gilligan's Island* was his uncle? Was it a coincidence that they had wanted him along on this adventure? Could this have all been a kind of crazy accident, or was something mysterious and wonderful unfolding here? He had never believed in God, but was there something happening here that was so mathematically improbable that it showed the hand of the divine?

The man sitting next to him had not said a word, even when dinner was served just as they were passing over Nova Scotia. But as Schwartz mused on the odd sequence of events over the last few days, he noticed that his traveling companion had finished his newspaper, reached into his briefcase, and taken out a book. The title of the book caught Michelangelo Schwartz's eye. It was entitled *Synchronicity: Why There Is No Such Thing as Coincidence* by Charlesworth Ephram III.

Schwartz decided to be brave and interrupt his laconic companion. "Why are you reading a book on coincidence?"

The man didn't look him in the eyes. But Wolf Eyes knew he had to say something. So he answered a question with a question. "Do you think it is a coincidence that I am reading a book on coincidence?"

Schwartz was not sure how to respond. But now he felt he had to say something. "I guess I was just thinking about coincidences. I was wondering if some coincidences have some meaning or pattern and if others just pop up by chance. But your book title suggests there is no such thing as an accidental coincidence. That would imply that there are no accidents. That would mean every conversation, everything that happens to us, is some kind of sign that is meant to convey some meaning beyond itself."

His companion didn't seem surprised. "So you were just thinking about coincidences and wondering if these coincidences have any meaning at all or if they are all just random."

Michelangelo Schwartz was under his spell and simply nodded yes.

"Would I be correct in guessing that, in fact, you have been thinking not about coincidence in general but about some important coincidences that have happened to you recently, and, when I opened this book, you wondered if that was another coincidence or if there was some pattern emerging? And, if that were so, and since you seem to be a thinking man, then you might have one last question. Would you like to ask that question of me now?"

Schwartz looked back in the darkened cabin and saw that William and Biff were fast asleep, along with the majority of the first-class cabin. He could talk freely.

"There is one question that does present itself. I recall Einstein once said that 'God does not play dice with the universe.' By that, he meant that there was a regular order to things and, perhaps, a more elaborate order than any of us have imagined. I must ask myself, is it a coincidence that you have booked this seat on this flight sitting next to me?"

His companion smiled. There was no getting away from it now. However, there was something charming and disarming about the man that he might have to kill very shortly. This was the first time in his long career he had ever spoken with a mark he was following. He was breaking every rule that he had relied on to keep himself safe, but, somehow, it seemed OK. There was something compelling about this exchange that made it OK.

"The great sages, prophets, philosophers, and ascended masters of all ages have agreed from the earliest mists of time until the present day," said Wolf Eyes. "They all believed that there are no coincidences, no missteps, and no wrong turns. Did you ever go to a Japanese garden and see the large, brightly colored koi swimming so elegantly? Do they ever make a wrong turn? Do they ever take a path they regret? Do they ever make a mistake? No. They are just swimming. We are like those fish, Professor."

Schwartz smiled. "How did you know I was a professor?"

"It's simple. You are wearing a worn plaid sports jacket with leather patches on the elbows in 2014. It has more stains than a tablecloth in a greasy spoon. No one but a professor would dare wear something like that."

Schwartz thought for a moment before he spoke again. "But, if there are no coincidences, does that mean that everything is preordained? If that is the case, we have no free will and, therefore, aren't morally responsible. Isn't that a bad thing?"

His companion smiled. This was getting pretty deep, but he seldom got a chance to have a regular conversation, and this was delightful for reasons he could not make clear to himself. He thought for a minute before he answered. "We can never know the difference between what we want to do and what we are meant to do. Because we can't make that distinction, we live our lives as if we have free will and are capable of making good or bad choices. Often, we think we have chosen well, but we are totally mistaken."

Schwartz was not quite following this thread. "What do you mean? We think we choose well, and we choose badly?"

"Let me give you an example. I would like to ask you a series of questions, which you can answer. I think you can pretty quickly get the point. When I give you a scenario, you tell me if, in your opinion, this event is good or bad. Let us begin by imagining that a young professor fell in love."

Schwartz decided to comply. And it seemed simple. "OK, I will play along."

His row mate went on. "Now, let us say that this love he has found is one of his students."

This was hitting a little too close to home for Michelangelo Schwartz, but he kept going. So he answered, "That would be bad."

His traveling companion continued. "Now, let's suppose that they act on this love, and they both become the happiest they have ever been in their lives."

"That would be good."

"Now, let us further postulate. This forbidden love gets discovered, and the professor loses his job as a result."

Schwartz could not believe he was having this conversation. "That would be bad."

His companion had not changed the expression on his face during this whole back-and-forth conversation. "But let us now fast-forward many years. Let us imagine that this same professor was forced to publish more works in order to salvage what was left of his reputation and, along the way, developed skills that were unique and valued. Let us imagine that these circumstances forced him to work harder, write more, and become more famous than he would have been as a professor who had spent his whole life in the same college. And let us further suppose that because of his scholarly reputation, he got involved in interesting things as an expert. So was that illicit love good or bad in the end?"

Schwartz was sure this man knew more about his life than he should. "How do you know all of this?"

His companion smiled. "Know what? I was just giving you an example using a professor because it is something that might happen in a college, and you are a college man. Professors have been chasing their students since Plato was getting oiled-up, naked in the gymnasium in Athens, next to those muscular young boys. I know very little, my friend. I was just waxing hypothetical."

Schwartz was not convinced. He now wanted to find out more about his companion. He reached out to shake his hand, but the man kept his arms folded.

"My name is Michelangelo Schwartz. I didn't catch your name."

The man smiled. He did not give his name. "Michelangelo Schwartz. What an evocative and interesting name! As I am sure you know better than I, Michelangelo is most famous for creating the ceiling of the Sistine Chapel. It is the heart of the Vatican, because it is where the new pope is chosen when an old one dies."

Michelangelo Schwartz was amazed his seatmate mentioned his first name in connection with the Vatican. Was this yet another coincidence? But his companion still had more to say. He thought for a few minutes before he put together his next words.

"But more interesting is your last name, Schwartz. Did you know that your name has been used in two very different ways? First, I am sure, with your New York or New Jersey accent, you must know it is a euphemism for a certain part of the male anatomy?"

Michelangelo Schwartz was afraid to ask. "Was that a swipe at New Jersey? What body part are you referring to?"

"Did you know that there are more than three thousand euphemisms for male masturbation? I bet, being a man of the world, you have heard a few."

In case you do not know, dear reader, "euphemism" comes from two Greek words, "eu" and "phone," which means "good sound." We use euphemisms for those things that are too painful to call by their real names. That is how strip joints have come to be renamed "gentlemen's clubs." That is why the Victorians called sex "amorous congress." Or when someone dies, we say he "bought the farm." Instead of saying someone is lying, we say that person is "economical with the truth." "Built for comfort, not speed" is a nice way of saying someone is fat. In New Jersey, they say "fallen off the back of the truck" for something they stole. We say, "Wham! Bam! Thank you, ma'am" instead of calling it a short sexual experience. Let's face it. Euphemisms are very useful.

Schwartz thought for a moment and began to recall a few of those expressions that every red-blooded man knew. "Of course, I have heard a few euphemisms for male masturbation. Let me see if I can list a few of the ones I know. How about 'spanking the monkey,' 'fixing your bayonet,' 'Custer's Last Stand,' 'shearing the sheep,' 'bashing the candle,' 'choking the chicken,' 'plunking your magic twanger,' 'flogging the bishop,' 'polishing your helmet,' 'slamming the ham'—"

His companion had heard enough and interrupted Schwartz. "Professor, this seems to be a subject on which you are well versed. I must admit I am impressed with your prodigious memory. But there is one expression I did not hear. Have you ever heard the expression 'shaking hands with Mr. Schwartz'?"

Michelangelo thought for minute and recalled that he had heard the expression. As a matter of fact, he had used it a few times himself.

"Yes, I have heard that expression used but had not thought about it in years."

"And, Professor, there is one more association I would like to suggest to you. Did you ever see the Mel Brooks film *Spaceballs*?"

Schwartz now knew where this was going. But Wolf Eyes went on.

"In that spoof on the movie *Star Wars*, Mel Brooks inserted an expression that now resonates in popular culture—"

It was now Michelangelo Schwartz's turn to interrupt. "'May the Schwartz be with you.'"

"And do you know what the 'Schwartz' was in that context? No longer did the term refer to 'choking your chicken,' but now, oddly enough, it referred to the most powerful force in the universe, the source of unspeakable power to those who possessed it. Here, the use of the word 'Schwartz' made it, in a sense, the Holy Grail we all seek."

Michelangelo Schwartz wanted to impress his companion. "Do you know where Mel Brooks got the idea 'May the Schwartz be with you' from?"

The man shook his head.

"Mel Brooks used that expression to honor his good friend, Sherwood Schwartz, a very famous Hollywood writer and producer. He's also my uncle from Passaic, New Jersey, and the man who gave us *Gilligan's Island*."

The man did not seem surprised. "There are some who see *Gilligan's Island* as a kind of anagram that cryptically gives us a glimpse into the true nature of the world. It can be looked at as a hologram of the human experience, if you will. The Skipper, Gilligan, the Professor, and the others are elements in a kind of *I Ching*, whose deciphering would open our eyes in new ways. It is a map of the journey of humankind. It is a kind of Scrabble game where the answer is 'there is a future, and here is the blueprint for the future of humanity.' It's a veritable tarot deck of possibilities for the human journey."

With that, the man leaned back in his first-class seat and closed his eyes.

The cabin was dark and quiet as the plane winged its way over the Atlantic. But, as Michelangelo Schwartz drifted off to sleep, he began to wonder how much of this whole adventure was accidental and how much was his destiny. He began to put the pieces together. He had forgotten the term "Shaking hands with Mr. Schwartz" and thought how ironic it was that his whole career had been ruined because he was unable to keep his Schwartz in his pants, so to speak. He then thought about the example of the philandering professor and the student that struck so close to home. He recalled the rumors he had read that placed the Holy Grail in the possession of the Vatican, a place forever associated with the painted ceiling of Michelangelo. This made the connection with his first name. He had also heard the expression "May the Schwartz be with you." He began to realize that the name Schwartz, in one context, was the Holy Grail that all sought. In the second context, it told him what had gone wrong with his life. He thought back to the Mel Brooks line. It was also quite amazing that the expression was in homage to his uncle Sherwood Schwartz. He wondered how improbable it was that this stranger could connect all of these dots in such an amazing and coherent picture.

He shook his companion awake, and as he opened his eyes, Schwartz said, "I have just one last question for you."

His companion looked at him with tired eyes. It was two o'clock in the morning. "OK, Professor Schwartz, but I am tired. So one question, one question only, and I am going to sleep."

"How could it be that you sat here, opened a book with the word *coincidence* in the title, gave an example right out my past, connected Michelangelo with the Vatican, and knew so much about my last name, both its vulgar meaning and its connection with the Holy Grail? Tell me the truth. What does it all mean?"

Michelangelo's companion did not say another word for the rest of the flight, even when he was leaving. But something important did happen after Michelangelo Schwartz drifted off to sleep. His companion reached over in the darkened cabin and placed a small device under the back collar of his jacket. That device was the size of a small fly and contained both a microphone and a GPS tracker. This meant that everything Schwartz said or heard would not be secret. The GPS in the chip would allow his companion to track his every move. But, before he went off to sleep, his cabin mate answered Schwartz's question with a single word. When asked why he was sitting next to Michelangelo Schwartz, he answered, "Coincidence."

8

In an ancient pub in Oxford, Schwartz meets a stuck-up Oxford don who puts them on the scent. We get a humorous history of the Glorious Revolution and learn about Rupert of the Rhine and how not to lose your head in a crisis. We learn that heresy rhymes with New Jersey. There is heavy drinking, complex intellectual discussion, spiced with crude humor, and a travel guide to Oxford.

Oxford, England.

The plane was banking in over London as the sun was coming up. Schwartz looked out the window as the first rays of daylight illuminated Saint Paul's Cathedral and Big Ben. He loved mornings in the British Isles. The traffic around London was heavy, so it took them a while to get to Oxford. Usually it would have taken an hour if the roads were empty, but these days they never were. They checked into the MacDonald Randolph Hotel, known to the cognoscenti simply as the Randolph. It was the most famous hotel in Oxford.

When they walked into the Randolph, they felt transported back to a more elegant and refined time in history. The staff was dressed in impeccable black waistcoats, white shirts, and black ties that harkened back to a formality that was hard to find in today's world. This hotel was a most wonderful haunt for the wealthy. It was built in the neo-Gothic style and had dark wood and stone throughout.

They checked into their rooms and made preparations for their noon meeting. Schwartz always liked to celebrate when he arrived in Oxford. After arriving on the morning flight, it was his habit to have gin and bitter lemon for elevenses, and Dubonnet before tea in the Morse Bar in the hotel. The Scotch whiskey selection was outstanding.

Michelangelo Schwartz had suggested the meeting take place at a pub that was revered by those who were literate and interested in history—the Eagle and Child Pub. He had spent many nights in this pub, engaged in serious drinking and conversation and chasing the various female co-eds that wandered in. Like the Greek god of wine, Schwartz himself would lead a merry band of drunken pranksters on nocturnal frolics through the winding streets of Oxford. The pub combined a great literary history with great beer. What more could you ask for?

The Eagle and Child had operated at the same location on Saint Giles Street in Oxford since 1650. Think of all of the pints of ale that had been pounded down there over the centuries. Now, that is tradition! Those undergrads and dons in the know coolly referred to it as the Bird and Baby or the Fowl and Foetus. During the English Civil War, when Oxford was the Royalist capital of England, the building that houses the pub served as headquarters of the Chancellor of the Exchequer.

The English Civil War was an important event in British history. When it was over, we had the institutions that still exist in modern Great Britain. The English Civil War got going near the end of the reign of a wacky and stuck-up guy, Charles I, who became king of England. When you had a divine monarchy or autocracy where nobody voted, it was the luck of the draw on who got to run the country. So people who were total perverts, jerks, or sadists could get the reins of power if they were born into the right family. Could you imagine someone becoming president of the United States just because that person was born into the right family? In France, a retarded guy once got on the throne. No joke. It has been widely argued that a member of the royal family was actually Jack the Ripper, who murdered prostitutes in London. So living under a monarch meant you might live under an incompetent and destructive leader that nobody trusted. Because we have elections in America that could never happen. Just kidding.

England was a Protestant country when Charles I became king in 1625. It took him no time to anger and cause fear in the English people. It was rumored that he was a secret Catholic in a Protestant country. Charles had his roots in the Catholic part of Scotland. So what was the first thing Charles I did? Naturally, he married a Roman Catholic lady, presenting the threat that his children, who would inherit the throne, would be Catholic, and started to swing the old incense in the Protestant churches. After so many religious wars that had destroyed the economy of England, people could not believe his chutzpah (not actually the term the English peasants used at that time). He appointed his corrupt drinking buddy, William Laud, to become the archbishop of Canterbury. When Protestants complained that the country was drifting toward Catholicism, the king had a reasonable response. He arrested everyone who complained and cut their ears off, even English lords. Next, he started to replace wooden tables in churches with stone altars. Protestants knew full well what incense and stone altars meant; the pope was on his way.

After losing a war with France (which took effort), disbanding the parliament, and alienating everybody, Charles I started going on and on about an idea that was really cool—the divine right of kings. This meant that a king was a king by God's will and that he could do whatever he wanted to, and anybody that criticized him was against both God and the state. Eventually, the whole thing blew up, and civil war erupted between the parliament and the king, and it involved the Irish, betrayal, Oliver Cromwell, a colorful relative of King Charles's named Rupert of the Rhine, and a couple of drunken Scottish lairds, who switched sides depending on the day of the week and who had the best whiskey. After Charles I was run out of London, he made his capital in Oxford for a while. Eventually, he lost his head in the argument. I mean, he literally lost his head.

England today has what they call a constitutional monarchy. That is probably no more absurd than what goes on in Washington, DC, which, at this writing, is totally dysfunctional. But Oxford had actually once been the capital of England for a while, just as the pope once lived in Avignon or some such French city.

Saint Giles was one of the main roads in Oxford. Balliol and Trinity Colleges were both on Saint Giles Street. Balliol College was founded sometime after 1262 and claimed to be the oldest college in the university, a claim disputed by both Merton College and the University College. It was founded by John de Balliol, a hard-drinking Scotsman, and the college has historically had a Scottish connection ever since. Its graduates include Christopher Hitchens, Adam Smith, and Harold Macmillan. Hugh Grant also attended, although it was rumored he got very nervous and stuttered badly during an interview.

Just a few blocks from there was the memorial to the Oxford Martyrs. If you ever walk through downtown Oxford, you will feel you are in a *Harry Potter* movie. As a matter of fact, many of the scenes of Hogwarts School were actually filmed in the colleges of Oxford. The streets were full of freestanding spires; here and there were stout wooden doors and leaded glass windows that seemed to be magic doorways to another time. There were bookstores and pubs everywhere, so one could tumble into them when feeling down or confused. It was heaven for Michelangelo Schwartz.

The Eagle and Child was near the Ashmolean Museum, where Saint Giles met the Magdalene Road. Schwartz and his companions were staying just a few blocks away in the MacDonald Randolph Hotel. You could come out of the hotel, walk past the Ashmolean, and, in a few minutes, you were at the pub. The Randolph Hotel was made famous in the novels of Colin Dexter's *Inspector Morse* detective series.

The Eagle and Child Ale House was owned by Saint John's College and was part of the college's endowment. You see, the plot of *Animal House* was not so far off. Imagine a college funding its endowment via an alehouse. This was one of the many reasons why Oxford colleges were in good financial shape while their American cousins were going broke. The Eagle and Child was located in a narrow three-story building that was painted yellow on the outside with the name in block letters. Over the front door, a sign hung that showed an eagle gently carrying a bundle with an infant in it. There were a number of theories about how the pub got its name, and we will leave it to your imagination to conjure up your preferred version.

When you walked in the pub, you could feel the history. For hundreds of years, Oxford dons and their students would sit here and muse over texts and current events. There was a bar to the right and a series of long tables in the main room. Off to one side was the Rabbit Room, where the Inkling's Literary Group would meet. The group included J. R. R. Tolkien and C. S. Lewis, among others. The others had first names and not just initials, and that tells you they were second stringers.

Oxford has been the home of many wonderful and odd people. Lewis Carroll was the pen name of Lord Dodgson, an Oxford don who wrote *Alice in Wonderland*. He taught mathematics, logic, and philosophy at Oxford; never married; and spent almost all of his time in the company of preadolescent girls, whom he was fond of photographing. We will leave it at that.

Erwin Schrödinger spent a good deal of time in Oxford. You may recall an experiment he did using quantum physics, famously known as "Schrödinger's cat," where he put a cat in a box, and, if the cat suffocated, it would be alive in an alternative universe, and, conversely, if the cat was alive in this universe, it would be dead in another. He backed this theory up with a ton of data from physics, a huge mathematical algorithm, and was supported by the best minds in quantum physics. But, outside of about five wacky professors, nobody else on the planet actually believed it. Ask yourself, would we bet our mortgage on that one?

Albert Einstein taught at Oxford. He had, apparently, figured out how the universe actually worked, but he had a hard time finding a pair of socks that matched and would often forget to bathe. He claimed he would not shower regularly because he was "lost in thought," but it was learned, after he departed Oxford, that the real reason was he was too cheap to pay his water bill.

T. E. Lawrence or Lawrence of Arabia was a sadomasochistic killer who had a proclivity for languages, maps, and self-mutilation. He has been called both the greatest Englishman of his time and a crazed madman. He was a true Oxford man.

The philosopher Jeremy Bentham studied here and went on to found University College in London. After he died, his skull and skeleton were stuffed into a look-alike of him that was kept in a cabinet at the college, and it was wheeled out for board meetings, where he continued to be recorded as "present but not voting."

The modern philosopher Thomas Nagel was a citizen of Oxford and was famous for a great philosophical article entitled "What Is It Like to Be a Bat?" (Have you never spent sleepless nights thinking about that question?) There is a reason why people avoid philosophers at cocktail parties.

Yes, the city had a great and noble history. But there is one thing we've left out. For centuries, it had been rumored that Oxford was a center of Illuminati activity. Cecil Rhodes founded a college in Oxford to recruit young Americans to form alliances with England and Old Europe. Francis Bacon, who was at Oxford long ago, was rumored to be the Supreme Ascendant Illuminated Master of the Illuminati. Both the Bilderberg Group and the Trilateral Commission met there regularly. Finally, Bill Clinton, Tony Blair, and Weird Al Yankovic visited it annually. Are you beginning to see a pattern here?

On the day that William, Biff, and Michelangelo headed for the pub, it was a lovely, rainy spring day in Oxford. The rain was so warm and slight that they didn't take any of the umbrellas offered to them by the doorman at the hotel. The pansies and daffodils were out in pots along Saint Giles. The walk from the Randolph Hotel to the pub was only a few blocks. Students and Oxford dons, weighed down with books and knapsacks, rushed past in their black gowns on their way to class. Some of the dons rode bicycles, and the noise of scooters was in the air. Oxford was always full of tourists, who choked the streets with their cameras and maps, trying to soak in the culture.

Schwartz went into the Eagle and Child first and found his favorite table in the back. He had visited the city many times before for conferences and done some research at the main library for his many articles. As it was before noon, the pub was all but deserted. The bartender was a round, old Englishman who looked like he had been pushing pints since the time of Henry VIII. His name was Haskins. He smiled as he asked if they wanted anything. Biff and William both ordered diet sodas, so they could focus. Michelangelo was never so dull, and, besides, he figured someone else would pick up the tab.

"I'll have a Smithwicks with a whiskey chaser."

The bartender didn't quite understand. "I see you are an American. Here, we drink the whiskey first and then call the beer a chaser."

Michelangelo did not want to appear disagreeable. "OK. Whiskey first, beer second, and another whiskey as a chaser for the first one."

William put his head in his hands and wanted to cry.

Just as the drinks arrived at the table, a woman in a great rush hurried into the pub. She was a plump and attractive forty-five-year-old, dressed in fashionable, preppy clothes. She was wearing black slacks with a gray sweater over her white shirt. She had on her teaching robes. She seemed every bit the Oxford don she had been for the last ten years. Her hair was jet black. She had hazel eyes, was an avid bicyclist, and wore round tortoiseshell glasses. Lindsey Orrogante was the Richard Fox professor of New Testament Greek at All Souls College, Oxford. She was a world-renowned scholar and a friend to Rome. Biff knew her from her photo and signaled her to the table. She sat down and shook hands in a stiff, officious manner. You could see that her brilliant career had been won at the expense of developing any social skills. She was not a woman who suffered fools gladly. Nor was she known to be diplomatic. While she was an academic superstar, she was not the best colleague. But, right now, she was anxious to tell her tale.

"The Vatican informed me that you three would be coming. I am not sure how I got involved in this whole thing in the first place, but I am involved. And, when they told me that you were the Schwartz of the poem, Professor Schwartz, I did a little research on you, as you write outside of my area of expertise. I must say, you have some unorthodox views on Dante."

Schwartz smiled. "Unorthodox? What an interesting word."

Professor Orrogante was all business. She scowled at him and got back to her story. She was always sending and not very skilled at receiving.

"It all started during the holiday break. I was doing some research at the Fels Academic Library at the Institut Catholique de Paris. As some of you may know, they have an excellent collection of not only New Testament Greek texts but also important ancient and patrimonial collections, cuneiform tablets, and ancient maps. While in Paris, I stopped by the Shakespeare and Company Bookstore."

Schwartz knew it well. Shakespeare and Company was to bibliophiles what Farrah Fawcett Majors posters were to seventeen-year-old boys in the 1970s. Professor Orrogante was pretty enough for him to try to impress her. Besides, he had never made it with an Oxford don. So he interrupted.

"Professor Orrogante, did you know that is actually the second Shakespeare and Company bookstore? The first was opened by Sylvia Beach in 1919 and was closed by the Germans when they occupied Paris in 1940. The current one on the Rue de la Bûcherie has been open since 1951."

Professor Orrogante looked at him with a disdain she usually reserved for her worst students, those who failed to do their assigned readings, and resumed her exposition.

"Don't be pedantic, Professor. Of course I know that. Now, as I was saying before I was so rudely interrupted, I was in the main room of the bookstore, and a man came up to me. It then occurred to me that I had seen this man before. I believe he and I had walked past each other on the Chunnel train from England to France. He walked up to me and handed me a book. It was *Le Morte d'Arthur* by Sir Thomas Malory. He told me I might enjoy book 6. But he said it in such a way that almost insured I would open it to that section. He then turned and walked out the door. I opened the text and recalled book 6 was 'The Noble Tale of the Sangreal,' where Malory gives us the famous story of the Knights of King Arthur's Round Table and their quest to find the Holy Grail.

"On the very first page of book 6 was a folded piece of paper, a bookmark with a poem on it. It was a curious poem. As I studied it, I realized it could be of importance. I then went to the Notre Dame Cathedral that very afternoon and met with the archbishop of Paris, who is an old friend.

He knows about such matters. I had made a copy of the poem and handed him the original. He forwarded it on to Rome. That is why you are here today. I have a copy with me that you may take with you."

Michelangelo Schwartz was skeptical and wanted to know more. "How do you know this guy was not some nut and this poem is not just his mad doodling?"

Lindsey Orrogante had an IQ of 140. She had never been comfortable being challenged by mere mortals. "It is not the poem alone. Since that day in Paris, I have had several conversations with those high up in the church and have learned the context. There are occasional high-up contacts between the Illuminati and the Vatican, just like there was a red phone between Washington and the Kremlin at the height of the Cold War. In one such contact this past winter, a member of the Curia in Rome was informed that there exists a faction in the Illuminati that feels it is time for the Holy Grail to be returned to the church. I was told that when the Illuminati gained possession of it on February 6, 1920, the balance was certainly on the side of the church. But since then, the rise of science, jazz, rock 'n' roll, and *Wheel of Fortune*, with Vanna White, have lured away the faithful from the church. Without the Grail, the Holy Mother Church was powerless to stop this erosion of values and faith. We suspect that the date of February 6 was chosen because that is the birthday of Adam Weishaupt, the most well-known Illuminati master. There are those in the Illuminati who feel it is time to rebalance the scales so that the harmony of their various enterprises can continue."

Schwartz wanted to milk her for all of the information he could get. "Their enterprises?"

"Scams like big oil, Wall Street, big pharma, higher education, and *The Fast and Furious* movie franchise. But in recent years the Illuminati feared that the crime, vice, and immorality of the common people had started to match their own, and that was unthinkable. It is one thing for Wall Street to be a lawless bunch of criminals ripping off everybody with no regrets, but when the average person starts to get into the act, society is in big trouble. Bear Stearns selling worthless derivatives to their private, wealthy customers is one thing. But when you get robbed driving to a black-tie dinner at the country club, that is a whole other kettle of fish. So a small splinter group, apparently high up in the Illuminati, wanted to make sure the balance was restored."

With this, she opened her leather bookcase and placed a copy of a handwritten yellow sheet in front of the three travelers. They read the poem together:

The cup that ends all human strife
And gives its bearer eternal life
Can be found not on the corners but in the middle.
You must come home to solve this riddle.

The holy man protects the books;
Beneath the star on pages he looks.
Along it runs a second street
That has a number that we must meet.

Now take the year the master was burned,
The same year lessons in love were first learned.
Subtract it from the year of the Vatican sculpture's birth
That gives us an eight anywhere on Earth.

This cup that can end all sorrow and grief
Has given the most laurel wreaths.
Dig there, and you will lose your breath,
Rule the world, and conquer death.

But before you can learn to sing this song
There is one man you must bring along.
This unworthy messenger alone can find the key.
He is living near the statue in the sea.

His first name is the father of *David* and the *Pietà*.
He loves baseball, Dante, and the theater.

His last name doesn't fit; it makes us scoff,
One of a million names for what Pius IX knocked off.

He comes not from Noah's old boat.
With grain alcohol, he keeps afloat.
Accused of Spinozistic heresy,
This acolyte hails from New Jersey.

The time has come for the Grail to change hands.
It has traveled across many lands.
Work on this riddle till your hands have warts,
But it will only be solved by a man named Schwartz.

As cool as finding the Holy Grail would be, Schwartz was still holding out on a chance for love with Lindsey Orrogante. He wanted to impress this fortress of knowledge and tradition.

"I can see how they got to me."

He finally got her attention. "I live in New Jersey, near the Statue of Liberty, 'the statue by the sea.' 'First name is the father of *David* and the *Pietà*.' That would be Michelangelo. The last name is one of millions of words for 'what Pius IX knocked off.'"

William was lost, although Biff and Professor Orrogante knew just what he was referring to. Lindsey Orrogante turned red with embarrassment and looked down. She knew well the reference. Biff turned toward William.

"In the 1850s, Pope Pius IX thought that many of the pagan statues in the Vatican were wonton and would lead to impure thoughts. They were the works of the great sculptors of Greece and Rome, and most of them were chiseled in the nude."

At this point, Biff hesitated out of good taste, and Professor Orrogante wasn't helping out. So Schwartz figured he would help Biff out and make the point plain and simple.

"What Biff is trying to get to here, but is too shy to say, is they had huge penises, so Pope Pius IX took a hammer and personally began to whack them off, in a manner of speaking."

Lindsey Orrogante was becoming irritated. "Professor Schwartz, that is not the phrase I would have chosen. Our Holy Father wanted the priests and nuns to keep their minds on higher things."

She was now glaring angrily at Michelangelo Schwartz. All of this analysis had made Michelangelo thirsty. Schwartz had finished his beer and two whiskeys and called for another round. William sighed deeply and shook his head in disgust.

Schwartz went on. "But there is a point here. There are millions of names for what Pius IX broke off: tally whacker, meat and two veg, Admiral Winky, giggle stick, hoo hoo, the Bald Avenger, the Bavarian beef stick, Doctor Cyclops, hunka hunka burning love, your John Thomas—"

Biff stopped him before he could get up a head of steam. "Yes, yes, we know. But what is the relevance of that line?"

Michelangelo smiled. "Have you ever heard the expression 'Shake hands with Mr. Schwartz'?"

Biff could not contain himself. "Oh, God."

But Michelangelo was not done. As he read the poem, he smiled in recognition.

"Not Noah's old boat, not the old ark but a new ark. Newark, New Jersey, where I was born! It also mentions baseball, Dante, and the theater. I have written extensively on Dante and the theater, and I am the biggest Yankee fan in the world. I have written articles on the history of the Yankees. As a matter of fact, I am counting down the days until opening day at Yankee Stadium, a day I never miss. So we will have to find the Holy Grail before the Red Sox arrive in the Bronx for opening day. Finally, it mentions Spinozistic heresy. Baruch Spinoza was a seventeenth-century Jewish Dutch philosopher. He was one of those Enlightenment thinkers that advocated for reason and logic."

Biff could not help interrupting. When he heard about any so-called Enlightenment rationalist who was considered a hero and a martyr for science, it made his Catholic blood boil.

"Schwartz, reason and logic sound good at first. That's right. No more faith! No more Holy Book. No more pope. But a little while after that the king of England, who had his last stand in this very city, gets his head chopped off on the basis of reason and logic, and then comes the French Revolution. Toothless, old hags with knitting needles get to see if the king and queen of France keep their heads or visit Monsieur Guillotine. After that, we get dope fiends, like William Blake and Lord Byron, running amok, talking about logic and reason. Shelley, a lecherous vegetarian, would sleep with anything in a skirt, and there were rumors he did not stop there. Did you know he was kicked out of University College, Oxford, because he wrote a pamphlet advocating atheism? Atheism! That, my friends, is where logic and reason lead. In those glorious days, the pope would have a few bottles of wine, get an idea, blurt it out, and we would all believe it without question. Oh, to go back to those simple days of faith! God, I miss those days!"

Schwartz broke in. "I am part Jewish, and I, like Spinoza, have been accused of heresy by the church. They even mention New Jersey by name at the end, just in case we didn't get it. It never occurred to me until now that New Jersey rhymes with heresy! New Jersey rhymes with heresy! How cool is that?"

William was very practical and wanted to move things along. "You got that all in a minute. But I am not sure how well heresy rhymes with Jersey. Now, while this is a good start, can you enlighten us on the rest of the poem and what it means?"

Michelangelo looked at the poem. It was dense and difficult to decipher. He had some ideas already on some of it, but if he was getting paid by the hour, with drinks and meals, he did not want to rush things.

"I am going to need more time. I would like to make a suggestion. I think Professor Orrogante and I should go back to her place and work on this. I think just the two of us together for a few hours could crack this."

Professor Orrogante was looking at her watch and yawning. "I would rather shove a sharp stick into my eye, Professor Schwartz. Besides, I never have sex with someone with a low IQ that I have known for less than an hour."

Michelangelo Schwartz wanted to be sure. "So, that's a 'no'?"

She got up, glared at them, and left the pub.

The bartender brought over the drinks. William and Biff had not touched their sodas. Michelangelo threw down another shot of Scotch whiskey. He shivered as the burning liquid made its way down his throat. He wondered why he so loved a spirit that was so hard to get down and tasted so bitter.

Biff was reading the poem over and over. "I can see why the church officials figured this poem refers to you, Schwartz. It seems clear. But why does it refer to you in particular? What is it about you that is so unique that only you will be able to decode this?"

By this time, Michelangelo Schwartz had a pretty good buzz going on. He remembered one more historical fact he wanted to entertain his companions with.

"Did you two know that Sylvia Beach, the ex-pat who founded the original Shakespeare and Company, home to Hemingway and Joyce, was also from New Jersey? I think that while we work on this, we should go to where Professor Orrogante got this poem—Shakespeare and Company in Paris."

William opened his eyes wide. "Paris? Why?"

Schwartz smiled. "You called this a quest. If we are on a quest, we follow the bread crumbs. Haven't you read your Homer or Sir Walter Scott?"

At this moment, Biff wished he had never met Michelangelo Schwartz in the first place. He thought for a few moments before he spoke. "Should we try to go today? There might be a late flight tonight."

Schwartz put down his drink. "No, there is someone I need to see this afternoon here in Oxford. Let's go tomorrow, first thing. Let's go back to the hotel to get organized, and, then, give me a few hours before dinner."

Shortly afterward, the three companions walked the few blocks back to their hotel. William said he was going to take a nap, and Biff got on the phone to Rome as soon as he was alone.

CIA Headquarters, Langley, Virginia

On the other side of the Atlantic Ocean, the sun was just coming up over the CIA Headquarters in Langley, Virginia. Director Glen Runciter was sitting at his spotlessly clean desk when Agent Joe Chip knocked on his door before opening it. The office had a marble floor, and there were no plaques or pictures on the wall. There was nothing personal in the large office, and the white floor had no rugs on it. A large picture window looked out toward the front of the building. Glen Runciter had dark hair, was of medium height, and carried himself like the former marine he would always be. Glen was on his first cup of morning coffee. There would be four or five more before noon. He looked up at Agent Chip. Joe Chip was a tall, blond Ivy Leaguer who went through prep school with the moniker "Chip Chip."

"Morning, Joe. What have you got for me?"

"Well, we were just going over the flight manifests to Europe yesterday, and it seems our Norwegian friend took the overnight to England."

Glen was interested. "Do we have any other information to go along with the flight manifest?"

Chip was looking at some papers as he spoke. "Not exactly, but here is something curious. Sal Greco was on the same flight."

Glen pushed back from his desk. "The Norwegian and Two Fingers Greco on the same plane? Are you kidding me? In our business, we can never assume something like this can be a coincidence. Are they working together? Maybe one is out to take out the other?"

Joe Chip had an idea. "Let's grab the phone records and e-mails of all the other people on that flight and all of the other flights to England yesterday. We have got to get our arms around this one quickly."

Glen nodded his head in agreement as Joe Chip asked one last question. "Do we want to go through getting a FISA warrant from the courts, so we stay within the law and are clean on this one, or should we just go ahead and start collecting the phone and e-mail data?"

Glenn looked out of the window with a bored expression on his face. He had been at the CIA for a long time. He was starting to dream about retiring to hunt and fish somewhere in the great American West. The caffeine was starting to kick in.

"Joe, as I think about it more, this is a hot one. Let's grab the e-mail contact lists, e-mails, chats, Facebook, Instagram, text messages, and tweets of everyone on that flight. Get their bank records and credit card histories as well. Grab them for the last year, and run them through the Raptor software. As far as a FISA warrant and the courts go, you know my feelings on that. We need to move things along, and we need to move things along at a good clip. You know what I always say at a time like this? I say, 'Fuck it. We are the CIA.'"

9

At the Bodleian Library in Oxford, Schwartz meets a hard-drinking Scottish laird named Earl Larry Bone. In this chapter, we learn about the failure of higher education, how Google is making us stupid, and the relationship between crop circles and the Saudi royal family. We are told that God invented whiskey so the Irish wouldn't rule the world. We get our first glimpse of a lost religious text, the Gospel of Moshe.

Oxford, England

Later that afternoon, in Oxford, Salvatore Greco looked through his binoculars and trained them on the front entrance of the MacDonald Randolph Hotel. He was across the street in a doorway, pretending to be a tourist. He held a map of Oxford in his hands. He didn't care that he was holding it upside down. The rain had stopped, and the sun was out. The streets were crowded with tourists.

Salvatore saw Michelangelo Schwartz come out alone. Schwartz was wearing his lucky jacket with the leather elbow patches and the mustard stains. Salvatore followed him as he walked down the street toward the center of town. He followed him past Blackwell's bookstore and past the White Horse Pub, both on Broad Street in the heart of Oxford. If Schwartz could bypass both a pub and one of the most famous bookstores in the world without turning in, he must be on a mission. Salvatore followed from a distance.

What Salvatore did not know was that Wolf Eyes was two blocks behind him, walking slowly and enjoying the spring air. Wolf Eyes knew how to live and how to enjoy each moment without letting the regret of the past or the anxiety of the future intrude. What neither Wolf Eyes nor Salvatore Greco knew was that they were on their way to one of the great places in the academic world, the main library of Oxford University. Had they known Michelangelo Schwartz, they would have known it was either books or booze. At his age, anything else was an effort.

The Bodleian Library was the central research library for all of the colleges of Oxford. While each college has its own libraries and artifacts, the Bodleian houses the largest and most prestigious collection. The bishop of Worcester is credited with funding the first library in Oxford in the fourteenth century. The libraries grew steadily, and, in 1589, a fellow of Merton College, Thomas Bodley, took up the cause to build and maintain a proper academic library. And on November 8, 1602, the first incarnation of the Bodleian Library was opened, a day celebrated by librarians worldwide. Not celebrated like Saint Patrick's Day in Chicago, but celebrated all the same.

It was Bodley himself who came up with the idea of the formal declaration users must declaim (at one time in Latin) before being able to use the reference collection. In the modern period, one could simply sign the form that had those words on it:

> I hereby undertake not to remove from the Library, nor to mark, deface, or injure in any way, any volume, document, or other object belonging to it or in its custody; not to bring into the Library, or kindle therein, any fire or flame; and not to smoke in the Library, and I promise to obey all rules of the Library.

In the early years of the seventeenth century, the Old Schools Quadrangle was built. It formed a courtyard through which scholars must pass to enter the library's main entrance. The courtyard was surrounded by the Tower of the Five Orders, so named for the five styles of architecture in which the towers were built—classical, Doric, Ionic, Tuscan, Corinthian, and Composite. The library was a place full of wonders and mysteries. The collections of the library were fabulous and contained a Gutenberg Bible and four—yes, count them—four copies of the original Magna Carta.

The flight from London to Paris was not until late the next morning, so Michelangelo Schwartz had the time and the energy to continue his research on the Illuminati and Grail. He went to the reference desk inside of the main entrance of the Bodleian and asked to speak to the head librarian, who was expecting him. The head librarian was himself a graduate of Oxford and a member of one of the most prominent families in Aberdeenshire. Earl Larry Bone could have stayed on his country estate or whiled away his life in the family's London town house facing Hyde Park. He loved books. He loved his student years in Oxford, loved university politics, and he loved to gossip. He didn't need the money. He was in it for the sizzle. In his sixties, he was as urbane and learned a dinner companion as you could find in the whole of the British Isles. Earl Larry Bone wore a seersucker suit, his trademark red bow tie, and a white shirt (Oxford, of course). He was of average height and weight and still had his wonderful head of thick brown hair. His blue eyes were playful behind his round black glasses. He had dined several times with Michelangelo Schwartz over the years and found him an entertaining raconteur.

Michelangelo Schwartz opened the large, old wooden door that led into Bone's office. It was crowded with books, maps, and every kind of memorabilia you could imagine. In the hundreds of years the Bodleian had been in existence, it had only had twenty-seven head librarians. It was a position any librarian in the world would have died for. Bone stood up and walked to the door.

"Schwartz, you old rogue, you! What a treat to have you back in Oxford!"

Schwartz walked over and shook his hand. "The Right Honorable Mr. Larry Bone, Earl of Stonehaven, Ellon, Portlethen, and Banchory, and Lord Protector of Turriff."

Mr. Bone never tired of hearing the litany of his titles and always appreciated hearing it from someone with a New Jersey accent. Schwartz was going to press his advantage.

"OK. Where is that Scotch whiskey you keep in here? Not the swill you ship to us suckers in the States but the good stuff you Scottish aristocrats keep for yourselves."

Bone was charmed by the crude yet erudite tone that Schwartz always took. In the world of English lords, Oxford dons, members of Parliament, and pampered students from the upper tiers of society, it was rare for him to hear the unvarnished truth, and Schwartz was just the man to deliver it. Mr. Bone walked over to his bookshelf and reached behind two large volumes of a first edition of T. E. Lawrence's *Seven Pillars of Wisdom*. He pulled out a bottle of the Glenlivet Fifty from 1962 that had spent eighteen years in American oak bourbon barrels and another three in European oak sherry barrels to sweeten and mellow it. These bottles had been in the wine cellar of the Earl of Stonehaven ever since. He put out two glasses and poured three fingers of Scotch in each. The Scotch had a deep caramel color and smelled of honey and vanilla. Schwartz gulped it down as if it was the first glass of water offered to a man who had spent three days without a canteen in the desert.

"Sacrilege, Schwartz, sacrilege! This whiskey is pure gold! This bottle is worth five thousand pounds!"

Schwartz smiled at his old friend. "That reminds me of a great joke. A man wanted to impress his mother-in-law, who hated him. So he was willing to go to any length to impress her. He went to a pet store and told the owner he wanted a gift that would knock someone's socks off. The owner of the pet store told him he had a parrot that spoke five languages, but the parrot cost thirty-five thousand dollars. The man went to the parrot and said, '*Parlez-vous Français*?' and the parrot answered, '*Oui, Oui, monsieur*!' The man was stunned. He asked a second question. '*Sprechen sie Deutsch*?' The parrot replied, '*Ja, ich spreche Deutsch*.' The man was delighted. 'I will buy that bird for thirty-five thousand. Send that parrot to my mother-in-law at this address, with a note saying it is from me! Thank you.' A few days later, the man met his mother-in-law on the street. He asked her, 'How did you like that bird?' She smiled. 'It was delicious! I wrung its neck, plucked its feathers, and cooked it at three hundred and fifty degrees in the oven for two hours, and it was moist and succulent.' The man was stunned. 'You ate it? You ate the parrot? That bird cost me thirty-five thousand dollars, and it spoke five languages!' The mother-in-law thought for a few seconds. 'Well, then it should have said something!'"

Bone broke out laughing. "Schwartz, it is always a treat to see you, even if you do not appreciate good Scotch!"

Schwartz toasted his host. "Then, I will be more measured on my second glass. Cute idea, keeping the booze behind the *Seven Pillars of Wisdom*, very urbane."

Mr. Bone laughed as he poured. "Schwartz, first, this is the finest Scotch there is, so calling it 'booze' is a sin, an absolute sin, my dear boy. Second, as you know, T. E. Lawrence, known to most people as Lawrence of Arabia, was an Oxford don himself. So it is a kind of compliment. You know the relationship between we Scots and whiskey."

"Larry, I am not sure I can grasp all of the subtleties of the Scots' relationship to whiskey, although I am sure it is intimate. But I think of that great line about your Celtic cousins across the Irish Sea. It has been said that God invented whiskey so that the Irish wouldn't rule the world."

Schwartz didn't have a lot of time, so he had to move things along. And time and money were two things Bone had in abundance.

"Larry, I'm here in Oxford working on a problem. A client has hired me to do a little research."

Bone was enjoying his Scotch as he looked up, and he seemed amused. "Let me guess, hmmmmmm...I bet you had no idea I was psychic!"

Larry Bone began waving his finger in the air in a circular motion. Then, he began to stare into his glass of Scotch with a very serious expression on his face. "Schwartz, I can see the future in a cloudy vision. It has something to do with Dante, Leonardo, or the Templars!"

Schwartz smiled at his refined friend. "With my background, that is a good guess."

"It's no guess, my boy. It's all we do here these days. I know you like that cricket team. What is their name again? Yes, I recall—the New York Yankees. But we don't have too many books on them here, so you would not fly all the way over here to see me for that. No, for us here at the Bodleian, it is the same thing over and over. Let me see if I can list them. It's either the Templars, the Grail, the Sinclairs, the notebooks of Da Vinci, the Illuminati, Jacques de Molay, blah, blah, blah. If it is not one of these, it is the other. They love it. It's all we do here now. It is all such a bore, my dear fellow, such a bore! Tell me you're not on this old chestnut, too. Didn't you sum it up a few years ago with a nice term when you presented a paper on the subject at the University of Cambridge? Do you remember the phrase you used when a member of the public asked you your views on the Holy Grail?"

Schwartz smiled. "Bullshit. I said it was all bullshit."

As he worked on his second glass of good Scotch, Michelangelo thought for a few minutes about his recent trips to bookstores. He thought about all of the books on all of these conspiracy theories. The more he thought about it, the more he realized that what Larry was saying was true. Conspiracy theories were everywhere. All of the best sellers were about dark conspiracies touching every element of society and religion. And, somehow, they were all coalescing.

"You're a librarian. You look at these trends all the time. How do you explain it?"

The Earl of Stonehaven took a few pulls on his Scotch. He was thinking how much he enjoyed this chaotic thunderstorm called Michelangelo Schwartz.

"Well, a number of things made it happen. More than twenty years ago, there was a book called *Holy Blood, Holy Grail*. The authors made the claim that Jesus was married and his children became the ruling families of Europe through the bloodline of Charlemagne and the Merovingian kings. They claimed that Mary Magdalene was the wife of Jesus, and they also claimed that the Vatican suppressed this knowledge to preserve its political power. No longer was Jesus the simple carpenter of the four Gospels. He now had a nagging wife, kids, rent payments, and that cabinet he was making for Pontius Pilate was a four-drawer model when it should have been a six. Now, this book contained leaps of logic, almost no evidence, and grammar so bad you would not believe it got past an editor. But it became wildly popular, and people all thought they were now in the know about the real history of the Catholic Church. That got the whole thing rolling. At the same time, some books were published about an archaeological find in the Middle East. In 1949, a shepherd in Egypt came across some old jars of first-century scrolls. For a long time, the church had suppressed them. These two stories somehow got linked up."

Schwartz knew the history of the scrolls. "Yes, the Nag Hammadi Library. That supposedly contain other accounts of the life of Jesus that contradict the four Gospels. I remember reading a paper on the Gospel of Thomas."

Bone smiled. "The Gospel of Thomas! My dear boy, that was one of the mild ones. Some of the more radical ones are still under wraps. I myself talked with a scholar, at the University of Tel Aviv, who has seen all of them. I bet you never heard of the Gospel of Moshe."

Schwartz shook his head to indicate he hadn't. Bone went on. "Not to bore you, but you know the First Council of Nicaea in 325 completed the work that had been going on since Emperor Constantine to include the so-called Synoptic Gospels of Matthew, Mark, and Luke and link them with the Gospel of John. They condemned every other account and put them outside of the tradition. In 367, Athanasius, the bishop of Alexandria, gave an identical list of what should be kept in and what should be banned. So we had the church telling us what was kosher and what was not. By the time we got to the Council of Trent, it was almost set in stone. Then, the Synod of the Hippo Regius in 393 tied the whole thing up in a bow. After that, all of the other gospels that were not included were banned, burned, or lost. So the Gospel of Moshe was lost for the ages. If that had stayed public, the world would have been a much different place."

Schwartz could not help but follow the conversation. "The world would have been a very different place? Would one book have so changed history? What is so unique about the Gospel of Moshe?"

"Schwartz, it is a whole different view of Jesus. If this had been included as the fifth gospel, wars could have been avoided, persecutions would not have happened, and the world would be a kinder and better place. Moshe of Nazareth tells us in the first line of his gospel that he ran a sort of deli across from Jesus's carpenter shop. Being near a major caravan route, he did a land-office business.

"We know that Moshe was a real historical figure because both Josephus and Philo of Alexandria mentioned him. Philo wrote that Moshe often had lunchtime speakers in his restaurant and had the best happy hour outside of Rome. And like Herodotus and the other ancient historians, Philo had some advice for travelers who happened to go to Moshe's. He wrote, and this is an exact translation, 'Try the knishes. They are fabulous.' In Moshe's account, Jesus is very fresh and different. It turns out that the great tradition of Jewish comedians who cut their teeth in the resorts of the Catskill Mountains were following in the footsteps of Jesus, whom they called 'the most influential Jew in history.' But you can see what the Catholic Church wanted to suppress in the Gospel of Moshe. Let me read a few lines."

He went to the bookshelf and took out a beautiful volume. He sat down next to his Scotch and smiled as he opened the book. "I now read from the Gospel of Moshe. 'And Jesus said, "Verily I say unto you, why do Jewish divorces cost so much? Because they are worth it!"'"

Schwartz interrupted. "Did they have divorce in Jewish law at that time?"

"Sure, they had divorce, Schwartz! A dowry of thirty shekels had to be returned to the family, but there were all sorts of ways for men to get out of it. Hell! Men made the rules, so they always wrote in a codicil on how they could weasel out. You might remember someone writing, some time ago, that if men could get pregnant, abortion would be a sacrament. But enough quibbling. Let me get back to the Gospel of Moshe. 'And Jesus said, "Verily, I say unto you, why do Jewish men die before their wives? Because they want to!"'"

Schwartz laughed, and Bone read on. "Here is a line that indicates that the Gospel of Thomas is not the only one that says Jesus was married. Listen to this line. 'And Jesus came to Canaan, and he spoke, "Lo, I say to you, my brothers, take Mary Magdalene, please!"' And, to further show he was married, how about this line. 'And lo, Jesus said, "I just came back from a pleasure trip. I took my mother-in-law back home!"'"

Schwartz could not believe his ears. "Larry, these are lines that made Jewish comedians popular for years. You mean they knew about this, and we didn't?"

"There are scholars of several arcane Jewish traditions related to the study of the Cabala that say it is part of their oral tradition, passed down by the Cohans, their rabbinical line. How about this next section? 'And the Lord said, "I take my wife everywhere, but she keeps finding her way back." A sick man came to Jesus and said to the Lord, "Oh, Holy One, heal me! I broke my leg in two places." And verily Jesus said, "Quit going to those places."' Or how about this one, Schwartz? 'I say to you, my brothers, when I read a scroll about the evils of Galilean wine, I gave up scrolls.'

"Moshe would sometimes add his own commentary. Apparently, because of his culinary talents, he was hired as the caterer for the Last Supper. He famously noted, when he was serving up the table that night, he noticed something unusual. I will read the exact line. 'When I saw the way Judas dived into the creamed herring, I knew there was something he wasn't telling us.'"

But then Larry looked up and got serious. He was coming to the most important line in the Gospel of Moshe.

"Schwartz, you know the Catholics base their whole faith in the pope on the interpretation of one line in the Bible. Jesus supposedly said, 'Thou art Peter, and upon this rock, I will build my church.' But there is more to the quote. What is interesting and humorous is that in New Testament Greek *Peter* comes from *Petra*, which is the word for rock."

Schwartz knew the quote well. "Yes. I can even finish the quote. 'And the gates of hell shall not prevail against it. I will give you the keys of the kingdom of heaven; whatever you bind on earth will be bound in heaven, and whatever you loose on earth will be loosed in heaven.' I know the quote well. The whole of the papacy, and, thus, the whole of the Catholic Church, rests on a certain reading of that line."

Bone looked down at the book and spoke slowly. "Read how the Gospel of Moshe gives a slight variation to the tale. 'And lo the Lord said, "Who wants to keep drinking with me? Shall we order another round of fine Judean wine?" But the apostles were sleepy and could not keep up. They begged him to stop. "No, Lord! We have had enough! Stop! No more!" And the Lord said, "Who can stay awake with me in the bitter night? Who can do a few more glasses?" But Peter, who sitteth at the right hand of the Lord said, "Yes, Lord, I can do a few more bottles! They say in Calpernia that I have a hollow leg!" And the Lord turned to him and said, "Peter, thou art my rock!"'"

Schwartz was stunned. If this ever got out, the whole basis of the church would be called into question! Schwartz was getting an education. But Larry returned to *Holy Blood, Holy Grail*, the book that had started the gold rush for the Holy Grail.

"*Holy Blood, Holy Grail* involved leaps of logic, suspension of disbelief, and a total lack of all historical knowledge. However, for some reason, like the reality show *Jersey Shore*, many years later, it captured the imagination of the world. Since then, there have been a hundred imitators who took that tale and expanded on it, fudged with it, and developed similar theories. There were several popular books that sold millions.

"Then, it gets worse. Along comes the World Wide Web. For the first time in the history of our species, anyone can publish anything they want. No longer are there scholarly editors who are careful about what they publish, who are careful about how they edit and how thoroughly they check the footnotes and scholarship. Fuck that! Now, any nut with basic computer skills can put up a web page or a blog. God, do I hate the word 'blog'! Suddenly, we are awash in conspiracy theories. There was a time that when you came to the Bodleian, you would find Shakespeare, Sophocles, and Joyce. Now, you get to read the thoughts of Cuthbert, the corner butcher, self-publishing a book on the Templars and how they went underground and are now living in secret in a small council flat outside of Blackpool. The difference between expert and amateur has disappeared. Everybody is an expert. Anybody can write about anything they want. There are no editors, no rules, and no standards of evidence."

This made a lot of sense to Schwartz. It was true that nobody was minding the store anymore. But his friend was not done with his analysis of what went wrong.

"Schwartz, add to this the fact that education worldwide has gone down the drain. Colleges wanted to educate more citizens, so they lowered their admissions standards, inflated their grades, and made sure almost everybody could get a degree. Colleges are judged on how many of their students graduate. So, to comply, colleges started giving everyone a piece of paper. After that, everyone got on the dean's list. Hell, it's like the Special Olympics. Over the years, these less well-educated idiots themselves became the professors. There was a time, Dr. Schwartz, when England ruled the waves. Now, she waves the rules. Once our colleges were among the finest in the world, and now, well, you know, you have been teaching.

"So, in time, this made a college degree useless. Having one today means nothing. No, I take that back. I would say a person who did not go to college is probably smarter than one who did. This drop in standards to include more of the vulgar hoi polloi, which means in Greek 'the vulgar many,' means the average person comes out of university knowing almost nothing about science, logic, or history. So, in a sense, they will believe almost anything.

"Now we add a little salt to the meal. Next, they get their grubby, little, uneducated hands on a computer and start using this demonic thing called Google that connects things that should have no business being connected. Those of us who were classically educated in the old ways know how to make connections. Those of us who read Lucretius, Cicero, Aquinas, and Bacon know to be careful using analogies, avoiding the *argumentum ad populum*, the *argumentum ad hominem*, and the *argumentum ad baculum*, and we try to reason with precision. We know how to make inferences. We know how to refute evidence. We know about the sixty-four syllogisms of Aristotle and how to construct an argument that is both valid and true. We were taught how to deduce correctly conclusions from premises. We were taught the difference between induction and deduction. We were taught to deconstruct vague connotations and put them into syllogistic form. But what good is that in today's world? None, my dear boy, none! We did a survey of students to see who took out books in all the libraries in Oxford. Do you know what we found? Those that took out the fewest books were those that went on to become British political leaders! Hell!

Ed Miliband, the leader of the Labor Party, was at Oxford for his entire college career. Good God, that boy didn't know where the Bodleian was. They say the only documents he knew by heart were the drink menus at the Bear Inn or the Lamb and Flag. Now he is on TV talking about the future of the European Union and revising our economic forecasting models. Schwartz, this is why we Scots drink."

Bone looked at his glass, took a good, long sip, and continued. "No, now, we have everybody thinking they're an expert and they can all discover the secret of the ages that has eluded the greatest minds of all time. How do they do it? Well, they start with a search for the Holy Grail. Then, we throw in the Templars, and then it gets good, real good. What do we have next? Let me see. Let's throw in a pinch of crop circles, a dash of the Kennedy assassination, two tablespoons of the KGB, one teaspoon of the Druids, one can of the CIA, two cups of alien shapeshifters, a pinch of the Trilateral Commission, the House of Windsor, the Bush-Saudi royal family connection, the Bohemian Club, the Rockefellers, and, just for some spice, let's add the Vatican and the Mafia. Oh, wait! Did I neglect to mention UFOs, reincarnations, and time warps? Oh, well, we can always throw that in later. It's a mess, dear boy, a total mess."

Schwartz had never thought about conspiracies in this way. "You forgot Obama's birth certificate. So, Larry, you have this all figured out. You blame a shoddy education system, stupid students who become stupid professors, no editorial gatekeepers, and Google."

"You have got it in a nutshell, Schwartz. One crazy idea connected to another. But let me edify you further on this important topic. Do you know how Google actually works? Right over at 1 Saint Giles Street is the Oxford Internet Institute. They are one of the premier places on the planet to analyze Internet policy, trends, and pitfalls. Last year, they had a conference, and one of the speakers was the main guy who tweaks the algorithm that makes Google searches run. I listened to his presentation, and I was stunned. Do you know how it works? The algorithm that runs Google searches modifies itself by adapting instantaneously to the popularity of search results. So the Google algorithm directs the next person to the most popular search that day. In both Google and Twitter, they call this 'trending.' So, when one person stumbles on something, the rest follow, like lemmings, plunging into an ocean of ignorance.

"Most popular also means most stupid. So it grows and grows. Let me give you an example. If I were to Google the name 'Michelangelo Schwartz,' I would get your name, but also a *Wikipedia* site for Michelangelo Buonarroti. This is because when most folks Google the term 'Michelangelo,' they are looking for him, not you. Of course, there would be other links on that page. Probably on the same page as Michelangelo Schwartz, they would get pointed to the most famous Schwartz, Sherwood Schwartz, that giant of American entertainment. Now, let us say I have free time, sitting at my desk, not doing my office work, and I click on the link for Sherwood Schwartz. Soon, I would be off on the whole Gilligan and the Illuminati tangent, and that would take hours."

Michelangelo was shocked at the mention of Sherwood Schwartz, his uncle from Passaic, New Jersey, here in the heart of the Bodleian Library. "You, the head librarian at the Bodleian, know about Gilligan and the Illuminati?"

Bone smiled. "My boy, we have a whole wall of books on the subject, and our own Dean Richard Raymond of Exeter College is the editor of the *Gilliganiana Journal*, published under the auspices of the Policy Studies Organization on Dupont Circle in Washington. That journal is devoted solely to that popular subject. The journal is published by Wiley, and the best academic libraries in the world all subscribe to it. We have an annual conference at Blackfriars Hall here in Oxford. Here, I have the conference proceedings right here."

Bone went to the bookshelf and pulled out a bound volume. He opened it up and started reading the titles of some of the scholarly papers. "Here we go. The first paper at the conference this past year was 'Gilligan as Ulysses: Sherwood Schwartz as the Modern Homer' by Professor Hans Vander Kauf from Utrecht University in the Netherlands. Next, we have 'Ginger: The First Feminist?' by Professor Anna Barker from Harvard. Here is a good one. 'Late Capitalism and Marx's Critique of Derivative Labor: Another Look at Thurston Howell III' by Howard Canaan of Middlebury College. But the big hit of the conference was this controversial paper by a senior professor at the Scripps Oceanographic Institute in the United States. It was entitled 'Nautical Musings: An Oceanographer Recalculates the Actual Location of Gilligan's Island.' The conference was so popular that we had to reject more than three quarters of the papers. People are really into this Gilligan thing. There are numerological interpretations, deconstructive approaches, anarchist readings, feminist critiques, phenomenological approaches, deconstructivist interpretations, Marxist interpretations, groups called the Tea Party for Gilligan and, amazingly, African Americans Who Love Gilligan. Schwartz, did you know that there are local chapters of this movement where they watch old episodes and discuss the hidden meanings?"

Schwartz had no idea that there was so much interest in his uncle's creation. Bone went on.

"*Gilliganiana* is very popular in college towns like Dartmouth, New Hampshire; Athens, Georgia; and even the University of Tokyo. There are even whole college courses in such unlikely places as Saint Rose's College in Albany or Mercy College in New York. The episodes about Wrongway Feldman and the episode where the cannibals capture Gilligan are the most popular among these groups.

"You may not have known this, Schwartz, but Wrongway Feldman was based on the real pilot named Doug 'Wrong Way' Corrigan. In 1938, and I am not making this up, Corrigan left Brooklyn. First of all, how hilarious is that for a starting point? He was on his way west to the air field in Long Beach, California. He did not make it to Long Beach, but he got close. He landed in Ireland instead."

Schwartz was amazed at the connections being made. Bone handed him the volume of proceedings from the conference. "Keep it, Schwartz; I have several copies."

Outside the building, across from the circular building they call the Radcliffe Camera, Wolf Eyes stood and took in the air of Oxford while using his earpiece to listen to the conversation. So far, there was nothing that caught his attention. He wondered what made this drunken Dante scholar so special that he had been dispatched to watch over him. The whole conversation about Moshe, Google, and higher education seemed like gibberish to him. So far, he did not get it.

Back inside the library, Schwartz took the book of proceedings and put it on the table. But he wanted to get back to talking about the Internet. "So Google is the engine driving random events into patterns that seem to make sense not even to you. If enough people think there is a connection, then the program accepts that and shares it with others. But then this makes patterns where there are none. And Google makes it look like everything is connected to everything else. Thus, the most common is the most true. It reminds me of the old joke. Mary and Barry got married. The only thing they had in common was the fact that they both were."

"Schwartz, I have a department meeting in a few minutes that has to do with next year's budget, which is the only meeting of the year I care about, so I will have to cut this short. I will put one fact to you. You may know that every year there is a meeting in Davos, Switzerland, of a shadowy group called the World Economic Council. Its proceedings are not published, and every important financial wizard in the world is in those meetings."

"Yes, Larry, I have come across the Davos Group. They are often mentioned in connection with the Illuminati, the Trilateral Commission, and the Bilderberg Group. It is suspected that the Davos Group runs the world economy from behind the scenes."

Larry smiled as he collected his papers for his meeting. "Well, Schwartz, so that no interlopers crash the meeting, they have a password known only to the members after they get past all of the initial security. That password is changed every year, and it is known to and shared with the most powerful people in the world. Bill Clinton was a Rhodes Scholar here at Oxford, and he comes back from time to time to visit. He and I had a drink last year, a few months after he had been at Davos. He told me last year's password because it had expired and was not a secret anymore. Do you know what that password was last year?"

"Larry, I am afraid to ask."

"Mary Ann or Ginger?"

10

We visit France, where there are several references to the courage of the French army, the quality of French wine, and the patience and gentleness of Parisian waiters. We visit a famous bookstore, find new clues, and meet Angelique, who joins the adventure.

Paris, France

Charles de Gaulle Airport is one of the busiest in Europe. The travelers' morning flight from Heathrow landed at noon Paris time. As they were making their way to a taxi, Schwartz thought about the greatness of France. He thought about the impossible Parisian waiter who'd mercilessly abused him a few years back, for more than a hour, at the top of his lungs for a slight mispronunciation of the sentence "*Qual è la parola in Francese*?" which can be translated as "What is the word in French?" He thought about the well-appointed and fashionable French women who make sure their lipstick matches both their shoes and handbags before they take their teacup-sized show dog out to take care of business before sunrise.

In his time in France, Schwartz had learned that the French kept the best wine for themselves, of which they drank three or four bottles a day, and the slop that was left over in the bottom of the barrel, they labeled "Chateaux Baron Laffite Rothschild." Then, they charged stupid yuppie stockbrokers in Los Angeles a thousand dollars a bottle. Because the French were smart, they'd tell their not-so-sophisticated American customers to hang on to those bottles for twenty years before they drank them. They called this "putting the wine down." So the Americans would build elaborate wine cellars, pipe in special air to control the humidity, and make sure the cellars were vibration-free. By convincing the Americans to wait, they made sure that by the time the Americans opened that bottle, smelled the harsh vinegar odor, and realized they had been swindled, the guy that sold the wine would be either dead or at another vineyard, working the same scam.

Shakespeare and Company is located at 37 rue de la Bucherie in the fifth arrondissement in Paris. It is located inside what was once a sixteenth-century monastery on the Left Bank of the Seine. You can see the towers of Notre Dame out of one window and hear the peel of its bells. Outside, you can see stacks of books on old wooden pushcarts that they can wheel in at night and an old front window crowded with books about philosophy and literature. The old cobblestone street has statues and flowers, as you would expect on the Rive Gauche. That bookstore has been home to Allen Ginsberg, William S. Burroughs, Rod McLuhan, Richard Wright, Jacqueline Suzanne, and Anaïs Nin. E. L. James, who wrote the best-selling *Fifty Shades of Grey*, has never been there. In fact, it is rumored she has never been in any bookstore.

If you walked into that store and didn't know any better, you would think you were in a novel by Victor Hugo or Charles Dickens. The bookstore has three floors crowded with books stacked in haphazard arrangements. Not the neat dust jackets of a modern American bookstore but tattered covers of secondhand books, hoping to return to a loving home.

The longtime owner of the bookstore, George Whitman, set up cots upstairs, so struggling artists, poets, and writers could sleep and eat at the bookstore. Over one of the passages on the first floor is a quote that George incorrectly attributed to Yeats. It contained the bookstore's philosophy: "Be not inhospitable to strangers as they may be angels in disguise." There is a wishing well in the center of the bookstore, where George put a sign that said: "Give what you can, take what you need, George." No wonder he once described the bookstore as a "utopian socialist collective masquerading as a business." There is but one more fact we must point out. Sylvia Beach and George Whitman, who founded the two Shakespeare and Company bookstores, were both born in New Jersey.

The three travelers stood outside the bookstore. A light rain was falling. The sky was gray, but the light was still beautiful. William was impatient and was not sure what they were doing in Paris when they should be making progress decoding a document.

"Schwartz, it is true. The book and poem originated here, but why do we need to be here physically? Shouldn't you be sitting down with a puzzle dictionary and a Greek lexicon, trying to make sense of the poem, instead of traipsing all over Europe?"

"Well, Bill, William, or whatever name you go by now, a week ago, I would have agreed with you. But it seems that whatever is going on here, and something is going on here, is more than meets the eye. It is way more than meets the eye. At every turn, there is a signal or sign. Now, a week ago, I would have said it was a coincidence or an accident. But, between the Illuminati, the Vatican, and God knows who else is at work here, I have come to believe there is a trail of breadcrumbs we are meant to follow, and follow it we will! Besides, think of it! We are in Paris, the City of Light! We are in a country where the president can live openly with a woman who is not his wife, and their relationship is simply described as 'French.' Besides, the wine is better here, if you like alcohol that has no kick. I suggest we go inside, separately, and see what happens."

William could not believe his ears. "Go inside, and see what happens? What kind of a plan is that?"

Schwartz smiled. He was a master of chaos. "It's sort of a Zen thing. Trust me. This feels like the right thing to do."

Biff did not feel like refereeing between William and Michelangelo. So he just walked inside. In a few minutes, William followed and then Schwartz. Michelangelo entered and found every inch of the bookstore packed with books, knickknacks, and all sorts of notes, papers, and mementos. It smelled of old paper, books, and the sweet scent of French food that was often enjoyed among the stacks. He stopped under one of the most famous arches of any bookstore in the world. He looked up and, for some reason, was sure that this was another piece of the puzzle. He stood looking up at what was written on the arch. "Be not inhospitable to strangers as they may be angels in disguise."

At that very moment, a young woman slipped up next to him. She was slim and attractive. She was wearing a beret, stylish black thick-framed glasses, and a beautiful blue slicker raincoat. She had black hair, brown eyes, and smelled like a freshly baked croissant. She was carrying a violin case and going through the books on the shelf next to him. She turned in his direction and smiled at him as she spoke.

"*Trouver ce que vous cherchez?*"

Schwartz smiled. He could read and understand French, but he was not going to embarrass himself by trying to speak it to a Parisian. That was a lesson that French waiters taught tourists with a blowtorch, pipe wrench, and cattle prod. So he answered in English.

"No. I have not, in fact, found what I was looking for."

She smiled. "Well, if you are a stranger here, why don't you try *The Stranger?*"

She reached in front of them and pulled a worn copy of the 1942 work, *L'Etranger*, by Albert Camus, from the shelf. Schwartz looked up again at the sign over their heads, and he took the book out of her hand. It was an old, secondhand copy from the Librairie Gallimard. Its owner had marked it up. Michelangelo leafed through it quickly. In the middle of the yellowed pages was a paper. It was relatively new and crisp. He unfolded it. It was written in French:

La bebe qui a construit la maison
Femmes et de la bière préférées
Mais il a enterré le trésor
Quand il l'appellerai à la maison

Schwartz may have been a drunk, a womanizer, and a man of questionable character, but he was a scholar who knew his French. He took a small leather notebook and a pen out of his pocket and wrote a translation in English:

The young child constructed his home,
Liked ladies and beer,
But he buried the treasure,
And it would call him home.

It made no sense to Schwartz, but he knew this was in the same style as the poem he had read in Oxford. Could this be yet another piece in the puzzle? Was this just some kind of accident? Like Google, was he making a connection where there should be none? Why did she hand this book to him? Who could have known they would be in the bookstore today? He was getting worried that there were other players who were five steps ahead of him, looking for the same thing. Could this be a clue to throw him off? Suddenly, he looked over at the young lady standing next to him. She smiled and spoke. "I like this bookstore. It has a kind of magic. Don't you agree?"

Michelangelo Schwartz was never a man to waste an opportunity. And this seemed to him to be the next step on a journey that was becoming more and more coherent. There was some kind of crazy logic and necessity he was beginning to feel. He realized that this woman standing next to him was not standing there by coincidence. She smiled back at him. "There is always magic if you know where to find it."

Then, he said the best thing a man could say to a woman in Paris. "Can I buy you a glass of wine?"

She smiled, shrugged her shoulders, and nodded yes. He took the book to the checkout, paid five euros, and they walked out together. William and Biff watched them leave and followed at a distance. What William and Biff did not know was that Salvatore Greco, the Vatican hit man, was following them. What Salvatore Greco did not know was that Wolf Eyes was following him. It was getting crowded.

About a block away was a little bistro that had black metal tables outside. Each table had a little vase on it with a few fresh flowers in each one. The spring rain had subsided, so they sat outside. William and Biff watched from a distance as the waiter, dressed in a white shirt, black bow tie, and a long apron over his black pants, brought a bottle of red wine and two glasses. They could not hear what the couple was saying, but they could guess. But they guessed wrong. His young companion had transfixed Michelangelo Schwartz. Schwartz had introduced himself. She did not give him her name. Instead, she launched into a discussion of books.

"I often spend time at secondhand bookstores. A secondhand book tells a lot about its previous owner. It is interesting to see which pages in a book were the most read, where a note was made, and where the reader put an exclamation point in the margin. In a sense, you get to know a person you may never meet, spend a little time with them, and live in their world."

This was getting way too heavy for him. Schwartz wanted to lighten up the subject. "Let me tell you a joke. Your English should be good enough to follow this. There is a bar in Tahiti with a slow turning fan, a thatched roof, a view of the ocean, a tropical look, and the whole deal. Into the bar comes this guy. He is wearing a beret; he has a pencil-thin moustache. He is wearing a black and white striped shirt, but he has a three-foot-tall purple-and-yellow parrot with a flame-red Mohawk on his shoulder. The parrot is wearing a pirate hat and has a patch on one eye. The man goes up to the bartender and says, 'Pardon, monsieur, but may I have a glass of your finest French champagne?' But the bartender can't take his eyes off the three-foot-tall purple-and-yellow parrot with a red Mohawk. So he finally has to ask the man what's the deal with the bird. The bartender walks over to the guy and asks, 'Where the hell did you get that thing?' The parrot looks the bartender right in the eye and says, 'In France! They got millions of them!'"

With that, Michelangelo Schwartz exploded in laughter as his companion looked at him with a quizzical expression. He realized that the joke had not gone over so well. So he responded to her original thought. "I am a book person myself and know the pleasure, the feel, and the comfort of a book."

She took a sip of her wine and looked deeply into his eyes. She was beautiful. He was becoming hypnotized. She spoke in a quiet voice. "What were you looking for in Shakespeare and Company? Anything special?"

At this point, Schwartz figured there was no point in hiding his cards. Somebody knew what was going on, and it wasn't him. She'd gone right for the book that had the poem in it. There was probably more to gain from playing his cards than hiding them. So he went with his instincts. That was what he had done his whole life, his whole disastrous life.

"I have been thinking about the Illuminati, the Holy Grail, and the balance of power between the forces of good and the forces of evil in this world."

She sipped her wine and admired the lilac bush that was blooming across the street. Its scent filled the air. Schwartz noticed that the mention of the Holy Grail and Illuminati did not elicit any kind of response from her. She thought for a moment before she spoke.

"These are large matters about which we can only speculate. But there is something I do know. My life has followed a path, and I believe that there is wisdom in that path. So I believe that everything happens for a reason, and I trust that reason."

"And what do you do when you are not wandering around in bookstores?"

She smiled demurely. "I do puzzles. I took my degree in mathematics at Cambridge but could not find a university job. They are very hard to come by here in France. So I began to write crossword puzzles. I was always good at solving them and playing Scrabble. So I began creating my own puzzles. It allows me to make a living and do as I like. So I can travel where I like, work on the road, and still make a living."

"Your English is perfect. I guess those years in Cambridge were wonderful. It is a charming city."

"Yes. I spent enough time there to become mildly proficient in both higher mathematics and English. They have a great tradition of mathematical and scientific thinkers, including Newton, Darwin, Babbage, Turing, and Stephen Hawking. While Oxford is rightly famous for the arts and literature, Cambridge has its own history and glory."

Michelangelo Schwartz decided that if there were no coincidences, he would take a chance. He took a paper out of his pocket and placed it on the table between them. He was going to share the poem with her.

William and Biff, who were watching from a distance, were startled. William's face turned red with excitement as he turned to Biff. "What the hell is he doing? Is he sharing the poem with her? Who the hell is she? Should we stop him?"

Biff was just as startled but more measured. "Let's wait."

Further up the alley, Salvatore Greco was looking through his binoculars as he talked to the Vatican on his cell phone.

"That's right. He has a paper out, and he is letting her look at it. I will keep you informed."

A hundred yards behind Salvatore, Wolf Eyes was also using his binoculars. Unlike Salvatore, he could hear every word through his earpiece that was tuned in to the listening device hidden in the collar of Schwartz's jacket. He was thinking that, later, he would have to inform his employer that things had taken an unexpected turn. Again, he noted the occurrence of conversations about the Holy Grail and the Illuminati, but he could not put it all together.

Schwartz and his companion looked at the poem:

The cup that ends all human strife
And gives its bearer eternal life
Can be found not on the corners but in the middle.
You must come home to solve this riddle.

The holy man protects the books;
Beneath the star on pages he looks.
Along it runs a second street
That has a number we must meet.

Now take the year the master was burned,
The same year lessons in love were first learned.
Subtract it from the year of the Vatican sculpture's birth
That gives us an eight anywhere on Earth.

This cup that can end all sorrow and grief
Has given the most laurel wreaths.
Dig there, and you will lose your breath,
Rule the world, and conquer death.

But before you can learn to sing this song
There is one man you must bring along.
This unworthy messenger alone can find the key.
He is living near the statue in the sea.

His first name is the father of *David* and the *Pietà*.
He loves baseball, Dante, and the theater.
His last name doesn't fit; it makes us scoff,
One of a million names for what Pius IX knocked off.

He comes not from Noah's old boat.
With grain alcohol, he keeps afloat.
Accused of Spinozistic heresy,
This acolyte hails from New Jersey.

The time has come for the Grail to change hands.
It has traveled across many lands.
Work on this riddle till your hands have warts,
But it will only be solved by a man named Schwartz.

She sat back and sipped her wine. Silences made him nervous. While she was sitting there, Schwartz remembered another French joke.

"OK. While you are thinking, how about another French joke? How many Frenchmen does it take to defend Paris?"

She shrugged her shoulders. Schwartz gave her the answer. "How many Frenchmen does it take to defend Paris? I don't know. It's never been tried!"

Again, he burst out laughing while she sat there, not breaking a smile. She turned back to the poem. "Professor Schwartz, the first line could be read as referring to the Grail, the cup that ends all strife. And there is obviously a reference to Michelangelo Schwartz, and, of course, they mention other Catholic things. We need to go to the heart of the Catholic world to get this unraveled. I have a suggestion. I am headed to Rome tomorrow. I know the director of the Palazzo dei Conservatori, which is one of the Capitoline Museums in Rome. A little while back they had an exhibition called '*Lux in Arcana*.'"

Schwartz smiled. "Light into the darkness."

She smiled back. "Yes. A little while ago, they hosted an exhibit of the Vatican Secret Archives that was meant to show the public that the Vatican was willing to be more transparent. The exhibit contained artifacts from the deepest regions of the Vatican. Many had never been seen before. There is a man there who I am sure can help you. The director of the museum, Antonio Cuccinelli, is a friend and knows more about the Vatican, its symbols, and its interests than anyone I know. In preparing for the exhibit, he spent years researching and thinking about these very things referred to in this poem. I think with the references here to Rome that is the place you must go if you want to understand the poem better."

Schwartz was quick on the uptake. He realized this whole conversation was no accident, and he was going to proceed forward. He would agree to any suggestion she might make.

"You have convinced me. Rome will be our next stop. I am working with two associates; I guess that is the correct word. Would you like to travel with us?"

She took a slow sip of her wine. "I have already made my own plans to get there. Let us meet at the entrance to the Palazzo dei Conservatori on the day after tomorrow at two in the afternoon. I will call my friend and make sure everything is arranged."

Schwartz smiled. "And your name is..."

She smiled back. "Angelique. My name is Angelique Serrureacle."

Schwartz had not given up on trying to make her laugh. "OK. How about one last joke?"

She sighed and sipped her wine as Michelangelo launched into it.

"What do you call someone who speaks three languages?"

Angelique answered, "Trilingual."

"OK. Then, what do you call someone who speaks two languages?"

"Bilingual."

"OK. Now what do you call someone who only speaks one language?"

She had no idea, so she shrugged her shoulders.

Schwartz gave her the answer.

"French."

He could see she was getting annoyed, so he broached one last request. "Angelique, I have a question that I have always wondered about."

She seemed agreeable. "Ask away."

"Is it true that when French women say 'no,' they really mean 'yes'?"

She thought for a minute before she answered. She looked him squarely in the eyes and smiled. "No."

Schwartz had to think about that for a while. He thought he might take another tack.

"Well, Angelique. I have a nice hotel room a few blocks away. I suggest we go there and really try to decipher this poem."

"Professor, surely you are not suggesting we sleep together after only knowing one another for half an hour. I am sure that is not the kind of man you are."

Schwartz slumped back in his chair. He took a long taste of the wine that was smooth and wonderful. It was not the slop they unknowingly served at the Plaza Hotel in New York. Shitski, he thought.

CIA Headquarters, Langley, Virginia

A few hours later, at the CIA Headquarters in Langley, Virginia, Joe Chip was again at the door of Glen Runciter's spotless office.

"Morning, Joe. What have we got?"

Joe Chip had a file he was reviewing. "Our Norwegian friend and Greco both spent two days in Oxford, and now both of them are in different hotels in Paris, near the university."

This was interesting to Glen. "It took us a long time to figure out who the Norwegian was. We have spent a fortune in manpower and surveillance to figure out his connections. We can't screw this up. What else have you got?"

Joe Chip gave a boyish smile. "Well, it turns out that three of the passengers on the same flight with Greco and the Norwegian also spent two days in Oxford. These three are now in a hotel a few blocks away from where the Norwegian and Greco are staying in Paris. There is some connection between these five people."

Glen leaned in. "Who are they?"

"Well, two of them, William Callahan and Biff Braunschweiger, work for an organization called the Anti-Catholic League of Brooklyn."

Glen knitted his brows. "The Anti-Catholic League of Brooklyn? Anything else?"

Joe Chip looked down at the file. "There is one more thing. The third man traveling on that plane is a former college professor named Michelangelo Schwartz."

Glen started laughing. "Are you making this all up?"

"Not only am I not making this up, but Professor Michelangelo Schwartz sat next to the Norwegian all the way across the Atlantic Ocean."

Glen Runciter got up and looked out the window to the front of CIA Headquarters. He had learned early in his time in the intelligence field that there are no such things as coincidences.

"Joe, I want every e-mail, every phone call, every name in their contact lists, and every time those three have sneezed or jaywalked in the last ten years. I want every Google search they have done, every library book they took out, and if they have any contacts with anyone we might consider a threat to national security. Get that on my desk in the next twenty-four hours. We need to keep better tabs on these people."

Joe was surprised. "Keep better tabs on these people? Hey, we keep track of everyone who has bought a copy of *1984* on Amazon and have them all on a watch list. And you don't want to know what we got on those who downloaded *The Hunger Games*."

11

We dine in Paris. Next arrive in Rome and visit Harry's Bar, where we meet Giovanni the bartender and learn what would happen if Tarzan and Jane were Italian. Finally, the gypsies (with surprising results) rob a drunken Michelangelo Schwartz.

Paris, France

That night, the three companions sat down at an outdoor café in the Latin Quarter of Paris for dinner. They drank copious amounts of Bordeaux wines, dined on delicately cooked lamb chops, and appreciated grilled vegetables that had been cooked to perfection and bathed in garlic and butter. French café music played softly in the distance, and the sounds of the city played a magic symphony. The wine made Schwartz feel poetic.

"You know, this reminds me of a joke. A man is on death row. On the morning he is due to go to the electric chair, a minister comes into his cell to comfort the man. He is asked if he has any last requests. He says to the minister, 'Yes, when they pull the switch, would you hold my hand?'"

William needed another drink.

They retired to the Marriott Hotel at 9 rue de l'Ancienne Comédie to spend their last night in Paris. All but Michelangelo Schwartz. He was a night owl who loved to wander the streets and meet new people. He was so fond of saying, "See what happens next."

Rome, Italy

The trio caught a morning flight to Italy. The flight from Charles de Gaulle to Fiumicino-Leonardo da Vinci Airport in Rome was short and surprisingly uneventful. The train from Fiumicino to the heart of Rome was the best way to come into the city. The airport was sixteen miles southwest of the city. The train took passengers to the central railway station in Rome that was appropriately named *Termini*—the end. They passed by farms and country houses in the beginning, and then the city came into view.

Rome was a city of bookstores, superior restaurants, shopping, and parks. It was a city where you could find wall-size pictures by Caravaggio in a very small church with little light, like Santa Maria del Popula. All through the city, in the great piazzas, there were stone statues with clear water shooting out from waterworks that were more than six hundred years old. There were obelisks the Romans liberated from ancient Egypt in their wars there. It was a city of ancient houses that had breathtaking ceiling paintings, with their trompe l'oeil effects. Rome was a city with more than five hundred Catholic churches. It was the city of the Colosseum, the Trevi Fountain, and the Spanish Steps.

It was springtime in the Eternal City. The sun was bright, and the air was clear. The Vatican Museum and the Vatican itself, with its pictures by Raphael, busts of the popes, and artifacts from all corners of the world, would be mobbed on a day like today. But the Vatican was not where they were headed. They were making for their hotel. Tomorrow, the trio was going to the heart of Rome, the Capital District.

They got a taxi from the Termini Station that drove at breakneck speed through the busy city and took them past the Piazza della Repubblica, past the Piazza Barberini, with its spectacular fountain, and up the steep hill called the Via Veneto to their hotel. Breakneck speed was the only gear in a Roman taxi.

The three traveling companions checked into the Rome Marriott Grand Hotel Flora at the top of the hill on the Via Vittorio Veneto. Wolf Eyes had arrived earlier and was staying in the Hotel Alexander not far away. Salvatore Greco was staying with a friend near the American Embassy at the bottom of the hill. In Rome, a man like Salvatore had many friends.

Michelangelo loved the idea of being on the Via Veneto. It brought back memories of the Federico Fellini 1960 film *La Dolce Vita*. He recalled Marcello Mastroianni in his cool Persol sunglasses following Anita Ekberg after she started wading into the Trevi Fountain in that film. When he saw that movie, he realized what he wanted to be in life, Marcello Mastroianni in a Fellini film, chasing Anita Ekberg in the Trevi Fountain. But since 1960, a lot had changed. The Via Veneto was not the hot spot it once was. Sure, there was Harry's Bar across from the Flora Hotel. A little way up the hill from the hotel was the Villa Borghese, with its fantastic Bernini sculptures. The Villa Borghese was once the residence of the nephew of one of the most corrupt Borgia popes. This pope was so corrupt he made his perverted nephew a cardinal. The house was filled with highly erotic, some would argue obscene, sculptures and the paintings of *The Rape of Lucretia*, *The Rape of the Sabine Women*, and *Hades Abduction of Demeter*. You get the idea. If you went in there for confession with that cardinal, you were in for a real surprise.

It was noon when Schwartz, William, and Biff checked into the Marriott. William and Biff went up to their rooms for a short nap. As soon as their doors closed, Michelangelo opened his and quietly tiptoed down the hall and down the marble stairs to the lobby and across the street to Harry's Bar. He had a full twenty-four hours before their next meeting. He walked in and took a seat at the elegant wood-paneled bar.

The bartender walked over and smiled when he recognized Michelangelo. "*Professore! Buon pomeriggio!* Long time no see!"

Schwartz was in heaven. He knew bartenders in every city in Europe.

"Giovanni, you old hound dog. Good afternoon to you. Good to see you, too, my old friend!"

Giovanni was a handsome young man in his late thirties, with blond hair and sparkling green eyes. He had an athletic build from biking all over the city. He was wearing a stylish knit shirt and a blue tie. Giovanni was a fixture on the Via Veneto.

"Professore, your usual? A Negroni?"

Schwartz grinned and nodded yes. He was in Rome, so why not enjoy the most Roman of cocktails? He felt as if he were on holiday even though he was working...well, sort of working. Giovanni mixed red Vermouth, Campari, and dry gin and put it on ice, with a twist of orange and a lemon peel. He shook the cocktail vigorously and slid it in front of Michelangelo. The professor picked it up and sipped it. He closed his eyes, and he was in paradise. The radio was on. Dean Martin was singing "Volare." Schwartz closed his eyes and sang along:

> *Volare,* oh, oh,
> *E contare,* oh, oh, oh, oh
> No wonder my happy heart sings,
> Your love has given me wings.
> *Penso che un sogno cosi non ritorni mai piu.*
> *Mi dipingevo le mani e la faccia di blu.*
> *Poi d'improvviso venivo dal vento rapito.*
> *E incominciavo a volare nel cielo infinito.*

Giovanni leaned over and smiled. "Professore, do you remember that woman you were with last time and how mad she got at you? She threw her Negroni right in your face. Do you remember?"

Schwartz winced. These were the kind of remarks he heard everywhere he went. "Giovanni, let us only talk of pleasant things."

"But, Professore, she was so beautiful!"

Schwartz smiled. "You can start making me a second Negroni, Giovanni. I think I am going to need it today."

Giovanni was busy behind the bar, cleaning glasses and singing along with Dean.

"Professore, I still remember some of those jokes you told me last time. Do you remember? I still tell them to my customers. How about this one? 'How does an Italian get into a legitimate business? By lowering himself in through the skylight.' That's a nice, eh?"

Schwartz could not help laughing at that old chestnut. So he figured he would join in. "OK, Giovanni, here is one for you. An Italian man who spent all of his life in Naples was walking along the beach, and he was praying. All of a sudden, he said out loud, 'Lord, grant me one wish!' Suddenly, the sky clouded above his head, and, in a loud, thundering voice, the Lord said, 'Because you have had the faith to ask, I will grant you one wish.' The man said, 'I often travel to Sicily on business. The boat ride is long and difficult for me. Build a bridge to Sicily, so I can drive over anytime I want to.' The Lord said, 'Your request is very difficult. Think of the logistics of that kind of undertaking. The supports required to reach the bottom of the Mediterranean Sea would be considerable! Think of all of the concrete and steel it would take! I would have to suspend my own laws of nature. That would go against everything I stand for. That is impossible, even for me. Take a little more time, and think of another wish, a wish you think would honor and glorify me.' The Italian man thought about it for a long time. Finally, he said, 'Lord, I have been married and divorced four times. All of my wives said that I am uncaring and insensitive. I wish that I could understand women. I want to know how they feel inside, what they are thinking when they give me the silent treatment, why they cry, what they really mean when they say nothing is wrong, and, Lord, help me understand how I can make a woman truly happy.' After a few minutes, God said, 'Do you want two lanes or four on that bridge?'"

Giovanni laughed so hard he could almost not stand up. Schwartz had another one. He figured now was a good time to use it. "How about this one, Giovanni? If Tarzan and Jane were Italian, what would Cheeta be?"

Giovanni thought for a minute and had a question. "Cheeta, the monkey? I don't know."

Schwartz retold the joke, so the punch line would not be lost. "If Tarzan and Jane were Italian, what would Cheeta be? The least hairy of the three."

Giovanni was not sure he liked the reference to hairy Italians, but he smiled just the same. He was a proud Italian, and he was not sure if that joke was told in the right spirit. Schwartz didn't seem to notice.

The cocktails were flowing, and the afternoon went by. After a little while, Michelangelo Schwartz looked down the bar and saw a thin man with a scraggly beard, who was dressed like a poor college student. He was wearing a T-shirt and jeans. He had metal rim glasses and was nursing a beer. Schwartz was very social, so he shouted out to him, "I bet you a cocktail that you are either American or Irish!"

The man looked up. "I am an American, but how did you know?

Schwartz smiled. "Because no self-respecting European would come into Harry's Bar in Rome dressed like that. That means you are either American or Irish."

The young man, who had brown eyes, was thin and in his thirties. He smiled and slid down the bar toward Schwartz. He didn't speak however. So Schwartz figured he would start the conversation. "My young friend, you look like you are in some sort of quandary. Can Giovanni and I here be of help?"

Schwartz turned to Giovanni and winked with a devilish smile on his face. The young man seemed hesitant. He looked for a long time into his beer. He was obviously upset about something, but Schwartz was not sure what it was.

"What would you do if you knew something that nobody else even guessed at that would make the front page of every paper in the world?"

Schwartz was curious, and he was thinking how everything that had happened to him so far had been a piece of the puzzle. "Are you a college man?"

The young man shook his head. "No, as a matter of fact, I am a high-school dropout."

Schwartz turned back to Giovanni and whispered, "If he is a high-school dropout, what could he know? What secret could he have?"

Schwartz turned to the young man and took out a coin. "Young fellow, here is how I do things. Let's flip a coin. I happen to have one right here. Heads, you tell the world what you know. Tails, you keep your mouth shut and live your life. I imagine, if you go public, it could make trouble for you. Am I correct?"

The young man sighed, "Yes" in a depressed way. He spoke in a quiet and nervous voice, "I have been going over this for a long time. I guess it's time to make a decision. I should make up my mind one way or the other."

Schwartz took a long drink. "OK, my young friend. Heads, you tell the world your story. Tails, you keep your secret."

The young man looked up. "OK, go ahead!'

Schwartz took one last gulp of his Negroni, tossed the coin in the air, caught it on his arm, and put his hand on top. He slowly took his hand away and looked up with a smile.

"Well, my young American friend, heads it is!"

Giovanni, the bartender, seemed excited. "It is heads! In Italian, we say, '*Non discutere con il destino.*' It means in English, 'You should never argue with fate.' So, signor, your path is now clear."

The young man finished his Peroni beer. He got up and took his knapsack. He walked toward the door. He turned one last time. "Thank you both. I thought I might not have had the courage to do this. You have made up my mind. I am going to do it. Thanks."

He turned to go out the door, and Schwartz yelled to him, "Young man, you're welcome. And you never said your name!"

The young man adjusted his glasses and gave a nervous smile. "Snowden, Edward Snowden. I do a little contracting for the US government."

After he walked out, Michclangelo Schwartz started laughing. Giovanni was cleaning the wineglasses but leaned over to the professor. "Professore, what is so funny?"

Schwartz was still laughing. "I don't know why I do the things I do. That coin did not come up heads. It was tails. I just lied to see what would happen."

Giovanni shrugged his shoulders. "Hey! What could it matter? I am sure that's the last we'll hear of him!"

When Schwartz left Harry's, the afternoon was still young, so he walked down to the bottom of the Via Veneto to the Piazza Barberini.

He was planning to grab a subway down to the Capital District and take a walk around the Colosseum and the Forum. As he went down the stairs to the subway, he noticed he was woozy. The five cocktails that Giovanni had so excellently prepared were taking effect. He wobbled a little bit.

If you have ever taken mass transit in Italy, you know the chaos, confusion, and total stampedes that occur when a train finally pulls in ten minutes late. By that time, the platform is packed with two hundred people, all trying to get in first through the only two doors on the train that are actually working. If you have ever seen Londoners queuing up neatly and in order for a bus to the West End, you will see a sight never viewed inside the borders of Italy.

On this particular day, the train pulled in, and there was the usual rush toward the train. Schwartz was carried along. But, just inside the door of the train, a large man stopped dead in front of him. A woman with a baby in a sling in front of her pushed Schwartz into the large man. Schwartz was yelling for the man to move, as the woman was yelling at Schwartz. All at once, he noticed her accent and smelled an unmistakable smell. He knew that scent, but from where?

Suddenly, the large man turned around and glared at him. The man yelled something to Schwartz in a language he did not know. It was not Italian. The man and the woman behind him suddenly vanished as the doors closed and the train jolted forward. Instantly, he placed that accent and that smell. He reached for his wallet and passport. They were gone. And so were the man and woman.

"Gypsies! Shitski!"

He was in big, big trouble. He got off at the next stop and reversed trains back to the piazza. He ran as fast as he could up the hill to the hotel near the top. The lobby of the Marriott was all white marble and dark wood. William and Biff were in the lobby there, talking to the woman behind the desk. She was on the phone. Schwartz rushed up to them. "We have to call the police! Those damn gypsies stole my wallet!"

The woman behind the counter looked up. "Dr. Schwartz, you want to call the *polizia*? They are on the phone for you."

He quickly took the receiver. His Italian came back perfectly in this emergency. "*Hai il mio portafoglio. Grazie. Saremo subito*. You are located near the bottom of the Spanish Steps? I will get a cab right now."

He turned to William and Biff. "They must have gotten my cash and credit cards and tossed it. But at least it is not a total loss."

The three grabbed a cab to the police station that was a five-minute cab ride away and went up the stairs. They sat on wooden benches in a waiting room, with a dozen poor Italians, until a tall man in a nice shirt and tie came in to collect Schwartz.

The office of Detective Mangieri was what you would find in any police station anywhere on the planet. A desk covered with papers and a workload no mere mortal could conquer. Detective Mangieri had a round Roman face, a Roman nose, a balding head, and was obviously fond of pasta.

"*Doctore*, you misplaced your wallet?"

Schwartz loved the style of everything Italian.

"I was at the Piazza Barberini, and a large man and a gypsy woman with a baby did the old hold and squeeze and got my wallet and my passport."

The detective was bored out of his skull and looked out the window. "Doctore, can you tell me what you had in your wallet?"

"About fifty euros, fifty dollars, several pictures of my several wives, and two credit cards that are probably at their limit."

The detective opened his drawer and handed Schwartz his passport and his wallet. Schwartz took a quick look, and all of his money and cards were there. Apparently, there was nothing missing. It was all there.

"Detective, this is amazing. How did I get all of this back?"

"Doctore, we had what you in America would call a sting operation. We were on the platform right behind the gypsies and handcuffed them the second they got off the train. But I will tell you, when the gypsies get a wallet, it is usually passed through many hands in the first two minutes, in case anyone is recognized. Your chances of getting this wallet back like this are one in a million. Doctore, you are what we might call in Italian a *bastardo fortunato*."

Schwartz smiled. "Yes, Detective, I have always been a lucky bastard."

That night, the three companions found a little restaurant on a side street just off the Via Veneto, with a wonderful waiter named Luigi, who steered them to a divine calamari, a better linguini, a perfect osso buco, and an air-filled gelato. It was all accompanied by pitchers of Chianti that were beyond divine.

They ate outside in the warm Roman springtime on a red-and-white tablecloth. Around them were the sounds of the Eternal City, honking car horns, and arguing Italians. They bathed in the sounds of the clatter of horses' hooves as carriages rolled by and the whining sound of the Vespa scooters. The meal was capped off with an espresso and black sambuca with three coffee beans in it. Those three beans represented the Holy Trinity—the Father, the Son, and the Holy Spirit.

Only in Italy would it occur to people to honor the church with an after-dinner drink. When they were finished, the three walked back toward the hotel. They strode up the steep hill, past baskets of flowers and the sounds of live piano music, as diners enjoyed their late meals. William and Biff actually made it back to the hotel. Schwartz took a detour to a place he had read about on a postcard he found on the street. It was a nightclub called Chica Chica Boom Boom.

12

We visit one of the most famous museums in Rome, where we decipher our first clues in our mystery. We learn about Dante, the fate of the Knights Templar, and why you should not drink cheap Chianti. We learn why Italian men are mamma's boys and what happens when an ostrich gets beheaded. Finally, the travelers are sent to see a blind librarian in Buenos Aires.

Rome,, Italy

The next day, the three had an elegant breakfast on the roof garden of the Marriott Grand Flora Hotel. Rome was built on seven hills, and the hotel was far enough up on one of these to afford a view of the whole city. The sun was shining, and the air was warm. As they sipped their espressos and nibbled on perfect Roman pastries, they could hear the church bells calling the faithful to mass. The table had a white linen tablecloth and a vase of beautiful yellow and orange tulips that were still in season. William and Biff both went on about how well they slept, while Michelangelo did not go into the details of his night at the Chica Chica Boom Boom. William was not sure things were progressing at the pace they should.

"Schwartz, why do we get the feeling you are dragging your feet on this and there are things you know but are not telling us?"

Schwartz was drinking in the sunlight and listening to the sounds of the Eternal City.

"William, if I was kidnapped and the kidnappers sent you my severed finger to show they had me, you would ask for more proof. Listen. I want to get this over as much as you. At this rate, I am going to miss opening day at Yankee Stadium, and I make it a point never to miss opening day at Yankee Stadium!"

Biff tried to calm the argument. "Gentleman, we are on a quest to change the balance of power in the world. Please restrain yourselves. Let's keep our focus."

In the early afternoon, the three took a short taxi ride down past the Via Della Repubblica in the Quirinale District to the Capital District. Soon, they were on the Via dei Fori Imperiali that ran in a straight line from the Piazza Venezia, passing by the Forum of Trajan and the Forum of Augustus to the Colosseum. The route took them past statues and fountains and through the heart of a modern city. It was a feast for the senses.

Traffic was just as Michelangelo had remembered it—total chaos with almost no rules and nobody obeying the few traffic rules there were. For some reason, Italians did everything very deliberately in slow motion, until they found themselves behind the wheel of a sports car with an engine that had three hundred horsepower in the middle of a large crowded city. Then, get out of their way.

The taxi let William, Biff, and Michelangelo out at the edge of the Piazza del Campidoglio, where they looked up at the Palazzo dei Conservatori. Michelangelo, not our protagonist but the famous Michelangelo, designed the piazza in 1536. Italian piazzas are breathtaking places full of handsome Italian men in red velvet Versace suits, designer sunglasses, and a fashionable three-day stubble. They sit at outdoor cafés with a cappuccino in a porcelain cup, smoking a cigarette and reading a fashion magazine. Their mothers make their beds, do their laundry, pay their bills, shop, and cook for them until the day they get married, at which time their wives take over those chores. Being an Italian man is not a bad deal, not a bad deal at all.

Pope Sixtus IV, who in 1471 donated his collection of bronze statues, began the collections at the two Capitoline Museums. In the center of the piazza was a large bronze statue of the philosopher-emperor Marcus Aurelius on horseback. Marcus Aurelius was a wise and kind emperor. He was not just an emperor of Rome but one of the great Stoic philosophers. He wrote how we should live not seeking pleasure or avoiding pain but doing what is right. He was one of the greatest leaders the world has ever known. But his parenting skills raised several questions. He left the empire in the hands of his son, Commodus, who was a total psychopath. Compared to him, Charles Manson looked like Mother Theresa. Commodus believed he was the reincarnation of the man-god Hercules. He often fought in the arena as a gladiator and never once lost, and you can imagine why. He once beheaded both an ostrich and a giraffe, to the horror of Roman citizens. The Roman senators who were forced to attend had to chew on laurel leaves to keep from bursting out laughing at their emperor, who, if annoyed, would cut off their heads for coughing the wrong way. Oh, to go back to the great days of Rome!

Angelique was waiting at the entrance. She was wearing jeans and a Sorbonne T-shirt. Her hair was in a bun, and she was carrying a satchel for her books. She looked like a young student. William purchased four tickets, and they entered the museum.

As soon as they entered, Salvatore Greco stepped out of the shadows and bought a ticket to get into the museum. Leaning on the base of the statue in the middle of the Piazza del Campidoglio was Wolf Eyes. He watched Salvatore and wondered who he was and whom he was working for. This was a more complicated assignment than he had first realized.

Once inside the museum, there was a beautiful courtyard straight ahead, with wonderful statues on both sides. Sunlight streamed down on the white marble statues and columns, but the companions went directly over to the left, toward the bookstore and gift shop, and up the stairs to the second floor. The office of Director Antonio Cuccinelli was in the rear of the building. His secretary showed them in. The office was large, with a white tile floor. The windows went all the way to the sixteen-foot ceiling. Light poured into the room.

Antonio was a handsome and trim man in his forties, who was dressed in a fashionable blue Italian suit and a stunning red Gucci tie. He greeted Angelique warmly, and she introduced the others. When she introduced Michelangelo, Antonio smiled. "Professor Schwartz, it is a pleasure to meet you face-to-face. I enjoyed your monograph 'The Influence of Boethius on Dante's *Vita Nuova*.'"

Michelangelo smiled and gave a slight bow as he shook hands. He had learned never to joke when another academic was honoring him. That was one of the moments he would pretend to be an adult. Antonio looked around the room. "Angelique tells me there is a document I might be able to help you interpret."

Michelangelo Schwartz took the lead. "Professor Cuccinelli, Angelique might have told you that I have a particular expertise that might help us decode a poem. A lot of the symbolism has to do with all things Catholic and the Vatican. With your exhibit of Vatican artifacts last year and the research you did to put it on, it may have given you some interesting insights to help us. So I would like to ask for your help."

The five sat at the large wooden table in the center of the room. The poem was set out, and the director read it:

> The cup that ends all human strife
> And gives its bearer eternal life
> Can be found not on the corners but in the middle.
> You must come home to solve this riddle.
>
> The holy man protects the books;
> Beneath the star on pages he looks.
> Along it runs a second street
> That has a number that we must meet.
>
> Now take the year the master was burned,
> The same year lessons in love were first learned.
> Subtract it from the year of the Vatican sculpture's birth
> That gives us an eight anywhere on Earth.

This cup that can end all sorrow and grief
Has given the most laurel wreaths.
Dig there, and you will lose your breath,
Rule the world, and conquer death.

But before you can learn to sing this song
There is one man you must bring along.
This unworthy messenger alone can find the key.
He is living near the statue in the sea.

His first name is the father of *David* and the *Pietà*.
He loves baseball, Dante, and the theater.
His last name doesn't fit; it makes us scoff,
One of a million names for what Pius IX knocked off.

He comes not from Noah's old boat.
With grain alcohol, he keeps afloat.
Accused of Spinozistic heresy,
This acolyte hails from New Jersey.

The time has come for the Grail to change hands.
It has traveled across many lands.
Work on this riddle till your hands have warts,
But it will only be solved by a man named Schwartz.

Antonio looked up at Schwartz. "OK. There are things with which I can help you. But first, I would ask you to tell me what you have discovered so far."

At that moment, Biff realized that with all of the bar bills, fancy dinners, and hotel bills, Michelangelo had told them almost nothing. But that was all about to change. Schwartz leaned toward Antonio and prepared to lay out all his cards.

"Well, as you can guess, the ending of the poem suggests that I alone can unlock the whole thing. I am not sure why this is, but whoever wrote this poem thinks that I have some secret or personal knowledge that will be of use. I have yet to figure out what that knowledge is. That said, I know 'who protects the books.'"

Antonio nodded his head in agreement. "Of course, Saint Jerome, the patron saint of libraries and reading."

Michelangelo nodded his head in agreement and jumped in quickly. "Yes, that is a simple one. But then it gets a little murky. 'The year the master was burned' and the year that 'lessons in love' were learned. Now, I may be wrong on this, but I believe he is referring to Dante's *Documenti d'Amore* that is commonly believed to have been written in 1314. I thought of this because it is a Dante reference and the poem asked for me, a Dante scholar, so that makes sense to me."

As Antonio was looking at the poem, he nodded his head in agreement. "*Si*. Professore, Dante's *Documenti d'Amore*, can be translated into English as *The Lessons of Love*. And now I may be of assistance, Professore. As you already have mentioned, we recently had an exhibit called *Lux in Arcana*, which displayed documents and artifacts from the Vatican's Secret Archives. One of those was the trial transcripts of the Knights Templar. Now do you see?"

Michelangelo Schwartz smiled. "Signore Cuccinelli, I see where you are going."

Michelangelo turned to the other three to catch them up on where they were. "At the end of the eleventh century, Bernard of Clairvaux founded an order of warrior monks to protect pilgrims on their journey to the Holy Land—"

William interrupted. "We call him Saint Bernard, Dr. Schwartz."

"Whatever! Anyway, these warrior monks are fantastic fighters and pure of spirit. They do not sin or know women."

William smiled. "So I guess you would not have been a member, Schwartz."

"William, I am trying to solve this problem, so let's move this along. The Knights Templar made their headquarters on the Temple Mount in Jerusalem, where the Temple of Solomon was supposedly built. Soon after they established their headquarters there, they began to excavate beneath the castle. We know the mine works went deep into the base of the mount. It was rumored that artifacts were found, very unusual artifacts.

It was claimed by members of the Templars that they had discovered the Holy Grail. In a short time, these poor warrior monks became the bankers of Europe and gained fantastic wealth and influence. The Templars became a force that rivaled the pope and kings. Nobody can figure out how they went from nine poor knights to the most powerful force in Christendom in such a short time. There were rumors of supernatural help. Some of these rumors involved the Holy Grail, and others involved a contract with Satan.

"In the beginning of the fourteenth century, King Philip IV of France was heavily indebted to the Templars. He asked them for another loan and was refused. So, in cahoots with the pope, the French king decided to bring the order down. On Friday the thirteenth in 1307, all of the Knights Templar were arrested, and their assets were seized. That is why Friday the thirteenth is still considered unlucky to this day. Under unimaginable torture that went on for years, many of the Templars confessed to being Satanists, homosexuals, and atheists—"

William interrupted. "I take that back, Schwartz. It sounds like you would have been a perfect member of the Knights Templar."

Schwartz had a retort. "Hey! I was like a medieval knight during my third marriage. Every night I went to sleep with a battle-ax by my side. And, William, I have one question for you. Did the aliens forget to remove your anal probe?"

William glared across the table. "Schwartz, you and I have some unfinished business."

Schwartz glared back. "William, you are a better man than I am. Think about that one."

As Biff waved his hand to calm the two warring adolescents, Antonio went on. "The twenty-third master of the Templars, Jacques de Molay, was burned at the stake on March the eighteenth."

Antonio was enjoying this and asked a question that he was sure Schwartz knew the answer to. So he turned and looked at Professor Schwartz. "March the eighteenth, what year?"

"March the eighteenth, 1314. The master was burned the same year Dante's *Lessons of Love* were learned."

Antonio smiled. "We are making progress. So we have a number 1314. Now, we are told to subtract that number from the year of the Vatican sculptor's birth. The sculptor can only be Gian Lorenzo Bernini, who created more statues in Rome than any contemporary. He was a favorite of three popes and had the reputation as the sculptor's sculptor. It can only be him. Bernini was born in 1598 in Naples."

While the others were thinking about these numbers, Antonio turned back to Schwartz. "Angelique tells me you are a fan of American baseball."

Schwartz nodded, but he was a little surprised that Antonio would mention baseball in this context.

"I don't get a chance to meet many baseball experts, and I would like you to look at a paper I am working on to present next year at a conference at the University of Louvain in Belgium. In my work on the Templar papers for the *Lux in Arcana* exhibit, I came across a curious document. It seems that when the Knights Templar were first formed, there were nine of them. One of their earliest training exercises for combat against the Saracens was some type of game where they tossed a ball inside what they called the diamond of truth."

Schwartz was interested. "Today, we call the field they play on the baseball diamond, and we have nine players on the field."

Antonio smiled. "I then noticed that the four bases formed a diamond much like the symbol of the Freemasons. Now, the Freemasons helped found America, and America is where baseball grew up. What do you think?"

Schwartz smiled. "Coincidence, my friend, sheer coincidence. I am a scholar of baseball. We know a lot about its origins, and, let me assure you, American baseball has no connection with the Knights Templar or the Freemasons. But, if you want to question weird things, I have a few questions for you."

Antonio smiled. "Go ahead, Professore."

Schwartz smiled. "Why is it the word 'monosyllabic' has five syllables?"

Antonio did not know what to say. But Schwartz was quick-witted and quick speaking. He was on to the next question. "Antonio, why is there no synonym for the word 'synonym'?"

Antonio was smiling but tongue-tied, so Schwartz fired away. "Why is there no other word for the word 'thesaurus'?"

William finished his math and got the attention of the group by raising his voice. "Take 1314 from 1598, and you get 284. What does that mean? Does this number ring a bell with any of you?"

Schwartz was not sure. It looked right, but there was still something that was troubling him. "Well, the number 248 has an eight in it, and the poem calls for an eight. That tells us we have the correct number. Does it mean 248 Jerome or Jerome 248? It must be a book by Jerome chapter 2 and verse 48. But what would that be? There must be more we need here."

He looked back at the poem and read out loud. "'The cup that ends all human strife and gives its bearer eternal life can be found not on the corners but in the middle. You must come home to solve this riddle.'"

Antonio furrowed his brow. He smiled as he began to think about what this might mean. "'Not on the corners but in the middle. You must come home to solve this riddle.' Now where is the home of the Holy Grail? It only had two homes before it went missing. There are rumors, of course, that it spent time in Scotland or France, but there are only two places that are its rightful home. Does it refer to Rome, the home of the Grail and the Holy Mother Church? Or does the middle referred to in this poem mean the Middle East, and that might mean that the current home of the Holy Grail is Jerusalem, the heart of the Holy Land. It must be one of these two. But which is it? We have made progress, but we are not there yet."

The four sat for a long time, looking at the poem until Antonio finally spoke. "OK. We have it. We have narrowed this down to either Rome or Jerusalem. On that, I would bet my very life."

They sat in silence for a long time, reading to themselves. Angelique leaned over to Director Cuccinelli. "Do you recall when Don Carlo Horos spoke here last year?"

Antonio nodded, and then his face brightened. "Of course, Don Carlo Horos. He can make the rest of this clear."

William leaned forward. "OK, who is this, and where do we find him?"

Schwartz knew the answers to both questions. "He is one of the world's leading experts on cryptology and cryptography. But that is not all he is. He is very old and almost completely blind. He has been blind for years. He is currently serving as the head librarian at the Biblioteca Nacional de le República Argentina, located in the Recoleta Barrio of Buenos Aires. But he is not just a great cryptologist; he has also written on Cervantes and Jane Austen. He knows his literature, his symbolism, and can decode things. Yes, he would be of help."

William was losing patience. "We are paying you because we were told you could solve this problem."

"William, I am solving this problem. We have made progress. We know more than we did a few hours ago. We know about Jacques de Molay, the year 1314, Bernini, Saint Jerome, the number 248, and the fact that we have to go home to find the Grail. So we now know it is either Rome or Jerusalem, but we don't know which one. We have accomplished all of this in one morning. But I have a question for Antonio. Antonio, can you set up a meeting with Don Carlo?"

Antonio smiled. "I perhaps could. But there is someone in this room who can help you even more. When he came here to speak last year, he was assigned a guide that he has kept up a correspondence with and who he has good feelings toward."

Schwartz turned to Angelique, and she nodded and smiled.

Antonio continued. "If you could convince Angelique to make an introduction for you or, better yet, to go along with you, I am sure he would give you all of the time you need. She showed him a small restaurant near the Campo de Fiori, and the two of them went back there night after night. He developed a great affection for Angelique, and I am sure that he would accommodate you. Besides, it is just the kind of thing he loves. And I would add that Angelique's Spanish is equal to her Italian and English."

Schwartz was daydreaming of Angelique screaming in ecstasy in all three languages. But he soon woke up and was back in the good old here and now.

"OK, Buenos Aires, Argentina, it is! We will experience Argentine steaks, rojo wine, the tango, and fernet."

Biff bit. "Fernet?

Angelique had traveled to Argentina several times. "Fernet is a liqueur popular in Argentina that has several herbs and is very potent."

Schwartz was falling in love, or whatever he fell into. "Not as potent as you, dear."

She smiled and looked around. "I can work from anywhere, so I do have a little free time. This is turning out to be interesting. I, myself, am a crossword fanatic, so it would seem that this is a little puzzle that would be fun to solve. But I want to say I feel that there is some force at work here that is bigger than all of us."

William and Biff did not like it, but they were now four and no longer three. This adventure was taking on a life and rhythm of its own.

Salvatore Greco was waiting outside. He had to wait for his instructions from the Vatican, just a few miles away. On the other side of the piazza, Wolf Eyes was listening to the transmitter. He knew everything they knew. He took out his cell phone and dialed the number.

"So far, they have the number 248, Saint Jerome, and they think it is either in Jerusalem or Rome. They are now headed to Argentina with the girl."

There was a pause on the phone.

"Go there ahead of them, and wait," a voice instructed. "Don't do anything. Continue to follow them. We will tell you if we need to change your assignment."

Wolf Eyes closed his cell phone and started off to the airport. He would be in South America ahead of everyone.

That night, Michelangelo, William, and Biff returned to see Luigi at the little bistro near the hotel. Angelique told them she had other plans. She was economical with her words and didn't explain further. The food at the restaurant was simple yet elegant. The pasta was made in the back by an old Italian grandmother.

Michelangelo Schwartz was appreciating the subtlety of the cooking and the presentation when Luigi leaned over. "Professore, you seem to me to be a man of culture. Would you like to know a little story, a little history of the wine you like so much?"

Schwartz nodded yes.

"Many years ago, the city-states of Siena and Florence could not decide who owned the region of Chianti, which lay between the two of them. So they decided that each town would start out a rider who would leave their town as soon as the cock crowed. The first rider to reach Chianti would claim the town as his own. Siena had a plump white rooster, but the Florentines, being very savvy, used a thin and hungry black rooster. The black rooster wanted to wake up the farmer, so he could have breakfast, and that black rooster crowed first. The rider from Florence started out long before the rider left Siena, and that is how Chianti came to belong to Florence. So, if you see a black rooster on the tape that goes over the neck of a bottle of Chianti, that is the kind of Chianti worth drinking. No black rooster, no good!"

Schwartz thanked him. He looked around and drank in the night. He felt the warm Italian air. Michelangelo Schwartz was breathing in the beauty of the Eternal City. He smiled when he thought of Detective Mangieri and what he had called Michelangelo Schwartz. He laughed out loud. "'Bastardo fortunato!' That has a nice ring to it."

13

Angelique, Michelangelo, Biff, and William arrive in Argentina, and we get a brief course on Argentine culture and food and a short history of the tango. We find out why library books on suicide are often not returned. The final pieces of the puzzle fall into place for Michelangelo Schwartz.

Buenos Aires, Argentina

The flight from Fiumicino-Leonardo da Vinci Airport to the Aeropuerto Internacional Ministro Pistarini in Argentina took just under fifteen hours. William made the ticket arrangements with Aerolíneas Argentinas. He also assigned the seats. So William sat next to Angelique, and Biff got the honor of spending fifteen hours watching Michelangelo Schwartz get plastered. Angelique spent the trip crafting new puzzles, while William slept. The flight was smooth and uneventful.

Ezeiza International Airport is located in the Ezeiza Partido of Buenos Aires. The airport is twenty-two kilometers or thirteen and a half miles southwest of the main city. After going through immigration and customs, they stopped at the window of the Banco de la Nación and exchanged their euros for Argentine pesos. They took a *remis*, which was the local limo, and headed through the countryside, past the slums, and into town. Argentina was a city of contrasts. They would soon move from the slums to a beautiful and modern downtown occupied by a very different population.

Soon, they were on the Avenida 9 de Julio Sur, one of the largest avenues in the world. The avenue had up to seven lanes going in each direction and was flanked on either side by parallel streets of two lanes each. There were two wide medians between the side streets and the main road. The street was named for Argentine Independence Day, which was July 9, 1816. There was a large obelisk on the avenue. The avenue was near the Río de la Plata, known in English as the River of Silver. From there, you could see Montevideo, the capital of Uruguay, just on the other side of the river.

Biff had a map that guided them to Caminito Street, but after walking down some winding streets, they found themselves facing a canal, and there seemed to be no bridges on either side. There was a man standing on the other side of the canal. Schwartz turned to Angelique. "Ask him how we get to the other side of the canal."

She shouted to the man on the other side. "*Cómo podemos llegar al otro lado del canal*?"

The man shouted back to her in Spanish.

Schwartz turned to her. "Did he say what I think he said?"

She smiled as she answered. "Yes, he said we are on the other side of the canal."

After some backtracking, the four found what they were looking for.

Caminito was one of the most visited streets in Buenos Aires. If you didn't know any better, you might think you were in Italy. All of the city's barrios had their own character. In the Boca Barrio, which had the Caminito at its heart, the large Genoese population, who had kept their traditions, highlighted the Italian influence. As a tourist location, it had all of the things you would expect. There was a street museum, bars, restaurants, and couples dancing the tango around the street when the weather permitted. You could hear the sounds of violins, guitars, and accordions playing tango songs.

The Argentines who lived in the Caminito area of the barrio were more European than North American. That meant they didn't like to eat on the run with a fast-food hamburger and a cup of bad coffee. They enjoyed drinking their *maté*, which was a coffee-like drink, all day long, through a straw. On the streets, you could have a *choripan*, which was a spicy sausage sandwich. Or you could have an Argentine hot dog, which they call a *pancho*. If you wanted something a little more substantial, there was always the *bondiola*, which was the Argentine version of a pork-shoulder sandwich.

The name *Caminito* meant "little walkway" in Spanish. Caminito claimed, like many neighborhoods of Buenos Aires, to be the birthplace of the tango. Legend had it that the dance so associated with this city was born in the brothels of downtown. The La Boca Barrio was one of the most colorful of all of the forty-eight Buenos Aires neighborhoods. The houses were painted in bright shades of red, blue, and yellow. There was art everywhere, and there was always a festive air about the place.

The four walked down the street and felt the uniqueness of Argentina. It was the beginning of fall in the Southern Hemisphere. The air was starting to cool. Schwartz could never quite get used to the idea that when it was summer in the United States, it was winter in Argentina. Music filled the air as they walked. The sounds were a strange mixture of European violin and accordion with a South American beat. The smell of great local beef filled the air. There were signs in Spanish, Italian, English, and German. There was a pride in this city that could be felt on every block.

Schwartz knew the reputation of the Argentines. "Argentines think the world revolves around them. They think they have the best women, the best fashion, the best wine, the best steak, the best music, and the best dancing. When they see lightning, they all look up because they think God is taking their picture."

They stopped right in the middle of the block next to an old red door. Angelique rang the bell. After what seemed an eternity, the wooden door opened, and the four companions went inside to get out of the cool evening air.

Don Carlo was an elderly man in a hot, stuffy apartment full of cats and books. He was a tall man, and his blind brown eyes were fixed straight ahead. He had a shock of gray hair and looked like a Spanish nobleman. He was wearing an old brown bathrobe over his shirt and slacks. Everywhere, there were Russian icons, old maps, silver items, and several native artifacts.

Michelangelo smiled. A blind man in a room full of books was a rich image. The apartment was small and crowded. It was not as luxurious as Schwartz had imagined it. There was a large, fat tabby cat that Don Carlo had named Robbie Burns the Kitty, so he would not be confused with Robbie Burns the Scottish poet. Next to Robbie Burns was a large and well-fed black cat who answered to the name of Frenchie.

Don Carlo sat down in a rocker, and the four travelers found places on the old chairs and sofas. There was cat hair everywhere. When Michelangelo sat in a small cloth chair, Frenchie sprang up and landed in his lap. The cat immediately settled in and started purring.

Don Carlo began. "I don't often have visitors. I like my silences. But Angelique was very kind to me when I lectured in Rome, and I would like to return the favor. When she called, she told me much of what she knew. I hope that I can help, but I am not sure that I can. I am also not sure why Dr. Schwartz is the only one with the key to this puzzle. That, in itself, is yet another puzzle. I would suggest we begin, if you would, by reading the poem out loud, so we might all think on this together. Can I offer you any *maté* or wine?"

Schwartz was not shy. "Don't you have anything stronger?"

The blind librarian smiled. "I have had a bottle of good Scotch sitting unopened on top of my small refrigerator in the kitchen for two years. I got it as a gift when I gave a paper about Robert Louis Stevenson, the Scottish author who wrote *Kidnapped*, at a conference at the University of Edinburgh."

Schwartz handed the poem to Angelique and headed to the kitchen. She began to read it out loud, slowly and carefully. Occasionally, Don Carlo would ask her a question in Spanish, and she would answer in Spanish. As Michelangelo attacked the bottle of Macallan, William and Biff listened intently.

When Angelique was finished, Don Carlo smiled and leaned forward. "You have all come a long way to see me. And I would like to think your trip has not been in vain. I think I may be able to shed some light into this darkness. But first tell me what you have discovered. And what interests me most is that you, Professor Schwartz, are the key to this. Now you must have thought about this. Could it be your expertise or something more personal?"

Michelangelo Schwartz felt hot. The apartment was very stuffy. He took off his jacket with the leather patches on the sleeves and slung it over the back of his chair. Michelangelo had not thought before that moment that it might not be Dante and his knowledge of the poet but something else. What would that be?

"Don Carlo, I am at a loss as to why I am named in this poem. My work on Dante and his time has been called eccentric, and I imagine there is something in my writings that I stumbled upon or suggested that hinted at the location of the Grail. I have published extensively on medieval symbols, and many of those theories have been called unorthodox. So far, it is my belief that somewhere, in one of my presentations or papers, I speculated about either the Grail or its symbols. That speculation is the key. I have been thinking about my presentations and my publications, and I have not yet found that key, but I am absolutely sure it is there that the solution lies."

The old blind man smiled. "Your search for a key that you yourself have lost reminds me of a story Herodotus tells us in his great work *The Persian Wars*. He tells us of a Persian monarch who sends a courier with a secret coded message to another kingdom. The messenger encounters all sorts of obstacles and difficulties but eventually delivers the coded message that can only be read by a person who has the key to unlock that code. When the code is unlocked, it tells the person who gets the message to kill the messenger who has delivered it. A great metaphor about codes, keys, and unworthy messengers."

Schwartz was smiling. "Let us hope that I am not like that unworthy messenger in Herodotus, and let us hope that by decoding the poem, I will not seal my own fate. Let us hope I am, as we say in Italian, a bastardo fortunato!"

As he said this, he wondered why Don Carlo, who was known for his insights as well as scholarship, had told this particular story. Did he know something Schwartz did not? Everything that had unfolded so far fit some pattern. Was this some kind of cryptic warning that he should stop his quest? Was this a warning not to solve the puzzle or deliver the message? Or perhaps this was simply a story told by an old man.

As he was musing, Don Carlo Horos spoke again. "Professor Schwartz, can you start us off? Can you shed some light on the darkness of this poem? Can you illuminate us with what you have already determined?"

Michelangelo Schwartz smiled. "Don Carlo, light into darkness, *Lux in Arcana*, a very nice way to begin."

He took a quick belt of Scotch. Schwartz thought they might share a laugh before they got down to business. "Before we get started on our real work, as a man who has spent much of his life in libraries, I have some questions for you."

The old man seemed confused but waved his hand for Schwartz to continue.

William stood up. "Don Carlo, we don't want to waste your valuable time. I fear our friend Professor Schwartz is about to unleash a tidal wave of bad jokes."

Don Carlo smiled. "We don't know each other very well. Maybe a little humor will help us in our work together."

Schwartz stood up and gulped down his glass of Scotch. He was trying to remember some of his best library jokes.

"Why can't you find any books on suicide in a library? Because they get taken out and never returned." Schwartz broke out laughing. The rest sat in silence. He went on to the next joke.

"How many librarians does it take to change a light bulb?"

There was silence. He was not shy, so he went on. "How many librarians does it take to change a light bulb? Change? Change!"

Don Carlo laughed and agreed. "Being a librarian for all of my life, I can see the humor in that remark. Librarians do not like change."

Schwartz was not finished. "What happens when you cross a librarian with a lawyer?" He didn't wait for anyone to answer. "You get all of the information you need, but you can't understand it."

Don Carlo was enjoying these jokes. So Schwartz had one more. "Why do so many libraries ban the book *Robin Hood*?"

Don Carlo knew that libraries really didn't ban the book *Robin Hood*, but he still listened.

Schwartz didn't wait for an answer. "Why do many libraries ban the book *Robin Hood*? There was too much Saxon violence."

Don Carlo did not get it. Angelique leaned over and spoke in Spanish, "*El sexo y la violencia*."

Don Carlo laughed. "*Comprende*! Saxon violence. Good! Very good, Professor Schwartz. Now, can we get down to this puzzle of yours? Angelique has told me a little bit, and I am most interested to learn more."

Michelangelo sat down and looked at both the poem and the paper that Angelique had handed him in Paris. He read both of them silently. When he was done, Don Carlo asked him to read them out loud one more time. After that, Schwartz summed up where they were, what they had learned, and what still eluded them.

"We have determined, thus far, that the saint who protects books is Saint Jerome. Next, it called for a number. It said take the year the master was burned, which is the same year we learned about the lessons of love."

Don Carlo smiled. "I assume, Professor, that because of your expertise, you quickly connected that with Dante's *Documenti d'Amore*. And, if I am not mistaken, the master would be a reference to the Templar master, somewhere around the same time."

Schwartz smiled. "I am now sure that our trip here has not been in vain. Not just around the same time but the exact same year—1314."

Don Carlo smiled and nodded in agreement. Schwartz went on. "Next, he asks us to subtract that number from the birth of the Vatican sculptor. Bernini was born in 1598. The difference of that subtraction gives us the number 284. We have an eight in the number, so we are OK. So we have Jerome and 284. We assume it is a text by Jerome, chapter 2, verse 48."

Don Carlo was humming to himself as he bobbed his head in thought. He was known for this little eccentricity. He was sometimes known to sing a whole Verdi or Puccini opera to himself as he worked or thought. The joke around the library was he could never sneak up on you. Employees could always hear him coming. They sometimes called him "*hombre zumbido*," the humming man.

Suddenly, he stood up, startling the four travelers. "Professor, I am not sure I would agree that the Vatican sculptor is Bernini as you say. Think of the first thing you see when you walk into Saint Peter's Cathedral. What is the crowd immediately to your right fascinated with? What are they all snapping pictures of?"

Biff knew the answer. "The *Pietà*, the statue of Christ in his mother's arms by Michelangelo."

Schwartz stood up. "Don Carlo, we were under the spell of Curator Cuccinelli, and I did not think this through thoroughly. Yes... Michelangelo. It might be Michelangelo. He was born in 1475."

Don Carlo smiled. "Correct. 1475."

Schwartz had a huge smile on his face. "*The Lessons of Love* is by Dante. The Vatican sculptor is Michelangelo. The poem also uses the word 'Schwartz.' I am becoming dizzy with the references that keep coming back to me."

The old librarian's thoughts were far away, and he was musing as he connected other things with that date. "My friends, do you know that 1475 is the same year that the oldest recorded game of chess was played, between Francesco di Castellvi and Narciso Vinyoles in Valencia? The game introduced us to what later came to be known as the Scandinavian Defense. Of course, the game of chess is much older, originating in India, perfected in Persia, and arriving in Spain with the Muslim conquests. But, in 1475, we have the first full game we know of that has been written down and left to posterity."

William was taking notes. He got the number first. "1475 minus 1314 gives us 161 not 248."

They all sat in silence for a minute. Then everything changed. Michelangelo Schwartz's face lit up with the biggest grin he had ever grinned in his life, and he stood up slowly.

"I've got it. My friends, I now know why I was essential to this quest. I now know how we have come this far, and, Lady and Gentlemen, I am now pretty sure that I know exactly, and I repeat exactly, where the Holy Grail is."

William objected, "But there is no eight in the number! The poem told us there would be an eight!"

Schwartz smiled. "Those three numbers—one, six, one—add up to eight."

Biff was not going to let this go. He stood up. "If you know, tell us. Damn it!"

Schwartz furrowed his brow in thought. "Just one question, Biff. Did you say the exact date the Holy Grail went missing was February 6, 1920?"

Biff nodded in agreement.

Schwartz smiled. "If I am correct, there is something astonishing I will have to share with you in the next twenty-four hours. But right now, I have to admit that it seems too fantastic to be true. I want to be sure, absolutely one hundred percent sure. There is one more person we need to speak to. In twenty-four hours, you will know everything I know."

William had many questions, but one burned in his mind. "OK. Where to next?"

"Cooperstown, New York. We are going to the Baseball Hall of Fame."

William's jaw dropped. "Are you kidding me? Tell me you are joking! The Baseball Hall of Fame?"

Schwartz was smiling. The argument had taken an unexpected turn.

Across the street, Wolf Eyes dialed his cell phone. "They are leaving Buenos Aires and are heading to Cooperstown, New York. He mentioned the Baseball Hall of Fame."

There was silence on the phone. In a minute, Wolf Eyes had new instructions.

"That's it. He is getting too close. Are you listening?"

Wolf Eyes was focused. "You have my full attention."

He listened for the code words they had agreed to at the beginning of this whole adventure. He listened for a long time before he heard it.

"Episode 432. 'Guess What? I'm a Man!'"

While Wolf Eyes was on the cell phone, he stopped listening to his earpiece that connected him to the transmitter. What he failed to notice was it had gone silent. In his rush to get to Cooperstown to solve the problem, Michelangelo Schwartz had hurriedly thanked Don and, in the excitement of his great realization, left his jacket behind on the back of the chair in Don Carlo's house. In that jacket was Wolf Eyes' ace in the hole. When Wolf Eyes looked at his GPS locator, he noticed the signal was not moving. Then Wolf Eyes realized he had lost his edge.

Michelangelo Schwartz's companions followed him closely as he raced to the waiting limo. Michelangelo Schwartz was excited.

"Biff, do you have any way to get us to the Albany area as quickly as possible?"

Biff got on his cell phone and made a few calls. A few minutes after he finished his last call, his phone rang with the ring of "In-A-Gadda-Da-Vida." He talked quietly with his hand over his mouth. When he hung up, he was smiling. Biff had used his connections to find a private jet in a small airport nearby that was available to fly north right away. The Vatican could call in *mucho* favors when it needed them.

After the limo had been en route for about twenty minutes, Michelangelo Schwartz noticed something. "Shitski! I left my jacket back at Don Carlo's home. We have to go back and get it. I need that jacket!"

William could not believe it. "We are not going back. Besides, that jacket is an old rag."

"William, that was my lucky jacket! But you can make it up to me. Lend me your phone."

Michelangelo took the phone, took out his notebook, and dialed a number. It was the number of a man who lived in Cooperstown, New York. He was the man who, if Michelangelo was right, had the last piece of the puzzle.

Salvatore Greco was still at the airport when his cell phone rang. It was Rome. He listened.

"OK, I understand. Cooperstown, New York. The closest airport is Albany. But it will take me a while to get there."

He listened again.

"I understand. So you think we may have the answer, but we don't know it for certain yet. Do you still need me?"

He listened intently.

"I will go to Cooperstown and await your instructions."

He knew the four were getting a private jet. He would be in Cooperstown long after Michelangelo Schwartz. Things had not changed. The Vatican had not made a decision whether or not they would use his services. The Vatican did not have the answer it needed yet. Right now Wolf Eyes and Salvatore Greco had two very different assignments.

Salvatore wondered why they were headed to upstate New York after all of the great cities of Europe and South America. What clue could be there? Salvatore had an advantage. Anything the Vatican knew, Salvatore would know in a few minutes. But it seemed as if his services might not be needed after all. From what Salvatore Greco had learned about Michelangelo Schwartz, he was not a very admirable character. In spite of his profession, Salvatore Greco was a religious man who tried to live a moral life. That was not true of Schwartz. Salvatore thought about the difference between the two of them. Salvatore donated money to the homeless, while Schwartz spent his dollars on the topless.

CIA Headquarters, Langley, Virginia, United States

At the CIA Headquarters, director Glen Runciter heard the knock on his door. He sat up straight. His desk was entirely empty, with the exception of a keyboard and monitor.

Joe Chip came in with his folders. Glen got right to it. "OK. Where are we?"

"Well, at this point, all six of them are in Argentina. A young lady has joined the two members of the Anti-Catholic League of Brooklyn and Professor Schwartz. She has been traveling under the name 'Angelique Serrureacle.' She does crossword puzzles for some French paper. There is not too much on her in the French database. But there is one more thing. In about two hours, Boris Zelenski will land in Buenos Aires as well."

That got the director's attention. Glen stood up. "Boris the Knife? He has not been out of Russia in three years. What the hell is he doing there? What do they know that we don't? We are getting behind the curve here, Joe. We have to keep up. Do you have the phone records, contact lists, e-mails, and phone calls from all parties?"

Joe looked down at his papers. "That's why I have not been in here for the last two days. We have been going over everything. I put the Delta Team on it, and they have come up with a lot. There are a lot of connections here that don't quite make sense. It turns out that one of the guys in the Anti-Catholic League, Biff Braunschweiger, is constantly calling disposable TracFone numbers, and Salvatore Greco is getting calls from the same number after every call."

Glen was thinking. "So they are on the same team, or, at least, there is some person who they both trust that is on the same team. Where does that signal originate?"

"Vatican City, Glen. Vatican City! But it gets more complicated. The other guy from the Anti-Catholic League of Brooklyn, William Callahan, the one that used to be a woman, is calling the same number the Norwegian is getting calls from. The signal is scrambled and keeps moving around."

Glen breathed deeply. It helped him concentrate.

Joe was not done. "We went through the contact lists of Callahan and Biff, and they both have phone numbers and e-mail addresses that we have traced to people high up in the Vatican."

Nothing surprised Glen after years on the dark side. "So the people running the Anti-Catholic League of Brooklyn are buddies with the highest-ranking people in the Vatican? Lovely. And one of them is double-crossing the others with the Norwegian. We need a scorecard to keep track of this one."

Things were really heating up, but Joe Chip was not done. "That's not all. Salvatore Greco had some of the same contact e-mails and phone numbers in his contacts, but he had them hidden under names like 'Mom' and 'Junior.' But they are some of the same people that Callahan and Biff have called recently."

Glen found this all very interesting. "And Michelangelo Schwartz? Is that really his name?"

Joe put his head down into the folder. "Well, he had none of these contact numbers or e-mails. We even went into his web browser, and, I must say, he has diverse tastes."

Glen sipped his coffee. "How diverse?"

"Well, in one day, a few weeks back, he visited the websites for 'Dante Documents in Italian,' 'Boccaccio's *Decameron Nights,*' a site for doing footnotes in the APA style, two sites for debt consolidation, and a site called College Girls Gone Wild. We did a search of his phone book and contacts, and there is a mix of academics, small-time pot dealers, bartenders, a taxi service he has apparently used a lot, and one number that we traced to Suzie Kim's Happy Ending Massage Parlor. I am not making this up."

Glen Runciter had heard it all before. "Dante and College Girls Gone Wild? Sounds like a typical professor to me."

Joe wanted to know what was next. "Where do we go from here? They are all on their way to Cooperstown, New York. All except for Boris the Knife, and I bet my bottom dollar he will be on his way there soon."

Glen had no idea where this was going. "I want you to call Carol, Pete, and Wally in Albany. Have them start out for Cooperstown. There is only one place there they would all be headed. I want bugs in every room of the Baseball Hall of Fame. Also, have them find out what hotel they check in to, and then make sure we have devices in those rooms the second they can plant them. What could they all be doing? What the hell is going on, and should we be worried?"

Joe Chip shrugged his shoulders.

Glen had one last piece of advice for his younger colleague. "I have only one memory of a college professor. Even though I went to college, I wasn't too impressed by them. But I remember an event not too long ago. I was at a restaurant one night in Purcellville, Virginia. A college dean had taken out a naughty professor who was involved with all sorts of shenanigans. The two were very loud, so I overheard the conversation. The dean said, 'You can't keep sleeping with everyone and breaking all of the rules. What do you think will happen?' The professor put down his beer and gave that uptight dean a reply I will never forget. That professor had no ethics, no self-restraint, and no shame. You know what he said in retort? 'You know what they say! The hotter the water, the stronger the tea.'"

14

We ride in a private jet from South America back to New York. Angelique finds out about sporting girls. Along the way, we learn about the drinking prowess of Babe Ruth, a curse on the city of Boston, and how it is possible to be a great professional baseball pitcher while on LSD. We learn that while Washington may be America's political capital, New York is the capital of saloons, steaks, and loose women.

A private jet, Buenos Aires Airport

Angelique was the first to board the small private jet, and Schwartz took the opportunity to sit across from her. For all of their travels, she looked as fresh and beautiful as the first moment he met her. He could not understand how someone so well traveled could look so young.

Angelique was smiling. She leaned forward, toward Schwartz. "I understood Paris, and I suggested Rome, and I see how we got to Buenos Aires. But why are we going to Cooperstown, New York?"

Schwartz smiled. "Cooperstown, New York, is the home of the Baseball Hall of Fame, and it is the home of the man we are going to see, Luke Brannigan, who has written the authoritative biography of my hero, the greatest American who ever lived."

Angelique looked out the window. "The greatest American who ever lived? Washington? Jefferson? Lincoln? Thomas Edison? Some might say that about Franklin Delano Roosevelt, who took America out of the Depression, won the Second World War, and established America as the preeminent democracy in the world."

Schwartz smiled. "None of the above. I am referring to the greatest of American heroes—Babe Ruth."

Angelique smiled. "Babe Ruth! Are you serious, Professor? We are flying to see a man who wrote a book on Babe Ruth? Wasn't Ruth a baseball player or something like that?"

"My dear, calling Babe Ruth a baseball player is like calling Mozart a piano player. But Babe was more than a baseball player. Let me elaborate."

He stopped to signal the tall, blond flight attendant. "Can you make me a Jack and Coke?"

"I can, and I will. One Jack and Coke coming right up."

He grabbed the flight attendant's arm and looked her deep in the eyes. "On second thought, make that a double. I am going to celebrate."

He turned back to Angelique. "Before you can understand the Babe, you must understand that he was, and is, the hero of every patriotic, red-blooded American male. He loved hot dogs, beer, loose women, and sports. He was that guy we all wanted to be. He was the greatest athlete of all time, and he never seemed to make any effort to do it. Somehow, and I have not figured out exactly how or why, he is at the heart of this whole adventure. That is what I realized in Don Carlo's apartment."

Angelique didn't understand. She turned toward Schwartz. "We are on the greatest and most fabled quest of all time, and that is to find the Holy Grail. The puzzle we have worked on has referenced Saint Jerome, a pope, Michelangelo, Jacques de Molay, and the Templars. We have been talking about Oxford, Paris, Jerusalem, and Rome. Why, then, would we start talking about American baseball? I think you are out in left field here, Professor, if I can use that expression."

Schwartz smiled. "I love it when you call me 'Professor.' But I have solved the riddle, and that is why we are going to Cooperstown. In the course of my whole life, I have never been sure of what I was doing. You see, my brain works differently than most other people. You may not know it, but in grammar school and high school, I was a terrible student. I was bored out of my skull, and the dim bulbs that were my teachers thought I didn't turn in my homework or study because I was stupid. I used to sit in class and make lists of the greatest left fielders of all time, or try, from memory, to come up with the five greatest left-handed batters in the National League. After school, I would walk to the library and read the *Encyclopedia Britannica*. I started with the first volume and just kept at it. So my education has been haphazard and odd. I am an expert on Dante, Grail legends, medieval symbols, chess, and baseball. And, amazingly enough, I think it is that witches' brew of expertise that has made me most fit for this quest."

Angelique looked up from her notes. "It sounds like you have put most of the pieces together."

Schwartz smiled as he sipped his Jack and Coke. "I am almost sure I have the answer. But I say 'almost' because I find it hard to believe what I think might be the answer. That is why we need to talk to one more man before I can be sure. Let me talk to you about the Babe, and, as I do, maybe we will come up with some fact or number that I have not thought of yet that might help us get the last pieces of this puzzle."

Angelique was always agreeable. "Agreed. Why don't you tell me what you think, and I will listen and take notes. Maybe we will come up with something together."

"Angelique, I have been hoping to come up with something together with you since you walked up next to me in Paris. But let me go over a few things. I think we are close to solving the puzzle. First, I probably have not told you that I am one of the biggest Yankee fans you will ever meet. Did you know that there have been fifty-three World Series, and of the thirty baseball teams in America, one single team has won the World Series twenty-seven times? That is the Yankees.

"Now, they are like the city they play in. New York is big, over-the-top, stuck-up, and full of itself. As I said, just like the Yankees. They have the biggest payroll and have often paid a fortune for the biggest names in the game. Because they have been so rich and so overpaid, fans of the smaller-market teams all over America, such as the Baltimore Orioles, the Pittsburgh Pirates, and the Kansas City Royals, hate them with a passion. Now, how did the Yankees get to be so dominant? The answer is one man and one man only, George Herman Ruth, known as the Babe, the Sultan of Swat, the Colossus of Clout, the Behemoth of Bust, the King of Swing, or, simply, the Bambino. He was born on February 6, 1895."

Angelique looked up. "You mentioned yesterday that the Holy Grail disappeared on February 6, 1920. I have heard that February 6 was the birthday of the founder of the Illuminati, Adam Weishaupt. Now you are telling me that February 6 is also Babe Ruth's birthday. How can that be?"

"Angelique, let me answer a question with a question. Do you think it was a coincidence you were in the Shakespeare and Company bookstore when I was looking for the next clue?"

She looked out the window and did not meet his gaze. He went on. "I don't think it was a coincidence that there was a man sitting next to me on the flight from New York to Rome who was reading a book on coincidence. I don't think it is a coincidence that these dates were chosen, and, finally, I know it was not a coincidence that I was chosen to unlock this puzzle. It was no coincidence because, in fact, I may be the only person in the world who could have put these pieces together. But if everything has been a sign of things to come, I worry about Don Carlo's story of the fate of the unworthy messenger. Will solving this puzzle be the last thing I do on this earth? I suspect you know more about that than I do, and I also guess you will not tell me it even if you know."

She did not look up from her note-taking but answered his question with a question. "You keep saying that you are the key to this puzzle. Why you? Why you alone in this world? Can you answer that question?"

Schwartz smiled. "That will be clear to you in the next twenty-four hours. Whoever wrote that poem knew that only by putting me on the case would it be solved."

She smiled. "OK, Professor. We have February 6, the Babe's birthday and the day the Grail disappeared. I have written that down. Now, you can get back to your story of Babe Ruth."

"He was born in the rough, run-down section of Baltimore called Pigtown."

Angelique giggled a little. "Pigtown, what a funny name."

Michelangelo was a true Yankees fan, and Babe was his hero, and he didn't want to hear that. "Anyway, he was born in Pigtown. Most of his brothers and sisters died early. His father owned a saloon, and he grew up in an apartment over the bar. He took his first glass of whiskey at age five and smoked his first cigar at age six."

Angelique scowled. "Isn't that a little young?"

Schwartz went on. "He was precocious and bigger than life in every way. Anyway, he started drinking and smoking, and he began to get in trouble with both his parents and the law. He would skip school, get drunk, and was what we in America call a 'juvenile delinquent.' He once said that if it weren't for baseball, he would either be in the penitentiary or the cemetery. At age seven, his father had enough and kicked him out of the house. He ended up in Saint Mary's Industrial School for Boys, a reformatory and orphanage."

"It sounds horrible."

"It was. When he was seven years old, his father signed him over to the Xaverian Brothers, who ran the reformatory and orphanage. For the next twelve years, the Babe grew up in that harsh industrial school. His family did not have him home for the holidays nor did they visit him on the one Sunday a month when visitors were permitted. In this environment, George Ruth acted out more and more and was at one point labeled as, and I quote, 'vicious and incorrigible.'"

Angelique had a sad look on her face that concerned Michelangelo Schwartz.

"But there is a light at the end of this long, sad tunnel, Angelique. At Saint Mary's, the Babe started to play baseball. And it turned out he was great at baseball. At a young age, he was drafted by the minor league Baltimore Orioles and ended up with a team called the Boston Red Sox. You may not know about baseball, but there are different positions."

Angelique tried to be helpful. "I have had the good fortune to know a little about baseball, not a lot but a little. So go on."

"Well, although he was the greatest hitter in baseball that held every record there was, he spent his first six years as a pitcher and only batted once in a while. Think of it. During his best years, when he could have been hitting, he wasn't even carrying a bat. So we don't even know how great he could have been with those six missing years added in. But it turned out he was a great pitcher. If he'd never picked up a bat once, he would have been a great baseball player. He pitched twenty-nine scoreless innings in the World Series, a World Series record that would stand for forty-two years. His World Series record was three and oh with a 0.87 ERA. His earned run average was 2.2770. There has been only one pitcher in the modern era to even come close, Mariano Rivera, another Yankee.

"When the Babe was with the Red Sox in 1916, he pitched nine shutouts. That record held from 1916 till 1978 when it was tied, not broken, by Ron Guidry. Oh, and I would be remiss not to mention Ron Guidry was a Yankee when he tied it. With Babe as their star, the Boston Red Sox won championship after championship. They were the greatest team in baseball. But then something happened. In December of 1919, he was traded to another team. That team was nothing great until the Babe arrived. That team was the New York Yankees. So, in 1920, the Babe left Boston behind and became a Yankee."

Angelique looked up. "1920. That is the year we have all been talking about."

Michelangelo smiled. "Not just 1920. But now connect the Babe's birthday, February 6, with the year he went to the Yankees, 1920. Are you beginning to see? Now try to keep up."

Angelique was making connections in her notes. She drew lines to connect dates and names. But a question still loomed large. What could a baseball player have to do with thc Holy Grail or the Illuminati?

Michelangelo was pretty sure he could make that leap of logic. But he needed to talk to one more person for a few missing pieces to the puzzle. "OK, Angelique. In 1919, the championship Red Sox got rid of the Babe. For almost a hundred years after that day, the Red Sox never won another World Series. When they traded the Babe, it began a run of bad luck that was legendary. It was called the 'Curse of the Bambino.' But when the Babc linked up with the Big Apple, there was trouble. Washington may be America's political capital, but New York is the capital of saloons, steaks, and loose women. The Babe and New York were made for each other.

They were big, brash, and full of themselves. Between 1920 and 1933, he never lost a game pitching for the Yanks."

Angelique smiled. "But he is better known as a batter?"

"Is the Babe known as a batter? He held every batting record there was. Let me give you just one example of what kind of batter he was. The World Series brings America to a fever pitch. It makes us bonkers. It was game three of the 1932 World Series, and the Yankees were playing the Cubs at Wrigley Field in Chicago. Babe had already hit one home run. It was the top of the fifth inning, and with one out, George Herman Babe Ruth came to the plate. The pitcher for the Cubs was Charlie Root, who hated the Babe. So the Cubs' pitcher started talking trash to the Sultan of Swat."

Angelique had mastered English but not American. She didn't know that phrase. "Talking trash?"

Schwartz smiled and leaned in. "Yes, you know, saying bad things about the other guy's mother and casting aspersions on his manhood. Anyway, the Chicago fans also got into it. They were booing the Babe, throwing popcorn boxes and beer bottles, and hooting insults at the great man. Babe strolled slowly to the plate. He never hurried, even in the tensest circumstances. Charlie Root threw a strike, and the Great Bambino held up his index finger to let the crowd know it was strike one. Shortly afterward, Charlie Root threw another strike, and the Babe held up two fingers to indicate strike two. The Chicago fans were going wild.

"Guy Bush was a pitcher for the Chicago Cubs who was not throwing that day. He was known as the Mississippi Mudcat, and he had a terrible history with the Babe. Guy Bush could not contain himself anymore and ran out of the Cubs' dugout. Bush yelled obscenities at Ruth, challenging him to a fistfight then and there. Bush's teammates followed him out of the dugout, grabbed him, and struggled to bring him back under control as pandemonium was breaking out in Chicago. Both benches were on their feet, shouting insults or encouragement. Everyone in the stands was on their feet, and it seemed like there might be a riot that could spill out onto the field. The police called for reinforcement, as it looked like the Babe was giving the city a heart attack."

Angelique had not followed baseball that much. "Three strikes are all you get?"

"Yes, three strikes, and you are out. And it was the World Series, and it was the Babe at the plate. He then did something that was meant not for the Chicago fans but for the ages. He made a gesture that helped make him a legend and made him seem bigger than life. He stood back from the plate, and on the beautiful, cloudless afternoon in 1932, he pointed at the center-field wall, four hundred forty feet away. A hush went over the stadium as everyone turned to see what he was pointing toward, but there was nothing there.

"Babe stepped back into the batter's box and took a few practice swings. The crowd and benches resumed their energy and began to scream and clap. The next pitch from Charlie Root was a curve ball meant to be strike three. But the Babe, the Bambino, the Great One swung that huge bat of his and hit the ball solidly. The ball flew over the infield, ascended into the outfield, and kept rising until the ball went over the wall. At that moment, everyone there realized that was the spot Babe Ruth had pointed to. The ball cleared center field near the flagpole, and that home run has been measured at four hundred and ninety feet. It was the longest home run in the history of Wrigley Field. It was Babe Ruth's last World Series home run. What a way to bow out of the World Series."

Angelique nodded in agreement. "So he was bigger than life."

"Just a few more points. During the 1926 World Series, the Babe got a request from a sickly child. Johnny Sylvester was bedridden and seemed to be dying. He asked Babe Ruth to hit a home run for him in a World Series game. The Babe promised the sick child he would, and the next day, he hit three home runs. Johnny Sylvester perked up, recovered, and grew up to be a happy and productive adult. The Babe loved kids and never denied his fans anything. He had lived as a poor orphan and never forgot that. But he did more for Johnny than just hit a home run. Babe hit the longest home run ever hit to this day, six hundred and forty-five feet. And I could go on and on, but I have not told you the most amazing part."

Angelique didn't understand. "So he broke every record, was an American hero, and was the greatest athlete of all time, but that is not what is most amazing?"

"You are correct, Angelique. What is most amazing is how he trained, if you could call it that."

Michelangelo asked to borrow Biff's cell phone to pull up a picture of Babe Ruth. Biff agreed and handed the phone to Michelangelo, who, in turn, handed the cell phone to Angelique, so she could see a picture of the Babe in his prime. She was shocked.

"He is fat and smoking a cigar, holding a bottle of beer, and has a girl in a bathing suit sitting on his lap."

Schwartz smiled. "You left out 'drunk.' Those who knew him said he was never sober a day in his life. It was said that the nickname Babe stood for 'Beer, Alcohol, and Broads in Excess.' He was the greatest athlete of all time, while, at the same time, he was drunk out of his mind. Can you imagine what would have happened if he was sober and actually trained? But that's not all. Do you know the English expression 'ladies of the night'?"

Angelique blushed before she answered. "I have never heard that expression, but I think I can guess what it means."

"Well, the Babe loved prostitutes. He knew every cathouse in every town the Yankees visited. But, even in this, he was the greatest that ever was. Once, in Saint Louis, he went to a house of ill repute and had relations with every single woman in the place. At dawn the next morning, he went next door and ate a dozen donuts. He then went on to hit two home runs later that same day. One of his famous quotes is 'I hate it when prostitutes make me pay. Don't they know who I am? I am Babe freaking Ruth.'"

Angelique was captivated by this tale. "How could he do all this drunk?"

"Oh, my dear, he was not just drunk. He was shit-faced drunk, obese, and spent most of his energy chasing women. His diet consisted of a sixteen-ounce T-bone steak and a dozen eggs for breakfast, washed down with a pitcher of whiskey sours. Then, it was about a dozen hot dogs and a few beers for lunch, a flask of whiskey, and a cigar during the game, and then chili and a few more beers before a visit to the cathouse."

"Are you saying Babe Ruth was a sex addict?"

"If he was alive today, he would be in Alcoholics Anonymous, Sex Addicts Anonymous, an ADD support group, Overeaters Anonymous, and that would just be his meetings on Mondays."

Angelique wanted to know more. "Was he ever married?"

Schwartz smiled. "He was married twice, and it was bad. Do you know during one of his marriage ceremonies, when it came to the part where you promise to be faithful, the preacher actually started laughing and asked Babe Ruth if he was kidding them?

"He also had some more great quotes. He is remembered for this one. 'Sometimes, when I think of all of the beer I drink, I feel ashamed. Then I look into the glass and think about the workers in the brewery and all of their hopes and dreams. If I don't drink this beer, they might be out of work, and their dreams would be shattered. I think is it better for me to drink this beer and let their dreams come true than to be selfish and worry about my liver?' Man, that is poetry! When I read that, I said, 'Dante, ha! Proust, ha! Flaubert, who cares!' That, my dear Angelique, that is poetry!"

Angelique was finding this all interesting. "So he was the most colorful athlete in history?"

Schwartz was a scholar, but he knew his sports. "There was one other athlete that gave him a run for his money in the category of 'colorful.'"

"Who was that?"

"Dock Ellis, who was an African American pitcher for the Pittsburgh Pirates. Let me tell you just a few of the thousands of stories that have been told about Dock Ellis. Dock Ellis refused to play high-school baseball, because he thought the high-school coach was a racist. While he was playing in the minor leagues, he once took a bat to a fan heckling him from the stands. But there are a couple of stories that sum up his antics. The first is that he was once maced by a security guard when he was trying to get into the baseball park, on a day he was scheduled to pitch, after he got into a screaming match with the officer. There is another story about a game on May 1, 1974. The Pittsburgh Pirates were playing their archenemy, the Cincinnati Reds. Dock was pitching. He hit the first batter with a ball. He hit the second batter, and then he almost took off the head of the third batter with a fastball."

Angelique did not know that much about baseball. "So his aim was a little off that day?"

Schwartz was enjoying telling this story. "No, just the opposite. His aim was perfect that day. He told someone before the game, 'We gonna get down. We gonna do the do. I'm going to hit these motherfuckers.' He then proceeded to hit five batters until he was pulled from the game. His plan was to hit everyone that came to the plate."

"But, Professor, wouldn't they lose the game if he did that?"

"Angelique, great men like Dock Ellis and Babe Ruth are bigger than winning or losing a single game. They are the immortals. They are after bigger fish to fry."

Angelique was curious. "And there are more stories about Dock Ellis?"

Schwartz was going to relish telling the next story. "On June 12, 1970, the Pittsburgh Pirates were in California to play the San Diego Padres. Dock Ellis mistakenly thought he had the day off, so he had taken a hit of LSD earlier that day. A little while later, his girlfriend picked up the newspaper and realized that Dock was scheduled to pitch that same day. He makes it to the stadium just in time for the game, but he was tripping his brains out. As he said years later, he was 'higher than a Georgia pine.'"

"Professor, don't a lot of athletes take drugs? What makes this so special?"

"Angelique, what makes this so special is what happens next. In baseball, a pitcher stands sixty feet six inches away from home plate and throws a ball into a strike zone that is about two feet square. That, in itself, would be an amazing feat, but there is a batter at the plate, waving his bat, trying to hit the same ball that was thrown into that small space. So the pitcher not only must get the ball into that exact small area more than sixty feet away, but he must fool the batter by throwing different kinds of pitches, where the ball speeds up, slows down, curves, rises, or sinks."

"It sounds very complicated, and it requires a lot of skill and precision. So how did Dock Ellis do pitching on LSD?"

"He threw a no-hitter. That means not one batter got one single hit off him that day. He was flawless. Twenty-seven batters came to the plate, and not one of them got a hit to make it on base. He pitched all nine innings hallucinating in Technicolor and managed to pitch one of the greatest games of all time. He said sometimes he thought the baseball was as big as a pineapple and sometimes it looked the size of a marble to him. He said he sometimes saw monsters in the stands, and he could not see the catcher's glove most of the time. He pitched one of the greatest games of all time when he could barely stand. Now, that is a great feat. Sure, Michael Jordan was a great basketball player, but do you think he could have made foul shots tripping? Do you think Jack Nicklaus could have made a hole in one if the golf course was turning plaid and glowing in translucent purple as he was teeing off? Do you think Jackie Stewart could have won the Monaco Grand Prix on a couple of hits of Orange Sunshine?"

"Professor, let's go back to Babe Ruth. Did he have children?"

"The Babe had two girls—and how they were born is a story in itself. Anyway, his partying eventually gets to him, and he gets traded to a minor-league team, the Boston Braves. On the last week of his baseball life, he hit three home runs in one game in Pittsburgh, hitting the last one clear out of the stadium and onto the streets outside."

Angelique had a question. "Why is he such a hero to you with all of those vices?"

"Can you imagine what he could have done if he was mildly sober and lifted weights once in a while and jogged now and then? In his heyday, he would leave the game, taking a taxi to Toots Shores Tavern in Manhattan, and start pounding down the gin and tonics and old-fashioneds. After that, it was off to McSorley's Old Ale House in the Village for brewskis. Around two in the morning, when the bars of New York were closing, the Babe headed out to find 'sporting girls,' one of his favorite expressions. At dawn, another T-bone and a pitcher of whiskey sours, and he was all ready to slam a couple more homers at the afternoon game at Yankee Stadium in the Bronx, the place they call 'The House That Ruth Built.'"

Angelique had a great memory, and she recited a line from the poem. "*La bebe qui a construit la maison. Femmes et de la bière préférées*. Professor, you first translated those lines as 'The young child who constructed the home and liked women and beer.' I take it you have another interpretation of those lines at this point."

Schwartz smiled. "I would no longer translate the first line as 'the young child that constructed the home.' I would now say, 'The Babe built the house' or better yet 'The House That Ruth Built.'"

Angelique thought for a moment. "That would be Yankee Stadium in New York."

Schwartz smiled. "Not just in New York. Do you know the show *Gilligan's Island*?"

She smiled. "It is very popular in France. Gilligan is as famous as those other great Americans, Jerry Lewis and Mickey Rourke. I, myself, have seen many episodes."

"Well, in one of those episodes, there is a flier known as Wrongway Feldman, who was always flying in the wrong direction. The name of his plane was a joke about Charles Lindbergh's plane, the *Spirit of Saint Louis*, the first plane to make a transatlantic flight. Wrongway Feldman had a plane also. It was called the *Spirit of the Bronx*."

15

We visit a small town in upstate New York and get involved with bugs planted by the CIA. We learn about Latin of the gold age and a certain exclusive club in Pittsburgh. A startling revelation explains the wayward life of Michelangelo Schwartz.

Cooperstown, New York

After refueling twice, the small jet landed at the Albany International Airport in upstate New York. Things were heating up, and the Vatican was not sparing any expense. At the airport, a white stretch limo was gassed up, and the engine was running. The chauffeur, Rudolfo (at least, that was what he claimed his name was), knew the area well. Angelique, William, Biff, and Michelangelo piled into the back of the limo as their bags were placed in the trunk. There were sandwiches and bottled water waiting for them. The car sped north, up Route 90, past Colonie and then at Rotterdam veered left onto Route 88, which ran through Cobleskill, quickly covering the seventy-four miles to Cooperstown.

Cooperstown was a small village of two thousand people located between the foothills of the Adirondack and Catskill Mountains. The town was named after Judge William Cooper, the father of James Fenimore

Cooper, who wrote *The Leatherstocking Tales*. It sat on Blackbird Bay on Otsego Lake by the Susquehanna River. It was most well-known for the Baseball Hall of Fame. The town was like a Norman Rockwell painting with its old downtown, pubs, and traditional restaurants. The town had a great history. Abner Doubleday lived there. He was a man who claimed to have invented baseball, a claim doubted by almost everybody except his very powerful family. It was the longtime home of the Clark family, who owned the Singer Sewing Machine Company, whose products were a part of so many American homes. The old homes were in the style of Georgian manors and Second Empire stone homes. Second Empire houses followed an architectural style that originated in Paris. They were tall with steep mansard roofs.

The limo was headed straight to the Baseball Hall of Fame. William wanted to stop at the hotel to check in, change clothes, and freshen up, but Schwartz wouldn't hear of it. They were close to the end, the end of something amazing.

The Hall of Fame was a large brick building on Main Street with red doors and the American flag flying. On the first floor of the Hall of Fame was the Plaque Gallery. The Plaque Gallery was the centerpiece of the Hall of Fame. It had oak walls full of plaques honoring the inductees from the history of baseball. There was a stone floor with long benches in the middle where you could sit and rest. Only one-tenth of 1 percent of any of those ever involved with the game of baseball ever made it into the Hall of Fame. On the ramp that went down Inductee Row, leading into the Hall of Fame Gallery, you could see the memorabilia connected with the careers of baseball's greats. In that room was the man to whom they had flown to Cooperstown to talk.

Sports legend Luke Brannigan was in his nineties. He was wearing a fleece pullover sweater with a Detroit Tigers logo on it and chino pants. He had tortoiseshell round glasses under a shock of white hair. He was thin and walked with a limp. He was one of the world's leading authorities on baseball and had written many books on the subject. When the group came in, he stood up.

"Professor Schwartz, right on schedule, as usual. You may have your faults, but punctuality is not one of them."

Schwartz took the lead. "Is there somewhere we can sit down and talk?"

Luke Brannigan smiled. "As I recall, you are a little partial to Cooley's Stone House Tavern. Let's not talk here. Let's get a drink. I think, before this day is over, one of us might need one."

William was not surprised. It was another town, and that meant another tavern. The five walked out of the Baseball Hall of Fame and headed over to Pioneer Street. Cooley's Stone House Tavern was an old two-story building that had a stone exterior and a green wooden porch. There, the ubiquitous Budweiser beer neon sign hung in the window.

When Wally and Carol, the CIA foot soldiers who planted the bugs, realized that the conversation would take place elsewhere, they quickly went to plan *B* and followed the five to the tavern. They waited till the five went inside, followed them in, and grabbed the next booth, so they could hear every word. They started texting on their phones the second they sat down. Soon, Glen Runciter and Joe Chip would know everything that was being said.

The inside of Cooley's Stone House Tavern was what you would expect of a pub in the Adirondack Mountains. There was a fireplace, pine paneling on the walls, and wooden floors. It smelled of great cheeseburgers and beer. This was Michelangelo Schwartz's vision of heaven. The five got a table. An older blond waitress approached their table, cracking gum with ruby-red lipstick on her lips and smelling like she had been dipped in a vat of cheap perfume. She wore her waitress outfit a little too tight for a middle-aged woman.

"What will it be?"

Schwartz could not help himself. "No rush. What's your name?"

She smiled at him and stared. "Trixie. What's your name, good-looking?

Schwartz smiled a sheepish grin. "Mickey."

William was not shocked. But the term "Mickey" was new to him. He leaned over to Schwartz. "Mickey? Since when is your name Mickey?"

Schwartz leaned over and whispered to William, "Hey! If she said her name was Countess Leonora, I might have said Michelangelo, but Trixie goes much better with Mickey, don't you think?"

As usual with Michelangelo Schwartz, it was getting complicated.

Biff intervened. "Let's order. I will have a Coke."

Schwartz was quick to order. "Jack and Coke, Trixie, you gorgeous vixen!"

She smiled as she blew a bubble with her gum. "My, my. Flattery will get you everywhere."

The banter went on as the drinks were ordered. As soon as Trixie was gone, Biff grew impatient. "Dr. Schwartz, can you please, *please*, help us move things along?"

Schwartz leaned into Luke Brannigan. "Your latest book was very controversial. It was savaged in the press, and academics panned it, but we are here today because I think you are on to something."

William was not keeping up. "What was your latest book?"

Luke Brannigan smiled. "It was a book I wanted to write for fifty years but was afraid. So, instead, I took the coward's way out. For many years, I wrote books on the history of the Louisville Slugger, the story of the first American baseball team, the New York Knickerbockers, and books on the Negro League, the World Series, and Ty Cobb. But my heart was not in them. My heart was in this book. This was the book I always wanted to write. So when I was the dean of baseball writers, with a great reputation and publisher connections, I was able to finally do it—write the book I always wanted to write."

William had not had his question answered. "And the title of your book is..."

Brannigan sighed, because he knew how his book was received. "The book is entitled *Babe Ruth and the Occult*."

There was a stunned silence at the table. Trixie returned to the table and started to pass out the drinks. She winked at Michelangelo as she handed him his drink.

Schwartz had a question for Professor Brannigan. "Luke, you and I have known each other for decades. There is no greater expert on baseball that I know of. But this book tanked your career and reputation. You knew full well what would happen when you published it, but you felt that you were ethically compelled to speak this truth. I know you have felt strongly about this, so I would like you to share with us some of your insights. And, my friend, I will tell you there are great things at stake here."

Brannigan sipped his Coke. "I have been hesitant to discuss this after the reviews and the reception, but, Professor Schwartz, I have come to respect your great knowledge and passion for baseball, especially the Yankees, over the years and hope I can shed some light. Let me begin with how I came to this subject. If you look at pictures of Babe Ruth, it is hard to imagine how he did what he did. He was overweight, an alcoholic, a sex addict; he was addicted to cigars and had a diet that should have killed him before he reached thirty. Yet, he set record after record and so dominated his sport that younger, more athletic men could only dream of doing what he was doing. Michael Jordan has been called the Babe Ruth of basketball; Tiger Woods has been called the Babe Ruth of golf. But Babe Ruth was not the Babe Ruth of anything; he was just Babe Ruth. So he defied all of the odds. It is rumored he had sex with more than five thousand women while drunk out of his mind. During this time, he broke every baseball record there was. There were reports that he drank heavily during the games, yet, day after day, he slugged homers at which we are still amazed today."

Biff was interested. "So you think there is a supernatural angle?"

Brannigan was nervous, but he continued. "Think about it. When he was with the Boston Red Sox, he was the greatest pitcher of all time. Even the greats of today cannot compare. He pitched more shutout innings in the World Series—THE WORLD SERIES!—than anyone before or since. The Red Sox won the World Series a few times. They were the royalty of baseball, and then came 1919."

William was doing his best, trying to follow this argument. "1919? What happened in 1919?"

"In 1919, the greatest pitcher in the history of baseball was only hitting every few days. Even though he had far less at bats than all of the players who played every day, he was still the batting champ. So he started another revolution. Forget A-Rod, forget Brett Favre, and forget

LeBron James. They all owe a debt to the Babe. In 1919, he told the Red Sox he would not play unless they doubled his salary and made him the highest-paid player in the world. The Red Sox could not afford this, so they traded him to the New York Yankees in the early months of 1920."

Biff could not help himself. "1920? 1920?!" He looked at William and smiled.

Luke Brannigan did not know what he was referring to, so he went on. "In 1920, the New York Yankees had never won a World Series. They were a bad team that was always going nowhere. But, in 1920, they got a new player. The Big Bambino moved to New York, and guess what? Suddenly, the Yankees were the toast of baseball, and they began a domination of the sport that has continued almost unabated until the present day."

Angelique did not know the history of the sport, so she asked a question. "What happened to the Red Sox?"

Brannigan smiled. She was following his argument. "Young lady, when the Boston Red Sox sold the Babe, everything went wrong. After dominating the World Series, they didn't win another for almost a hundred years. It has become known as the Curse of the Bambino. It was like they had a spell on them. Let me give you one example, young lady. In the 1986 World Series, the Boston Red Sox were heavily favored. The first team winning four games wins the World Series. Game six was at Shea Stadium in Queens. The Sox were up in the series three to two. If they won game six, they would be World Series champs and finally break the Curse of the Bambino. The game went into extra innings and after the top of the tenth inning, the Red Sox had a two-run lead. All they had to do was get three outs, and they were World Series champs. What happened in the bottom of that tenth inning lives in baseball lore. Bus Saidt, who was the sportswriter for *The Trenton Times*, typed these words, 'I'm sitting here, and I still don't believe it.'"

Biff was fascinated. "Go on."

"Well, the Red Sox were up five to three. With two outs, the Mets had Gary Carter at the plate with two strikes. The Mets were down to their last strike, with the bases empty, and down by two runs. The Red Sox were finally one strike away from glory. The Mets star, Keith Hernandez, went back to the Mets locker room and sat alone, lit up a cigarette, and opened a cold beer. He was going to watch the rest of the game on TV by himself. It was over. In the Red Sox dressing room, champagne that had been on ice was opened. The corks were popped, and the cups were spread around. The Red Sox pitchers who came into the locker room early embraced and cried. The man who managed the billboard at Shea typed in the words, 'Congratulations, Boston Red Sox, 1986 World Champions.' As soon as Gary Carter got that last strike or flied out, he would put that billboard up.

"It seemed that they had finally broken the Curse of the Bambino, and they broke it in the hated city of New York. But, then, something happened. Gary Carter got a hit and got on base. The next two batters both got down to their last strike, yet, amazingly, both got on base. A wild pitch then tied the game at five to five. The stage was set. Mookie Wilson, a fan favorite with the Mets, was once again down to his last strike. He took ten pitches as the crowd was going wild.

"Then, the unthinkable happened. The pitch was right on target, and Mookie did not get the entire ball. A little dribbler bounced down to Bill Buckner, the sure-handed first baseman of the Sox. It seemed to everyone watching the game that Mookie had failed. It was a routine play for any little-league child to scoop up the ball and tag Mookie out. It was all over. Then, inexplicably, a miracle occurred. That simple, easy ball bounced through Bill Buckner's legs and rolled into the outfield. That drove in the winning run. The Mets had won. It has been called the Miracle at Shea. The Mets also won game seven, and the curse continued. Schwartz, do you recall an odd story about what happened in the first inning of that game by the Red Sox dugout?"

Schwartz knew his baseball history. He thought for a while and smiled. "Yes, I remember now. Something odd went on in Shea Stadium that day. A black cat came out on the field and danced before the Red Sox dugout."

Luke Brannigan smiled. "Coincidence?"

Schwartz smiled. It was all making sense. "Luke, you believe that in 1920, the Babe goes to New York and with him goes the magic. And, Luke, my old friend, correct me if I am wrong, but you are saying it is magic."

"Magic indeed, Professor. Did you know Babe Ruth was excused from most training camps in both Boston and New York? He didn't know what a push-up was. He probably didn't jog a mile altogether in his whole life. He would have sex with five hookers in one night, drink a gallon of beer, eat two dozen hot dogs, and was the best guy on the field. How would anyone explain it? It goes against the laws of physics!"

Schwartz was thinking. "Now, what you say is logical. Anyone who has ever seen a picture of the Babe would find it amazing that he was able to even pick up a bat, let alone do what he did. But is there actually evidence of an occult connection?"

Luke Brannigan smiled. "Schwartz, you are a scholar, and you know my work. You know how careful I have been with my research, my footnotes, and my indexes. As I was writing my earlier books, I had access to all the documents here at the library of the Hall of Fame. I also used some of the great university libraries around the country. With latex gloves, I paged through all of the great diaries, letters, and notes that never made it to the sports page. I began to think that there was more to Babe Ruth than met the eye. For example, the Babe is often thought of as not too bright with a lot of muscle. As you know, he grew up in an orphanage. But there is something you may not know, and it might surprise you."

Schwartz was going to bite. "And what would that be?"

"His private journal was written in Latin. And not just any Latin but that of the golden age."

Schwartz was stunned but jumped in so that the others would know just how amazing this was. "The golden age was the period just before the emperor Augustus. It was named by German philologists as '*das goldene Zeitalter der romischen literature*' and includes Julius Caesar's *Commentarii de Bello Gallico*, Cicero's *De re Publica* and Ovid's *Metamorphosis*."

William was confused. "So this drunken, philandering baseball player could write in Latin?"

Schwartz thought for a bit. "That may not be as far out as it seems. He spent fifteen years at Saint Mary's, and there Brother Matthias Boutilier mentored him. Ruth called him 'the greatest man I ever knew.' Well, Brother Boutilier loved two things—baseball and Latin literature. Before he taught baseball after school, he was the school's Latin teacher. Being a Catholic school, and since the mass was in Latin in those days, the subject was mandatory. While

Babe was a troublemaker and an outsider, he did spend hours and hours with Brother Matthias. Mr. Brannigan, are we on the same page here?"

"Professor Schwartz, exactly right. I myself was educated in Catholic schools and knew enough Latin to get started on this neglected journal. It was neglected for a simple reason. Baseball scholars are usually not scholars as a professor might understand that term. So, when these sportswriters, many with low IQs, like Marv Albert and Mike Lupica, came across it, they had no idea where to begin. When others with just a high-school education came across gibberish they didn't understand, they would just blow over it. Most of them have ADD. If you have ever watched ESPN, you will notice there is never a segment over three minutes long. That is as long as those guys can focus. I imagine that if sportscasters like Harry Caray or Ralph Kiner actually saw this stuff, they would scratch their heads and turn the page. So I copied a number of pages, went home, got out my *501 Latin Verbs*, *Greensleeve's Latin Grammar*, and the *Oxford Latin Dictionary*, and I went to work. As I dug down into the journals, I became more and more fascinated."

Schwartz now understood where this was going. "In your book, you said you found incantations, medieval references, and talk of the Templars. But, somehow, when scholars went to check your sources, the journals had vanished. So it was your word alone, and it got ugly."

Luke became sullen. "Yes. As you know, the A. Bartlett Giamatti Research Center inside the National Baseball Hall of Fame has more than three million documents. Ruth's Latin notebooks were almost never taken out and studied. But a week before my book was released, the journals disappeared. Because I was the only one who had cause to examine these documents, no one else can corroborate my claims."

Schwartz smiled. "I knew Bart Giamatti when he was president of Yale. This was before he became the commissioner of baseball. I was a National Endowment for the Humanities postdoctoral fellow there, and, as you know, Bart was a scholar of the Italian Renaissance. His son Paul, later the famous Hollywood actor, was just a child at the time. Bart and I talked Dante and baseball. He knew both as well as I did."

William wanted to join the conversation. "Paul Giamatti? I loved the movie *Sideways*."

The four looked at William in silence, and Luke Brannigan turned back to Schwartz. "Ruth was into something weird, in fact, so weird that no one in the history of baseball has followed this trail down the rabbit hole. But, when you think about it, it makes sense. Arthur Conan Doyle had his detective Sherlock Holmes say something that has always impressed me. He said, 'Once you eliminate the impossible, whatever remains, no matter how improbable, must be the truth.'"

Schwartz waved his empty glass at Trixie as he continued his questioning. "So, while it is improbable that the Babe was involved with something very esoteric and ancient, there is no other explanation as to how he could perform in the shape he was in. Thus, as impossible as it seems, it is the only logical explanation."

Luke Brannigan was not done. "But there is more. There was a meeting after a Red Sox game, before the Babe came into his prime. The Sox were in Pittsburgh to play the Pirates, and Babe headed out after the game for dinner in a private room at the Twentieth Century Club. The Twentieth Century Club is one of the most exclusive private clubs in Pittsburgh. At that dinner was former president Teddy Roosevelt, Pierre-Auguste Renoir, and John Henry Heinz. Renoir had kept his trip to America secret, so there are only scant hints about his visit in any of his biographies or art histories. A drunken Babe Ruth autographed the menu for one of the waiters after the Babe used it to doodle while the others talked. His attention span was shorter than a Minnesota summer. That menu is in the library at Duquesne University in Pittsburgh. I examined that menu, and these are the words that were written, 'Grail, Molay, Da Vinci, Rothschild, the Satan of Swat—"

William interrupted. "Mr. Brannigan, don't you mean the Sultan of Swat?"

Brannigan smiled. "The Babe wrote, in that meeting with Heinz, Roosevelt, and Renoir, the words 'The Satan of Swat.' Something else was being offered, and something else was being received. Something dark and unholy was taking place. Do you know why he took the name the 'Sultan of Swat' just a few weeks later? It was a coded anagram. The name is an anagram for 'No awful stats."

Angelique smiled. She could not help speaking up. "So his name is a code for what he would do in life. Because he had the best statistics in almost all categories, he took a name that signaled what he would be famous for years later."

Biff sat back. "This is astounding. This is amazing. I can't believe this. You are telling us that there is some connection between Babe Ruth, the Illuminati, and the Grail?"

Luke Brannigan looked surprised. "I can understand how you would get to the Illuminati with what I said, but why would you mention the Holy Grail?"

Schwartz looked around. Biff had spilled the beans. But it did not matter anymore. Michelangelo Schwartz had all of the information that he needed. In the next booth, Wally was on his Blackberry, texting the words "Holy Grail" back to Joe Chip at the CIA Headquarters.

"If you all would not mind, I would like a little time alone with Luke Brannigan here," said Schwartz. "I think we are close, and I think he and I can finish this up within the hour."

Brannigan smiled. "Professor Schwartz, I think we do need some time alone. Because no matter what you think you know, there is one piece of the puzzle that I am sure you do not know. It is something I came across while writing my book, and I wrote you sometime back that there was something we needed to talk about, but it had to be face-to-face."

William and Biff wondered what could be so explosive that it could only be presented face-to-face.

Michelangelo Schwartz stood up. "I am going to take a walk with Luke Brannigan. We will be back shortly. I would ask you all to stay here and have some lunch. And, Biff, while you are at it, get me Trixie's phone number."

Brannigan and Michelangelo Schwartz went outside. As they walked in the chilly spring air of upstate New York, Brannigan directed the walk.

"Schwartz, I moved here years ago to be near the library at the hall. I have spent thousands of hours going over documents no one else has touched in decades. It was in doing the research on Ruth that I dug down into all of his papers and found things others had missed. But I did something I have not confessed to anyone until today. During one of my countless sessions in the library, a letter, yellow and cracked, fell out of one of Ruth's journals. That journal had not been opened for fifty years. It was a letter addressed to him. I read it, and it so moved me that I did what no scholar should ever do. I tucked it into my jacket pocket and took it with me. Yes, I stole an artifact from a library, something I have never done before in my life. But there is a reason I did this. This document will be interesting for you to read. I have not shown it to a soul or written about it, but I want to share it with you."

The two walked down Pioneer Street toward Crazy Cupz Coffeehouse. Nearby, the two opened a weathered door and ascended an old wooden stairway to a second-floor apartment where Brannigan did his writing. It was immaculate, the home of a writer. Luke Brannigan pulled out a chair, and Schwartz sat down. Brannigan put down a glass in front of Schwartz and filled it with a very nice sherry.

"Schwartz, you are going to need this."

Michelangelo tasted it and looked up. "I am all ears."

"Schwartz. First, tell me what you know, and I guarantee I will tell you something you do not know."

Schwartz took out the two poems and put them down on the table. He went over what he had learned and what he suspected. He showed Brannigan how when you subtracted the death of the head Templar, Jacques de Molay, from the birthday of Michelangelo, you got the number 161. He was looking for an eight, but one plus six plus one equaled eight, so he had his eight. He explained the saint of the books was Jerome.

Brannigan smiled. "Saint Jerome and 161, eh? Is that when you got it?"

Schwartz smiled, because William, Biff, and Angelique would not have made the connection.

"That's why I am here in Cooperstown with you, Luke. When I saw Jerome and 161, I realized where it was and why it was me, the unworthy messenger. Yankee Stadium is located at Jerome Avenue and 161st Street in the Bronx, New York."

They went over the rest of the poem and the sheet from the bookstore in Paris. Brannigan smiled. He waited a minute before he spoke.

"The child that constructed the house, the House That Ruth Built, Yankee Stadium, and all the rest. And you must come home. Home for the

Grail is not Rome or Jerusalem; it is buried under home plate in Yankee Stadium. That home of champions, that holy ground for baseball fans, that place of so many last-minute miracles, and miracles we now know they were."

Luke Brannigan sat down in shock. "That would explain the cryptic messages, and it explains Yogi."

Schwartz was following, but he wanted to get it clarified. "Explains Yogi?"

"Of course! Amazing! Don't you see, Schwartz? After Ruth came the Yogi Berra years. He has a ton of World Series rings and set records for catchers that still stand today. He seemed a simple soul, but, day after day, he would say profound Zen things."

Schwartz was smiling. "Luke, like when he said, 'If you come to a fork in the road, take it'?"

Luke smiled. "How about 'it isn't over till it's over'?"

Schwartz was trading Yogiisms. "How about 'that place is so popular nobody goes there anymore'?"

Luke was not done. "One of my favorites. 'I didn't say all of those things I said.'"

Schwartz was next. "'This is like déjà vu all over again.'"

Luke was laughing as he spoke. "'I knew I was going to take the wrong train, so I left early.'"

Schwartz was not to be outdone. "'Baseball is ninety percent physical; the other half is mental.'"

Luke smiled. "We almost forgot this one. 'The other teams could make trouble for us, if they win.'"

It was Michelangelo Schwartz's turn. "'You should always go to other people's funerals; otherwise, they won't come to yours.'"

Luke smiled. "Let's end with this gem. 'If the fans don't want to come out to the ballpark, you can't stop them.'"

Schwartz finished his drink and smiled as he spoke. "Yes, you are correct. Simple Yogi had thousands of quotes using the most profound logic and such complex sentence construction that they amazed and confounded those with PhDs in grammar and philosophy. Yes, Yogi was not the bumbling and confused ballplayer he wanted us to think he was. He was giving us Zen riddles—koans, as they are called by the Japanese Zen masters, whose purpose was to open our minds to a new kind of reality. It was not about baseball at all but the principle of noncontradiction that lies at the heart of all argument.

"Every great logician, from Aristotle to A. J. Ayer, has told us that you cannot hold two contradictory ideas at the same time. But Yogi showed us they were wrong. Every single one of them was wrong! Plato, vanquished! Aristotle, dismissed! Aquinas, finished! Yogi showed that he was the most brilliant philosopher of all. What a critique of the history of philosophy, done in such a way that we didn't even see that curve ball coming. Do you know that in the acceptance speeches of US presidents the name quoted the most in the last fifty years was not Washington, Jefferson, or Lincoln but Yogi Berra? I am beginning to see the light."

The two men spent a little while longer looking at the poem, and Schwartz spoke, "They, then, had my name here. They thought that I was the only one who could solve this puzzle, and now I know why. I was the only one with an extensive knowledge of the Holy Grail, its history and lore, and, at the same time, was a rabid baseball fan who understood the Yankees. You know, I have always wondered how they could win year after year after year and almost never be out of the pennant race. Now, I know. They have had supernatural help."

Brannigan smiled and refilled Schwartz's glass. "That is not quite all, my friend. Do you remember, some years back, you and I met at an affair the night before the Yankees Old Timers' Game at the Oak Bar in the Plaza Hotel in New York? We talked Yankee trivia, and you went on and on about Babe Ruth. Do you recall?"

Schwartz remembered. "Yes, my parents were Yankee fans. My mother never missed a game on the radio. She was fanatical about her admiration for the Babe. She raised me to love what she loved. I have spent my life following the Yankees and have read every book about the Babe that has ever been written. I've even published a few articles on him myself."

Luke Brannigan put on his latex gloves and went to a folder in the bookshelf. Using a pair of tweezers, he took out an old piece of paper.

It was cracked and yellowed. Luke carried the letter he retrieved carefully to the table. He laid it in front of Michelangelo Schwartz.

"Schwartz, that night at the Plaza Hotel, you told me about growing up in a Yankee household, and I remember you told me your parents' names. I remember them not only because I have a great memory but because those names were so unusual."

Michelangelo thought for a second on the names Bridget and Shlomo but didn't know where this conversation was going. Brannigan sat across from Michelangelo, who had the letter in front of him. Schwartz looked down. The handwriting was familiar to him.

Brannigan spoke, "Read it out loud, my friend. And read it slowly. But take a drink first."

Schwartz finished his sherry, looked down at the letter, and spoke slowly. "February 6, 1948." Schwartz looked up at Brannigan. "This was written on his birthday in the last year Babe Ruth would be alive. He would not have another birthday after this one."

Luke smiled. "Correct. Continue reading, my friend."

Schwartz began again:

> Dear Babe,
> First of all, I want to wish you a happy birthday. Second, I want to share with you something special. You probably don't remember me, but I am pregnant with your child. I do not ask you for money, and I do not ask you for anything. I know it is yours because I have not slept with my husband, Shlomo, in over a year.

Schwartz sat back. He knew the handwriting well. It belonged to his mother. This was a letter from his mother to Babe Ruth, telling him she was with child, written two months before Michelangelo Schwartz was born. He continued to read:

> He will be raised as a Yankee fan. And I will always have him as a reminder of those sixty seconds of magic on that

> night in the service elevator of the Algonquin Hotel, where I worked as a chambermaid. I will always remember when you pulled me into the elevator and heard my accent, you made a little joke. You said, 'What is the definition of Irish foreplay?' And then you said, 'When the husband says, "Brace yourself, Bridget!"' That put me at ease a little, even though you never asked me my name, which, by a miracle of fate, is Bridget. A little of you will always be with me.
> Love, Bridget Schwartz

Schwartz was stunned. Luke Brannigan was smiling. "You see, there have been no accidents here, no coincidences. It has all come full circle, like a Dickens novel. You, the illegitimate son of Babe Ruth, have been chosen, somehow, some way, to finish your father's work. Do you understand what I have just shown you?"

Schwartz took another swig. "I now understand why I have lived the life I have, why I have also been termed 'incorrigible.' Like Babe, I love baseball, booze, and the ladies. For the first time in my life, I understand who I am."

CIA Headquarters, Langley, Virginia

Meanwhile, in Langley, Virginia, things were heating up. There was a frantic knock on the door of Director Runciter at CIA Headquarters. Joe Chip hurried in.

"Sir, you are not going to believe this. Wally called from Cooperstown, and guess what? They are talking about the Holy Grail and the Illuminati."

Glen Runciter looked grim. He looked up at Joe Chip for a long time before he spoke. "I will take that file from you, Joe. You are relieved from this case. I want you to make sure that Wally, Pete, and Carol are to report directly to me, and keep this compartmentalized. I don't want anyone outside of us to have anything else to do with it. Do you understand?"

Joe Chip did not understand. "So I am off this case?"

Glen got up and walked Joe Chip to the door. "You are off this case. I would like you to take a two-week vacation. Take Jane, and go someplace warm where you can swim and get some sun. I will ask you to speak to no one of this. Before you go, I would like all of your files and notes from the last two weeks...and one last thing..."

Joe Chip smiled. "Let me guess. This whole thing never happened."

Glen smiled and showed him the door. Glen walked back behind his desk and picked up his phone. He pressed the scramble button. He dialed and waited.

"This is Glen Runciter. Please tell the big man the following: 'Episode 132. "I am in Love with a Gay Stripper."'"

He put down the phone and laughed to himself about the title of that *Jerry Springer* episode. But, right now, he had only three words on his mind.

"Holy shit, Batman!"

Cooperstown, New York

Michelangelo Schwartz and Luke Brannigan walked back to Cooley's Stone House Tavern. Schwartz sat down with Brannigan alongside of him and began to tell the three others what he suspected and what he had learned. The others listened closely as Michelangelo spun his tale. They sat in stunned silence when he was nearly finished.

William spoke. "So you think that the Holy Grail is buried under home plate at Yankee Stadium? How could that be? Wasn't the old stadium torn down and a new one built across the street a few years back? So that would show this story can't be true."

Luke smiled. "I was thinking about that on the walk over here. You might recall a rather odd incident. New Yorkers were very spooked after September 11, 2001. The whole city has been paranoid ever since, and you can understand why. One night, just before the old stadium was torn down and the new one erected, something rather odd happened. Schwartz, do you recall the story?"

Schwartz smiled. "Yes, there was worry about a bomb or something, and several blocks were shut down for an entire night. In the morning, it turned out the entire infield, including home plate, of the old Yankee Stadium had all been dug up, and the new stadium was off-limits. Now, that makes more sense to me. That was the night they moved it to its new home."

Biff and William were smiling. They had gotten what he wanted. Schwartz was now expendable. Biff wanted to move things along so he made a suggestion.

"I suggest we grab some rooms at the Marriott on the way out of town and get some sleep. We can get you all back home pretty soon."

Schwartz was finishing his drink. "I think we all owe it to ourselves to take a trip to New York City. I would like all of us to visit Yankee Stadium. I think you owe me that."

Brannigan could not contain himself. He walked over to Schwartz, hugged him, and kissed him on the cheek. "Just think of it, Michelangelo Schwartz. You are Babe Ruth's illegitimate son."

Schwartz did not think about it, but there had been times in history when a kiss on the cheek meant an act of betrayal.

Schwartz took the last sip of his Jack and Coke. He burped loudly. "Luke, he is my father."

16

We visit one of most famous dive bars in America and are introduced to the McGonigal twins. We learn about the expression "belly up to the bar." We find out what Michelangelo Schwartz had in common with Teddy Roosevelt and David Bowie. An ambush in Greenwich Village has a surprise ending.

Cooperstown, New York

An hour after the travelers had left for their hotel, Luke Brannigan's cell phone rang. He picked it up.

"*Si*, Cardinal Reunite. *Mo era solo qui e aveva la chiave*."

Luke Brannigan was many things, but he was, first and foremost, a good Irish Catholic. He was a former altar boy, and he never missed mass. He was a regular at confession and Monday night novenas and prayed his rosary on a daily basis. Critics had panned his book *Babe Ruth and the Occult*, but it had caught the eye of the Catholic Church. He had spoken with them a few times about it, but they never connected that book to the Holy Grail until an hour ago, when a phone call from Biff Braunschweiger to the Vatican put the puzzle together.

Luke listened for a few minutes.

"Your Eminence, he now has the key, and I suspect he might try to use it himself."

He listened again to the cell phone.

"I am your loyal servant, Your Eminence. Whatever the Mother Church decides, who am I to question?"

He listened again.

"A good spot might be a place that Professor Schwartz favors. There is a tavern in the East Village, McSorley's Old Ale House, that is a watering hole he knows well. It is in kind of a quiet area, and that would be a good spot if it were, say, just after nine and before ten, when the place gets hopping."

When he hung up the phone, he felt bad. He sat down and poured a sherry. Schwartz had never done him any wrong. Schwartz was a good fellow. They loved the same things. And yet he had sold him out. Brannigan thought for a long time. William and Biff would both lead Schwartz to the slaughter, and he would have no idea until he got to the slaughterhouse. Then, he realized that he had both betrayed Schwartz and kissed him on the cheek, just as Judas had done in the garden on that fateful night two millennia ago. He thought of all of the parallels and became dizzy. He thought of Schwartz, who was in over his head, who had no friends in this thing, and who didn't have a clue. The unworthy messenger had decoded a message that would cost him everything.

The limo arrived at the Marriott Hotel. The tired company headed to their rooms to rest and shower. All, that is, with the exception of Michelangelo Schwartz. Within the hour, Angelique, William, and Biff were all in their rooms for the night. Michelangelo Schwartz sat in the lobby with a Utica Club beer in his hand, looking at all of the baseball photos on the walls of the hotel. He was, after all, in Cooperstown, a place of holy pilgrimage for those who loved the game. There, on the wall, was a picture of the Babe. It was that picture where the Babe is wearing a huge crown and has a smirk on his face and a bat resting on his shoulder.

Schwartz reflected on his wayward life. He thought about his drunkenness and his philandering. He thought of all of those times when Sister

Bill was running a faculty meeting and he could not keep from cracking up. He could never keep it in his pants or keep his smart-aleck mouth shut. He thought of his father, the Babe. He thought of that famous poem, "Pitcher," by Robert Francis. In that poem, Francis showed us the art of pitching. He told of the grace and poise of the pitcher, whom he described in the poem as "not errant, arrant, wild." Later, in the same poem, was the beautiful and often-quoted line about what a pitcher, a good pitcher, did. His craft was "making the batter understand too late."

He looked up at the picture of the Babe with a bat on his shoulder, winking at the camera with a big grin on his face. At that moment, Schwartz was proud of the life he had lived. He had never learned to live inside the rules, but neither had Babe. He could not resist a beautiful woman, but that was in his DNA. He loved his booze, but, as Freud once said, "Biology is Destiny." It all became clear, and it was beautiful. Michelangelo Schwartz had a tear in his eye as he lifted his Utica Club in a toast. He smiled. "Thanks, Dad."

The next morning, there was a knock at Luke Brannigan's door at his apartment in Cooperstown. He was wearing a wool sweater and sipping a cup of herbal tea while sitting at his computer. He went down the old creaking staircase and opened the door. There stood a man with translucent gray eyes, who was staring at him.

"Mr. Brannigan, you don't know me, but I believe you have some information I need."

Miami International Airport, Miami, Florida

Salvatore Greco never made it to Cooperstown. He was in Miami when he got a call on his cell phone from Rome. He listened to a familiar voice.

"They are on their way to New York City. They are due to fly out in two days to Rome. The professor's services are no longer required. We have the information that we were lacking. They will be in New York tomorrow night. We would like you to go there and fulfill your holy obligation."

Salvatore knew what that phrase indicated. He blessed himself with his eyes closed. Now, he wanted to be sure he had all of the information he needed.

"New York is a big town."

"We have taken care of that. He will be at McSorley's Old Ale House in the East Village. He will leave there shortly after nine tomorrow night, using the front door. We suggest you be there ahead of time to make sure the meeting is successfully set up."

Salvatore was thinking as he listened. He had a question. "Are you sure he will be there?"

He listened to the answer.

"McSorley's Old Ale House, New York, nine tomorrow night."

Salvatore needed to pick up a sniper's rifle from the basement of the Opus Dei house in Riverdale in the Bronx. You would be amazed to see what else they had in that basement. This was going to be the last night in the life of Michelangelo Schwartz. Salvatore smiled, knowing he had information that gave him an edge. What he didn't know, and what he couldn't know, was that Wolf Eyes was driving to New York City in a rental car, on his way to McSorley's Old Ale House to also complete his contract on Michelangelo Schwartz. Before he died, Luke Brannigan had given Wolf Eyes the information he required. It was going to be an exciting night at McSorley's.

The same plane that carried Salvatore Greco from Buenos Aires to Miami had another passenger, known to some as Boris the Knife. Salvatore and Boris moved in separate universes and would not know of each other. However, at the KGB headquarters, there were computer experts trying to assemble puzzle pieces they only faintly understood.

New York, New York

McSorley's (yes, that was what it was referred to by the locals) claimed to be the oldest Irish bar in New York City. This claim was easy to defend, as Irish barkeepers were notorious drunkards themselves and, thus, bad record keepers. It was easy to dispute which bar was first. But McSorley's could make a claim. It had stood on the same spot on 15 East 7th Street since before the American Civil War.

How many times have you seen an Italian bar or a Chinese bar or a Jewish saloon? Yes, there was no doubt about it, the Irish liked their spirits. McSorley's was in what was, for a long time, a very questionable neighborhood in the East Village. You may ask what the definition of a "questionable neighborhood" in New York City means. It means you have a fifty-fifty chance of making it home on any given night without your wallet being stolen and your face bashed in. McSorley's was what any city guide would call a dive bar, but it was one of the coolest dive bars in America. Old newspaper clippings covered the walls, and there was sawdust on the floor.

This dive bar had hosted Iggy Pop, Teddy Roosevelt, Robert De Niro, Boss Tweed, E. E. Cummings, John Lennon, David Bowie, the Situation, Woody Guthrie, Brendan Behan, Norman Mailer, Arthur Miller, Hunter S. Thompson, Mickey Mantle, Amy Fisher, and Joey Buttafuoco. As a matter of fact, it was in McSorley's that Joey Buttafuoco first made this famous claim: "I never laid a hand on her." And that just scratched the surface of the famous patrons who had walked through those doors. And, of course, as a run-down watering hole in New York that used to stay open till dawn, it was a favorite of the Babe himself.

Until 1970, women were not allowed in the bar. There was no ladies' room, and it was a men's-only saloon. The National Organization for Women, rather than focusing on domestic abuse, sexual slavery, or equal pay, spent a fortune suing the bar to let women come in. We are not making this up. They, eventually, had to put in a women's room. Criminal!

McSorley's had two beers, light and dark. Your choice! On the bar rail were a pair of handcuffs put there by Harry Houdini himself. There were wishbones hanging over the bar, left by GIs off to fight in World War One. They were to come collect those wishbones when they got home. The wishbones that were still there were those whose owners never made it back to collect them. The Irish bartenders gave the place an old-world charm.

Biff had gotten a text on his cell phone earlier that day. "Suggest McSorley's. Be there early, and make sure our friend walks out the front door exactly at nine. Make sure he walks out alone. Steer clear of the Irish Mass."

He took William aside and showed him the text. William was not as swift as Biff.

"Irish Mass?"

Biff leaned in and whispered, "'Steer clear of the Irish Mass.' It is a code that means steer clear of the Irish Catholic from Massachusetts because it was bad to be next to him in Dallas."

William squinted. "Does that mean what I think it means?"

Biff looked straight ahead. "It means four of us will go to McSorley's, and three of us will leave. Let's hope, anyway, that three of us leave."

William smiled. He was not sure this was a good idea, but it was too late now.

Of course, when Biff suggested that they go to one of the Babe's favorite haunts, Schwartz could not resist. They had a light dinner at the Marriott Marquis Hotel in Times Square and grabbed a taxi. They went south, toward the Village. The taxi stopped in front of McSorley's, and Angelique, William, Biff, and Michelangelo got out. Schwartz liked McSorley's and was happy that Biff suggested they show the place to Angelique.

They walked inside and smelled the beer that had been spilled on the floor over the course of 150 years. They found a small table for four and sat down. A waiter approached with a thick Irish brogue.

"Light beer or dark? Your choice."

They all ordered.

Angelique looked around. "This isn't a very fancy place. Why do you like this place, Professor?"

"Two reasons. The first reason is that picture behind the bar. The famous sports photographer Nat Fein was a regular patron here, and that is the original print of that famous photo. It was taken on June 13, 1948. It is entitled *The Babe Bows Out*. It was a rainy afternoon at Yankee Stadium when they retired the Babe's number. That meant no Yankee would ever again wear the number three. Ruth was dying from cancer and appeared at home plate during a ceremony marking Yankee Stadium's silver anniversary. Bob Feller, the great pitcher for the Cleveland Indians, loaned

Ruth his bat to lean on because he was having trouble standing. I have always loved that picture. But there is a more important reason we are here. This was one of Babe Ruth's favorite watering holes. In America, we have an expression 'belly up to the bar.' Do you know it?"

Angelique shook her head.

"Well, the expression 'belly up to the bar' was first heard in this bar. There are no stools at the bar. You stand, just like in the old days. And it was the Babe whose belly was always at that bar. And when he couldn't stay on his feet anymore, he would sit in this very chair I am sitting in now."

She smiled. Michelangelo Schwartz sipped his beer. He had never been happier in his life. Things were going swimmingly for the first time in his life. He could not have guessed what was going on outside of McSorley's Old Ale House.

At West End of East 7th Street, Salvatore Greco was sitting in the front seat of a rental car, with a good view of the front of McSorley's. Next to him was a sniper rifle that was loaded and ready. Darkness had already fallen. When Michelangelo Schwartz walked out that door, he was a dead man. Salvatore never missed. He had never used a second shot in all these years. Until the time came, he had his binoculars in one hand and a rosary in the other. He was mumbling Hail Marys and Our Fathers to calm his mind.

William was feeling worse as the evening wore on. Schwartz was a cad and a liar, but there was something fun about having him around. William was feeling regret for betraying Schwartz and the church. He had been lying to Biff, lying to Schwartz, and lying to himself. He wanted to clear his conscience. He had been playing both sides in this game.

"Schwartz, you and I have not always gotten along. But, in the end, I want to say you turned out OK."

Schwartz was smart, and he knew a change in tone when he heard one. "What do you mean 'in the end'?"

William looked away. "You know, the end of our little adventure here."

Schwartz leaned into the table and tried to look William in the eyes. But William was avoiding his gaze. Schwartz raised his voice to get William's attention.

"I didn't know it was over."

William sipped his beer and looked away. Schwartz sensed something was wrong, but he did not know what it was. His gut was almost never wrong, and it was growling and making noise. He looked at his watch. It was 8:50 p.m.

At the east end of the darkened street, Wolf Eyes pulled up in his rental car. He parked away from the streetlight in the dark. He opened the small briefcase and began assembling his rifle. He also had a perfect record. He also had never even had to fire a second shot. Luke Brannigan had told Wolf Eyes all he needed to know. Shortly, Michelangelo Schwartz would walk out the front door, alone. Wolf Eyes had brought along the book he'd bought at the airport before he'd flown to England, just in case he got bored—the same book he was reading on the plane when he sat next to Professor Michelangelo Schwartz.

Inside McSorley's, a man was leaning against the bar, drunk on his feet. Another patron staggered next to him to refill his beer mug. As he waved the mug, he spoke with a thick Irish brogue. "My good man, bartender, how about a refill for a good Irishman?"

The man leaning on the bar woke up when he heard this. He was drunk, but this got his attention. He spoke in a loud voice with a slurred Irish brogue, "Saints be praised! I'm Irish, too!"

The first man was just as smashed as the second. "I'm not only Irish. I am a Donegal man."

"Saints be praised. I am a Donegal man, too. What parish?"

The first was so drunk he had to think a minute. "Saint Rose's by the Bay of Donegal."

The other drunk was getting excited. "Saints be praised! I am from Saint Rose's by the Bay of Donegal, too!"

The waiter came over to the table where Michelangelo Schwartz and his pals were sitting. The waiter looked at the two drunks now talking excitedly at the bar and shook his head in disgust. He started laughing as he spoke, "It is going to be a long night. The McGonnigal twins are drunk again."

Schwartz raised his glass. "Faith and Begorrah!"

William didn't understand. "What do you mean? Faith and Begorrah?"

Schwartz leaned in. "Those were the first twins I ever slept with on the same night!"

William started to laugh, but it was an empty laugh. The beer glasses were all empty. Biff looked at his watch. It was 8:58 p.m.

Biff stood up. It was time. He gulped. He had lived a life of deception, but this was about to become something much more real and much darker.

"Let's go back the Marriott Marquis and have some cocktails. I will take care of the bill. Schwartz, can you go outside and call a cab?"

William stood up and still did not look at Schwartz. He spoke in a faraway voice. "I have to visit the little boys' room myself. Catch you outside."

Schwartz had a bad feeling, but he could not put his finger on it. He finished his beer and got up. Angelique was at the bar, admiring the artwork and fighting off drunken New Yorkers. Michelangelo Schwartz looked at his watch. It was 9:01 p.m. He got up and walked toward the front door alone. He pushed the door open and stepped out into the cool night air. It was a beautiful spring night in the City That Never Sleeps. He could hear the car horns blasting in the distance, and he could smell urine and dog poop. God, he loved New York.

He did not notice a red laser dot when it appeared, dancing on his right cheek. A half second later, another laser dot appeared on his left cheek. He stood oblivious, enjoying the night. He thought of the whole incredible journey. He thought that William might not be that bad after all. He laughed when he thought about his life. It was the happiest he had ever felt in his life. It had been a life well lived, from the brim to the dregs. Suddenly, he felt himself flying through the air, back into the bar, just as his ears exploded. All went black, and he saw stars and comets glowing. The last thing he felt was his head exploding.

When he woke up a minute later, he was on the floor inside the front door of McSorley's. Was he hurt? Was he dying? Was he still alive? He looked up and saw Angelique standing there, smiling. He was furious and confused.

"What the hell are you doing? You could have broken my neck. Was that you? It felt like I was picked up and hurled. Don't tell me you did that? What's going on here?"

She did not say a word.

He got to his feet and felt the lump on the back of his head. He was woozy. He got up and noticed William and Biff were standing together, looking sheepish. Schwartz now knew what his tummy was telling him earlier in the evening.

He peered out of the door, and all hell seemed to be breaking out on the street. People were running and screaming. Everyone at the bar was looking out either the door or the window. Everyone seemed curious, except William, Biff, and Angelique. He turned back to William and Biff. He realized something was terribly wrong, but he didn't know what it was. Schwartz felt anger rising as he spoke. "Something is going on outside, and you two don't seem the least bit interested or the least bit surprised."

William and Biff looked at each other and seemed to have no ready answer. For a long time, they didn't answer. Finally, Biff spoke haltingly. "No, no. We are surprised. Really!"

Schwartz just stared at them for a minute. You can't bullshit a bullshitter.

He turned and looked at Angelique. "You know I am still a few steps behind whatever the hell is going on here, but thank you. I guess it was no coincidence we met in Paris."

She smiled and looked at him with a gentle but knowing smile. She finally spoke. "I think our journey with your two companions is over. They have what they wanted from you. But you have learned from this journey as well, Professor. If you think this through, you must have one last question. I think there is one more person you would like to talk to."

Schwartz was amazed. She was a better chess player than he was. She was two moves ahead of him.

"Yes, there is one more person I must speak to, but I don't think you can make that introduction. I don't know anybody who can make that introduction. Do you know who I am talking about?"

"Professor, I am perhaps the only person in the entire world who can make that introduction on such short notice. But I am at your service. It is time to finish this. Shall we go?"

"Before we go, I will tell you this. That day when we had our first wine on the Left Bank, you told me your name was Angelique Serrureacle. In English, we could say your name meant 'the angel who had the key to the lock.' Right then and there, I had some confidence you would be of assistance. I just never realized how much you would help."

She smiled. "I think it is you, Professor, who has found the key that will unlock the door. It is time for us to go."

Schwartz nervously peeked out the door. Outside, there was chaos. People were running everywhere, and a police car had pulled up with its lights flashing. An officer got out. A man ran up to the officer. The officer kept him at arm's length. The officer always started with the same comment.

"We got a 911 call for shots fired on this street with a person possibly injured."

The man who'd run up to the policeman was breathless and excited. He spoke with a thick New York accent. "Yes, but it's not just one person injured. I think there are two men who shot each other while they were sitting in cars at opposite ends of the street."

Schwartz walked out into the street. At both ends, crowds were gathered. Schwartz and Angelique walked to his left. Biff and William walked to the right. There, William and Biff saw the last thing they expected to see. Slumped over the steering wheel was Salvatore Greco, with a rosary around his neck and a rifle still in his hand. William blessed himself. Biff did not know what exactly had gone wrong, but something went terribly wrong. He tugged William by the sleeve, and they slipped into the darkness of the New York night. Next to them, in the crowd, stood Boris the Knife. It was getting too hot for him. He was near the end of his career, and he was no longer going to take any chances. He turned and walked away quickly. In forty-eight hours, he would be back in Russia.

At the other end of the street, Schwartz pushed his way to the front of the crowd, and there was a man who had been shot in the head. It was a clean wound in the forehead, so Schwartz could clearly see the face. He recognized that face. It was the man who had sat next to him on his flight to England. A rifle was lying in the road next to the car. The man's wolf-gray eyes were open and not moving. On the seat next to him was a book entitled *Synchronicity: Why There Is No Such Thing as Coincidence*.

17

The dean of the College of Cardinals learned his craft from watching *The Wizard of Oz*. A hat reveals a surprise. Michelangelo Schwartz hears the confession of the pope. We find out what a vice-president of the United States might be doing in the Bronx after midnight.

Vatican City, Rome, Italy

The office of the dean of the College of Cardinals in the Vatican had a white marble floor that was lined with bookshelves made of oak. They went from the floor to the ceiling, as did the two huge windows. Outside, the Roman sky was gray and cold.

Cardinal Reunite was sitting in his office in the Vatican when there was a knock on the door. He was expecting two visitors. He was nervous but knew he had to have this meeting. It was Angelique and Michelangelo. Cardinal Reunite rose, smiled, and embraced Angelique. He did not shake Michelangelo Schwartz's hand. He knew where that hand had been. The two sat down in the two chairs in front of the desk, and the cardinal seated himself back in his chair. He rocked nervously as he began.

"My child, when I heard you were coming, I thanked God. Look at you! It has been years, and you haven't aged a bit. But then, what did I expect?"

She smiled demurely. But, as usual, she never said much. "Your Eminence, this is Dr. Michelangelo Schwartz. I know you are already familiar with him. It is important that he see the Holy Father, and he needs to see him today."

Cardinal Reunite opened his eyes wide in shock and shook his head side to side to indicate that was impossible. "Nobody sees the Holy Father today, not nobody, not no how!"

Schwartz interrupted. "No, Cardinal, I think you have him confused with the Wizard of Oz."

Reunite smiled. "Is that where I got that line from? I have been saying that for years to deny audiences with his Holy Father, and nobody else ever complained. Anyway, it cannot be done on such short notice. He is, after all, the spiritual leader of hundreds of millions."

With that, Angelique stood up. She walked over to the cardinal, who seemed nervous as she approached. She leaned over beside him and whispered in his ear. She was looking at Michelangelo Schwartz as she spoke. He furrowed his brow in thought. His eyebrows rose, and he smiled as he spoke. "Why didn't you say that in the first place? That's a horse of a different color!"

With that, he quickly walked out of the office and closed the door.

As they sat in the office of Cardinal Reunite, Michelangelo Schwartz had a thought. "Angelique, I wonder what would happen if we asked Google where the Holy Grail was?"

She shrugged her shoulders. "Go ahead. There is no harm now."

Michelangelo Schwartz pulled out his smartphone and spoke into it. "Google, where can I find the Holy Grail?"

A mechanical voice answered slowly. "The Holy Grail is believed to be buried somewhere in New York City."

Schwartz looked at Angelique in amazement. "Just think of all of the trouble and time we could have saved if we just asked Google!"

Michelangelo had one more question for Google. He spoke into his phone. "Google, where did you get that information?"

His phone answered in a mechanical voice. "Siri told me."

Angelique looked out of the window into Saint Peter's Square. It was filled with wandering pilgrims even though it was raining. Michelangelo Schwartz was musing about all of the twists and turns of the last few days.

"You know this whole thing turned out well. But I never got paid by William and Biff, so I am still strapped for cash."

Angelique smiled. "I was thinking about that story you told me about having your wallet taken by the gypsies and, amazingly, getting it back. So at least you have what was in there."

At that moment, Michelangelo Schwartz realized that in all of the excitement about getting his wallet back, he had not gone through it thoroughly. He took his wallet out and began taking out each item. In the back of the wallet was something he did not recognize. He took out the small card and looked at it. He turned white. He looked up at Angelique, who sat there, composed, as always.

"This was not in my wallet when the gypsies took it on the subway."

"Professor, are you telling me the gypsies actually gave you something? What is it that has your attention, and is it something you could have put in there and forgotten about it?"

Schwartz was cocksure. "This is not something I would have forgotten about. This is a baseball card."

Angelique was still looking out the window as she spoke. She was smiling. "I would imagine that in your life you have had many baseball cards. Perhaps this is one you had and forgot about."

"Angelique, this is not something I would have forgotten about. This is a 1914 card for the Baltimore Orioles, put out by *The Baltimore Sun*. This is Babe Ruth's rookie card, and it is in mint condition. There are only about a dozen of these in existence. This is worth a fortune. In my hand right here is the money I will need to retire and begin the next phase of my life."

"And, Professor, what would that next phase of your life be?"

"New Jersey gets cold in the winter, and, because you have to drive everywhere and I drink heavily on a regular basis, I am forced to drive drunk often in bad weather in a car that is falling apart. So I always thought I needed to be in a place where I could avoid both. There is a little town in Florida, thirty miles north of Miami and on the ocean, called Delray Beach. You can walk to everything, and there are dozens of bars there. Delray Beach has tropical weather all year around, and there is a little bar there called the Hurricane that has a happy hour of cheap two-for-one drinks that goes on every day but Sunday. There is a sassy bartender named Shelly that keeps the jokes and the rum flowing. For me, that would be heaven."

Angelique smiled as she echoed his last word softly. "Heaven."

In a minute, Cardinal Reunite came back in. "I am amazed. It is most unusual, but the Holy Father said he would see both of you. Angelique, we still are in your debt here, and the Holy Father can give you a few minutes. Do you both need to get polished up and get your hair done—"

Michelangelo Schwartz interrupted. "No, that is also from *The Wizard of Oz*."

The cardinal smiled as he guided them out of the door, and the three walked down a long corridor. There were marble statues on both sides, nude with the exception of well-placed fig leaves. It had been many years since they lost their Schwartz. The cardinal's shoes clicked and echoed against the tall ceiling. In front of two large wooden doors, two Swiss guards stood at ease, with lances in their hands. They snapped to attention as the three approached. One of them opened the door, and the three went in.

Angelique went in first. The room was large, and light was coming in from the floor-to-ceiling windows, even though the sky outside was gray and a light spring rain was still falling. There were large glass doors that led out to a balcony. The room had large chests with many drawers, and a number of gold and jeweled artifacts were on display. The pope and his assistant were in the room. The pope was getting ready to go out on the balcony and bless the multitude below in Saint Peter's Square. The pope was dressed in a white gown and white beanie.

Michelangelo Schwartz was amazed when the pontiff smiled with recognition and held out both hands to Schwartz's companion. "Angelique, my child, when I heard it was you, I knew I had to see you, so I put off my daily appearance for just a few minutes."

He held her hands with his elbows locked and gazed into her face. "It has been a long time, but I always say you never change."

He then turned toward Cardinal Reunite and his young assistant. "Could you leave the three of us alone for a few minutes?"

Cardinal Reunite was not happy as the two left the room. But Cardinal Reunite backed out, bowing, and closed the doors quietly. Michelangelo Schwartz was alone with Angelique and the pope.

Suddenly, the Holy Father looked up and scowled. "Well, Professor Michelangelo Schwartz, here you are in Rome. We meet at last, face-to-face, mano-a-mano, as they say."

Schwartz didn't know what to make of this. In New Jersey, when you heard someone use the expression "mano-a-mano" and one of the manos was you, it was time to run.

The pope continued. "As you know by now, Professor Schwartz, when our scholars first looked at the poem, the first thing they realized was that it called for one single man to solve the riddle. You recall the line 'work on this riddle till your hands have warts, but it will only be solved by a man named Schwartz'? That, along with other clues, led us to you. Before I brought you up to the other cardinals, I took the liberty of getting to know your record. I learned a lot about you, but I didn't anticipate how this would end. But we are now very near the end of this whole affair. I hope you have come to make your confession and make your peace with the church."

Schwartz stepped forward, but the pope did not extend his hand.

"Your Holiness, before we get to the end, there are a few small questions and one big question I need answered. First, how did you know it was me that was needed for this quest? Schwartz is a common name."

"Our scholars went over all of the details. Our intelligence agencies and our academics concurred. We then did crosschecks with Interpol and the FBI, so we are all on the same page. And, when I read the line that said the 'unworthy messenger,' we knew it was you."

"Your Eminence, this journey was not just a mission for the church but a mission for myself, a journey of self-discovery."

The pope walked closer to him. "My son, the Holy Mother Church has many friends. I have learned something in the last few days that has made everything clear. I have learned that while your last name is Schwartz, your father was not Shlomo Schwartz."

"Holy Father, it seems many people have been ahead of me in this adventure. But, along the way, I learned who I was, where I came from, and why my life's path has been as it has. I have lived my life drinking, chasing women, and living large. But I am my father's son. It all makes perfect sense now."

"Good, my son."

Schwartz stepped closer to the Holy Father. "Finally, once I found out where the Grail was and wanted to go dig it up, forces conspired to stop me. I can understand why the Illuminati would not want it found. But I must know why you also did not want me to succeed. That is the big question I need answered. It seemed that at least one of the two men you sent along as my companions made sure I was in the sights of an assassin as soon as I discovered the location of the Holy Grail. I thought I was sent to find the Holy Grail and return it to its home in the Vatican."

The pope went over and looked out the window for a long time, lost in thought. Finally, he had collected his thoughts. "Since February 6, 1920, we did not know where the Grail was or who the Supreme Ascendant Illuminated Master was. We realized a few days ago that the Supreme Ascendant Illuminated Master was not a Rothschild or a Rockefeller but Babe Ruth himself. The only thing he had in common with those other two is that his name begins with an *R*. It all began to come clear then. We then understood about the Grail. For generations, some of our scholars thought the Grail was in Sinclair Castle in Scotland. Others speculated it was back in Jerusalem. Some thought it was in Rome, and some even speculated it was in Washington, DC. Our scholars all assumed it would be in some place of power. So, when you discovered it had been buried under home plate at Yankee Stadium in the Bronx, I realized we could not dig it up."

Schwartz did not understand. "Why could you not dig it up if it was in Yankee Stadium? That is the mystery. Why did my linking the Grail to Yankee Stadium seal my fate? If it was in the White House or Kremlin, you would want it returned. Your Holiness, that is the one question I am here to ask and, I believe, only you have an answer to. The church wanted me to help find the Holy Grail. I helped. But when I told you all that it was buried in Yankee Stadium, my life was suddenly in danger. I can understand that the Illuminati would not want me to succeed, but why would you, the Vatican, not want me to succeed?"

Angelique stepped forward. She apparently knew something that Schwartz did not. She put her hand gently on the Holy Father's arm. "Holy Father, confession is good for the soul. And that is true for all of us, even you, Your Eminence."

The pope smiled at her. "As usual, you are right, my child. Confession is good for the soul."

The pope turned to Michelangelo Schwartz. As he did, Angelique quietly took a few light steps backward as the two men stared at each other. She opened the door and slipped out of the room. She closed it quietly behind her. Outside, she saw Cardinal Reunite pacing nervously. She smiled at him. "Give them a few more minutes, and then go in. It is going to be OK."

She turned and walked gracefully down the marble corridor that led out of Saint Peter's. She did not look back.

Back in the room, the Holy Father sighed and looked at Michelangelo Schwartz. "I understand two men were following you and your progress. After the unfortunate event in New York, we did some investigation, and we realized one had been dispatched by the Illuminati. He was meant to keep you from the Grail. It is disturbing to us here in the Vatican that he was following you, because that means someone in the church, very high up, has a loyalty to the Illuminati and was feeding them information. We suspect now that it was our own man, in a manner of speaking, William Callahan. You know what the church fathers once wrote: 'Never trust a man who was once a woman.'

"But you are correct, my son, about our intentions. When we thought the Grail could transfer power from Beijing, Zurich, Washington, or Jerusalem to Rome, we did not mind. If you had found the Grail in any of those locations, the church would have been eternally in your debt, you would have been paid, and your life would not have been in jeopardy. But when I was told that you had discovered the Holy Grail had been under home plate in Yankee Stadium for all these years, I could not let you dig it up. That was the one spot we could not desecrate or violate. When you told us it was in Yankee Stadium, I knew you had to be stopped, no matter what the cost."

Schwartz did not understand. "Desecrate or violate? Holy Father, I don't understand. When you found out it was buried in Yankee Stadium, why would you not want it dug up and returned to its home in the Vatican? Why would you, the pope, the shepherd of tens of millions of souls, leave the most holy and powerful artifact in the Bronx and not bring it to Rome? Why would you not use that power for good?"

The pope looked for a long time at Michelangelo Schwartz. He sighed deeply, turned his back to him, and walked over to a large dresser. The pope took a key that was on a gold chain around his neck and unlocked a large maple drawer in the bottom of the dresser. He took off his beanie and put it on the table. The pope leaned into the deep drawer. When he emerged, he was wearing a baseball cap. He turned toward Schwartz. Schwartz gasped in amazement. The cap had a New York Yankees logo on it.

"Professor Schwartz, you have bragged you are the biggest Yankees fan in the world. But, my son, I beg to differ. You may be the biggest Yankees fan in America, but the world is a very big place. While my body has belonged to the Holy Mother Church, my heart has always been with the Yankees. I can name the first two hundred and sixty-six popes in order, but I can also name every member of the 1927 New York Yankees in their batting order, which was known as 'murderer's row.'"

Schwartz could not believe it. "Forgive me for not taking you at your word, Holy Father, but that is a little hard to swallow. OK, let's see if you are telling the truth. If you are a real Yankees fan, in that 1927 lineup, who hit after center fielder Earle Combs?"

The pope smiled. "That's an easy one. Second baseman Tony Lazzeri."

They began to banter about the 1927 Yankees, oblivious to the crowd gathered below in Saint Peter's Square, waiting in the spring rain to be blessed by the Holy Father so that their sins could be forgiven, and there were also a few souls who hoped they could be cured of their cancer.

A little while later, in that same light rain, Angelique walked along the bridge near the Vatican that started from the Castile Sant'Angelo, the Castle of the Angels. She stopped on the bridge that went over the Tiber River. She looked up at a statue of an angel that had been carved by Bernini. It was masterfully executed. She looked over the river and smiled. She had enjoyed meeting Michelangelo Schwartz, and she smiled when she thought of him. The time she'd spent with him had been a whirlwind of jokes, fun, and adventure. She wondered why he had had such a hard life when his was the kind of life everyone should want to live. People were funny. She would leave Rome tomorrow. There was a pressing issue in Moscow that needed her attention. Meanwhile, she was headed over to see Luigi. She had never had such a fantastic cannoli.

Back at the Vatican, Cardinal Reunite could not wait any longer. He had been pacing and looking at his watch for the past fifteen minutes. The pope was already late for his audience on the balcony with the faithful in Saint Peter's Square. Cardinal Reunite knocked on the pope's door and burst in. Schwartz and the pope were laughing over by the window and hugging each other in tears. Schwartz was talking.

"Your Holiness, how about the time Reggie Jackson and Billy Martin started a slugfest inside of the Yankee dugout? What a night!"

The pope almost could not keep his breath from laughing. "No, no... how about Pedro Martinez of the Red Sox throwing a seventy-year-old Don Zimmer to the ground in the American League Championship Series at Fenway in 2003? But you know what, Schwartz? They say you should forgive all, but A-Rod might be the exception!"

Schwartz slapped his knee. "Your Holiness, first of all, call me Michelangelo. We are pals. But A-Rod! Oh, my God! Last season, he had more drugs in his system than a pharmacy!"

The pope had tears in his eyes as he looked up at Cardinal Reunite, who was standing there, stunned. The pope pointed at Michelangelo. "More drugs than a pharmacy. That's a good one! Michelangelo, you kill me!"

Schwartz was still laughing. "Yes, and you almost killed me! Literally!"

The pope was doubled over in laughter and had tears in his eyes as Cardinal Reunite tried to restore order.

"Holy Father, your flock awaits. You must make an appearance. Please, I beg of you."

The pope had come to appreciate Michelangelo Schwartz. "Schwartz, before you go, may I ask one favor?"

Schwartz was quick to forgive. "Anything, Your Eminence."

"May I have the autograph of Babe Ruth's illegitimate son?"

Schwartz took out a felt pen and picked up the pope's white beanie that sat on the table. He signed it "Michelangelo Schwartz, Babe Ruth Jr."

"Now, Your Eminence, may I ask something in return? I would like to go out on the balcony with you when you bless the crowd. It must be a rush."

The pope was laughing. He asked himself if this was how the good thief asked Jesus for forgiveness on the last day of his life and was allowed in heaven after a life of sin and crime. It was refreshing to have someone treat him as a human being and not just the pope.

"Sure, Schwartz! Come on! This will be a first for both of us."

Cardinal Reunite stepped forward in a panic. "Holy Father, I must protest in the strongest terms. You cannot take a tourist on the balcony with you for the blessing. In fifteen centuries, this has not been done. I beg you, Your Eminence."

The pope turned to the cardinal. "Keep your shirt on, Stan. I am sure the Big Guy will understand."

The pope's young assistant opened the French doors to the balcony, and the pontiff and Michelangelo Schwartz walked out to the cheers of the crowd. The pope raised his arms in greeting, and Schwartz stood behind him, grinning. As great as this moment was, it was occurring to Michelangelo that he needed a drink. He would be paying a visit to Giovanni at Harry's Bar on the Via Veneto later that night.

Two hundred feet below, in Saint Peter's Square, stood a newly married couple from America. It was the second marriage for each of them, and they were having their honeymoon in Rome. The bride did not look her fifty years. She spoke to her husband. "I am so glad we found each other. I am proud to be your wife."

Her new husband looked back at her with loving eyes. "Yes, my dear, but I am sorry you didn't take my name. That would have been perfect if I could call you Mrs. Wilkins."

The tall, blond bride blushed. "Thanks, Mr. Wilkins, but no thanks. After my divorce, it was murder taking back my maiden name, and I vowed I would never change it again."

Her husband looked at her and beamed. "I love you anyway, Lulu Lefay!"

Around them, the rain was falling, and, suddenly, a yell went up from the crowd as they looked up. They kissed for a minute, and Lulu Lefay looked up, and she could not believe her eyes. She squinted in disbelief. Suddenly, she screamed, "Oh my, God! Who is that up there in a Yankee cap with Schwartz?"

Yankee Stadium, Bronx, New York

That night, faraway in America, the Illuminati made their move. Under the cover of misty darkness, a group of men began digging at home plate in Yankee Stadium. Two men in expensive suits peered down into the hole. Their names were Chuck and Dan, also known as the Coke brothers. The Grail had to be moved, and it had to be moved before dawn. Dan Coke shined his flashlight down in the hole and wanted to speak to an older bald man who was part of the digging crew.

"How is it coming, Dickie boy? Any progress?"

Dick Cheney wiped the sweat from his brow and looked up. "I can't believe you are making me do this. I have had four heart attacks, and I was vice-president of the United States!"

Chuck Coke answered, "Shut your pie hole, Dickie, and keep digging. We will decide who does what! Don't forget who calls the shots around here. We needed people we wouldn't have to kill, and that is a short list. Besides, you big boys can use a little exercise once in a while. Hell! On our ranch in Texas, we work all the time."

At that moment, Dan Coke's cell phone rang, and he answered it. "Yes, we are moving it tonight. No, the Vatican has not moved on it yet.

We can't figure it out. But I will let you know as soon as they do. We will have it in its new home by nightfall tomorrow."

They shined the flashlight down in the hole, and there, next to Dick Cheney, was Glen Runciter, director of the CIA, digging away.

Dan encouraged him. "For God's sake, put your back into it, Runciter. We haven't got all night here!"

When you are near the top of the CIA, you have led a complicated life. The world was a dark and tangled place, and, sometimes, people who were good at chess played more dangerous games. In his time at the CIA, Runciter had overseen delivering suitcases full of hundred-dollar bills to Iraqi warlords, gotten Britney Spears tickets for the kingpin of a Mexican drug cartel, and rewritten the golf scores on John Boehner's golf card. He could make anything disappear, like the night a drunken Karl Rove staggered onto the stage at the New York comedy club and began with the joke "Take the Republican Party, PLEASE!" That never made the papers.

But now he was focused on the topic on hand. About six feet underground, his shovel hit something. The shovels were banging against something metal. There was a lot of excitement in the hole. Dick Cheney found a laminated card on top of the box. It was weathered and covered with dirt. Dick handed it up to Chuck Coke.

Chuck Coke took the card and shined his flashlight on it. From down in the hole, Runciter yelled up, "What is it?"

Chuck Coke wiped off the dirt and mud, so he could read it. "It's an old driver's license."

Dick Cheney now wanted to know. "Does it have a name on it?"

Chuck Coke squinted as he looked more closely. "Jimmy Hoffa."

THE END

Dr. Frank McCluskey earned his PhD from the New School for Social Research before becoming a National Endowment for the Humanities Post-Doctoral Fellow at Yale University.

McCluskey currently lives in Delray Beach, Florida, where he is hard at work researching the best rum bars in South Florida.

We hope you enjoyed our story. Stayed tuned for our next book, where Michelangelo Schwartz takes on Texas, Southern politics, and the mystery of the Alamo. See you then!

CPSIA information can be obtained at www.ICGtesting.com
Printed in the USA
BVOW08s1121240814

364013BV00010B/59/P